DATING
THE
Enemy

new york times bestselling author
NICOLE WILLIAMS

Dating the Enemy
Copyright © 2018
Nicole Williams

ISBN-13: 978-1-940448-24-4 | ISBN-10: 1-940448-24-7

To everyone who's ever been broken by love,
but refused to be defeated by it.
Love on.

CHAPTER
One

"**F**or being an alleged expert in all things of a romance-related nature, your love life sucks."

"Thanks for the reminder. *Friend.*" I nudged my "alleged" friend, Quinn, as we moved up in line at our favorite place to grab breakfast before heading into work.

"Telling it like it is. That's what *friends* are for." Quinn blew me an air kiss before scoping out the display case of crack cocaine in pastry form. I wasn't sure why she scanned the selections every morning—we'd been ordering the same thing for the past three years. "You know what today is, right?"

"Yeah, it's March fifteenth."

She saw right through my act. "Also known as the one-month mark after hooking up with Steamy and Dreamy. If you don't hear back from him by today, you might as well—"

"Yeah, I know, Quinn." To distract myself from the mention of a certain male, I focused on the chocolate-filled croissant that had my name on it.

"I'm not saying that to be a bitch. You know that, right?"

"I know."

"There's a reason we follow certain rules when it comes to the male species and it's to protect us from the douchecanoes of the world." Quinn's sneakers squeaked against the tile as we moved up.

Only a few back from the cashier. I could almost feel my blood sugar spiking. "This guy, I don't know. He was different. Definitely not one of those douchecanoe types that are taking over the world."

Quinn shook her head. "It's like a damn plague."

"A swarm of locusts."

"A swarm of douchecanoes, whose only compass is the aim of their dick." When the older woman in front of us gave us "the look," Quinn the traitor pointed at me and muttered, "Relationship Troubles."

"He wasn't like that," I said, quieter so as not to add elevated brow number two to the tally. It was still early.

"You haven't heard from him for a month."

"*Almost*," I said promptly. "Almost a month."

Quinn's eyes lifted to the ceiling. "You spent a whole what? Five-ish hours with him?"

"No." I gave her an insulted look. "Almost nine hours."

She waved at me. "Excuse me. That's damn near a long-term relationship. Definitely long enough to ascertain the man you dove into bed with after a couple of drinks was not one of those one-night-stand, dick-compass douchecanoes."

Elevated eyebrow number two.

It was going to be one of those mornings. And it was only Monday.

"There was a connection." My fingers curled around my pearl necklace, twisting the smooth orbs. It was an old habit, worrying at my grandma's necklace. I was lucky I hadn't rubbed them all down to nubs by now.

"Yeah, I took sex ed in fifth grade. I'm familiar with *that* connection." Quinn employed her hands to demonstrate an act that was inappropriate for a café with finches on their curtains.

"Not *that* connection. The other one. The important one."

"Says the romance writer who's so hopelessly romantic she wrote an article about a fish falling in love with a duck."

My mouth fell open as I squared myself in front of her. Quinn was pretty much my total opposite: tall, thin, dark hair cut to her jaw, complemented by dark eyes and skin. She dressed totally different from me as well. She lived in sneakers—the trendy, bright kind—never wore anything from her waist down unless it was a pair of jeans, and her chest was always covered in a T-shirt with some emblem or saying or picture on it.

Quinn's pinkie went beneath my chin to close my mouth.

"First of all, I am not a romance writer. I am a journalist. One who researches and writes about topics of an amorous nature."

"A romance writer," she mouthed slowly.

My arms crossed over my pale pink cardigan. "Second, I'm not a hopeless romantic. I'm a hope*ful* romantic. And third—" I glared at her when she gave an exaggerated yawn—"that article was well-documented."

"It was a fish—a rainbow trout, if I remember correctly. And a mallard duck." From the way she was blinking at me, it was like she was waiting for me to be struck by a lightning bolt charged with reality.

"If you actually read the article, you would have realized I didn't say it was love the way we humans know it, but a connection nonetheless. One that made no sense but could not merely be written off to coincidence." My nose wrinkled as I said that last word. The coincidence people. That state-of-mind. Believing nothing happened for a reason, and that fate was a fallacy. What a sad way to spend one's existence.

"It's really a miracle they haven't committed you yet." Quinn patted my cheek before pulling cash out of her pocket. We were next in line.

"Okay, okay. I know the duck-fish article was out there, but people eat that stuff up. And you can't deny there's something going on when a duck feeds the grasshoppers it catches to a foot-and-a-half-long trout."

Quinn's head tipped. "And that's supposed to convince me of true love how?"

"It's supposed to convince you, and my readers, that there's one special someone for everyone."

"And what am I supposed to do if my special someone is a scaly underwater dweller with fins?"

I patted her cheek. "Then learn to swim."

We'd just made it to the counter when a different employee moved into the cashier spot. Quinn had been in the middle of adjusting her bra strap when she saw him. When he saw her too.

Our favorite crack cocaine dealer—also known as Justin the Jacked—cracked a smile that made the planet tip on its axis for half a second. He had the height of a basketball player, the beef of a football player, and the face of one of those Norse gods. He stuck out in a café filled with sweets and women, although I was confident half of the women who visited Flour Power every morning came for *his* buns, not the flaky kind Amie baked fresh every morning.

Quinn had to grab my arm for support when his flashing green eyes landed on her. As if a guy like him needed to have twinkling eyes to top off the man sundae already layered in his dish.

"Love the shirt today." Justin's eyes dipped to the faded logo on Quinn's shirt.

Quinn was struck mute. Only her eyelids were moving.

Justin rang in our orders without asking. "Damn shame the Sonics aren't around anymore. Best team in the NBA."

Quinn said? Nothing.

I drove my elbow into her ribs when he reached inside the case to grab our croissants.

"I love you." It burst out of her mouth loud enough that half the cafe heard it.

"I mean, I love them. The Sonics." She pointed at her chest before covering the Super Sonics logo with her hands. Which more looked like she was cupping her breasts.

The croissant Justin had just snagged from the display fell out of his tongs. "Shit." He dug back into the display, his gaze still aimed at the inadvertent boob squeezer.

"Stop groping yourself in front of the person responsible for serving our breakfast," I whispered to her. "He drops one more and we're going to have to go halfsies on the last one."

When Quinn glanced down and saw the positioning of her hands, not even her flawless brown skin could conceal the blush that flamed into her face.

He managed to get two chocolate croissants tucked into paper sacks, safe and sound, before making our coffees. As he stirred cream and sugar into mine and milk into Quinn's, he glanced at Super Sonic Squeezer.

"I managed to snag a couple of tickets to the Knicks game this weekend." He swallowed, his big hands having a difficult time fastening the lids on our coffee cups. "It's not the Sonics, but I have an extra if you know of anyone who might want to tag along with me."

Quinn was staring at his hands, probably wondering what every woman in here was—were all of his appendages as massive? Another elbow to the ribcage broke her from her reverie. "I can't think of anyone, but if I do, I'll make sure to let you know."

My eyes closed as I resisted the urge to beat my head against the glass display. Quinn had the flirting IQ of an amoeba. Not that I was a whiz in that category either, but good grief, the guy with ginormous body parts was asking her on a date.

Justin's forehead wrinkled as he slid our coffees across the counter. "Okay.

Thanks?" He actually looked dejected as he made our change, those green orbs not nearly so sparkly when we said goodbye.

As we wove through the line of women toward the door, I leaned in. "You should probably spend more time reading my column. He just asked you on a date and you responded by offering to find someone else to go in your place."

"What? He didn't ask me out." She shoved through the door, picking an end off of her croissant. "Guys never ask me out."

"That one just did. The very one you've been crushing on hard the past year." I checked my watch to see if we could walk to work or if we had to jog to it. It was a walk day. I motioned at her with my coffee cup. She'd been one of my best friends since I'd moved to the city, and was amazing in every way. "And what do you mean guys never ask you out? You're brilliant and beautiful. Witty and fun. The total package. What guy wouldn't want to go out with you?"

"I'm a sports writer. I have short hair. And I wear sneakers." She held up her foot. "Girls ask me out, not guys."

"People don't automatically assume you're a lesbian because you like sports and sneakers."

She huffed. "My parents think I'm a lesbian."

We shared a sigh as we milled down the busy sidewalks of New York. Not even the buttery, sugary goodness of our morning tradition could lift our moods.

We commiserated our lacking love lives in silence together for a few minutes, and then Quinn gave me a serious look. "Okay, so after today, no more of this wishing and waiting you've been doing the past month. Deal?"

"What wishing and waiting?" I asked, playing clueless.

She rolled her eyes. "If he doesn't call you or try to make contact today, he's gone. His file goes into the trash and you empty that puppy, got it?"

"Already done." My eyes crossed when I checked the tip of my nose. Still the same size.

"Just write it off as an experience-gainer and keep moving forward. He's not the only hot stranger you'll run into in the middle of a snowstorm, Hannah."

"Absolutely not. I'm sure I'll find myself stranded in Chicago after all the flights are canceled, subsequently leading to all of the nearby hotels being fully booked, and forced to spend the night on the snowy streets, when I bump into a man who makes ovaries and other parts throb. We share a few drinks and laughs, before he gives me the best three orgasms of my whole life." I took a breath. "Totally the kind of thing that happens every few months."

Quinn slung her arm around my shoulder as we moved inside of the building the *World Times* was housed in. "Why is it so hard to find a good guy these days?"

"Are you asking Ms. Romance the journalist or Hannah Arden your friend?"

"You say that like they have differing views on the subject."

"They don't. I'll just be sure to end my response with an XOXO, Ms. Romance if you want the journalist response."

Quinn groaned as she punched the up elevator button. "You hopeless romantics make me nauseous."

"Hope*ful* romantics," I clarified again, trying to discreetly tug on the elastic waist of my tights. They were doing the slow creep down my ass, and if I didn't do the regular yanking and wrangling, they'd be down to my knees by lunch. I didn't know why they bothered with making them in different sizes. The Cs felt as snug as the As, managing to cut a purple indentation into my waist every single day.

I wasn't overweight according to my physician and BMI calculations, but I was practically obese by Manhattan standards. In this city, a size ten was considered chunky on a leggy, tall woman, and I had to stretch my neck to hit five-four. I liked my body though, and I knew that was what mattered. But sometimes I wished other women liked their bodies enough to actually nourish them so I didn't look like the abnormality in a nightclub.

"Do you smell that?" Quinn sniffed the air when the doors closed, once the elevator was packed to capacity.

"Body odor?"

"Promotion. I can smell it from forty floors away." She took another whiff, giving me an excited look.

"I don't want to jinx it." I took a slow breath, feeling that bubble of excitement in my stomach when I imagined Mr. Conrad sitting me down in the conference room and offering me the head of the Life and Style department. I'd been waiting for this day since I decided in middle school that I was going to become a journalist. I didn't think this opportunity would come my way until I'd reached my forties at least, but the position was opening up and my column was the top read and commented on online article every week.

At least, the top read and commented *regular* contributor.

"What time are we celebrating tonight?" Quinn asked.

"And by celebrating, you mean what time are we all meeting at my place to watch *Pride and Prejudice*, Colin Firth edition, and wonder how much longer our own Mr. Darcy will take to enter the scene?"

"It's P&P night? I might have to take a pass. Last time we watched that, half the women started crying. *Before* the movie started." Quinn cringed. "I'm waiting for all of your periods to sync. Any day now. You're all a cult."

"It's okay. We love you despite you being a reluctant romantic. We accept you as you are."

"I'm not the reluctant one. It's the men of the world who are. Specifically, when it comes to me." Quinn scanned the elevator, her gaze lingering on the subjects of the male species, more captivated by their phones than the woman who had just grabbed her boobs. After a couple of seconds of going unnoticed, Quinn gave up with a sigh. "Why couldn't I have been born with the wiring that dug chicks? My love life would be so much more gratifying. Not to mention existent."

I fought a smile as we shoved through the mob of bodies when the elevator doors sprang open on the fortieth floor. "There's one perfect someone for everyone. Forget about the rest."

Quinn's snort wasn't soft. "Peddle your lies some-place else."

My shoulder lifted, as I was used to the barrage of criticism I took for being one of those rare types who still believed in happy endings and soul mates. "I'm looking forward to the day you meet him and realize I've been right this whole time. I accept apologies both in written and verbal forms."

As we whisked through the doors of the *World Times*, I felt something different in the air. That hint of anticipation—both nervous and excited—settled around me as I moved past the front desk toward the conference room.

"And I only accept one kind of apology when we're old spinsters on our death beds and you realize it was me who was right all along."

"What kind of apology is that?" I asked, chucking my empty coffee cup inside the garbage can as we passed it. I missed. I should have known better than to assume I had the athletic talent necessary to get a small cup inside a large hole from two feet away. Gym class had been my own personal hell on earth, my gym teachers spawns of Satan himself.

Quinn shook her head as I crouched to retrieve my cup from the floor and try for the garbage can again. She was one of those sporty types who could lob a carton of milk from twenty yards back and sink it in every time. "The kind that involves lots of shameless groveling."

"You're impossible."

Instead of detouring to her cubicle, she stayed with me until we were outside the conference room. "You're impossibler."

"That's not a word."

"Yet you believe in lots of things that aren't real, so don't dog me on one word that might not be." Quinn turned toward me, dropping her hands on my shoulders like she was about to give me a pep talk at halftime. "Go get that promotion, Miss Arden. Show the world pink angora and runs in pantyhose can get the job done just as much as a smart pantsuit."

"Crap. I've got a run? Already?" My head twisted over my shoulder to find, sure enough, a run peeking up through the back of my suede heels, already stretching to mid-calf.

"Forget about the run—you're about to be offered a kickass position and have your salary doubled. I, on the other hand, have a sterile cubicle to return to, where I'll be forced to write about why my beloved Mets lost their preseason game last night, after which I'll check my social media accounts over lunch like everyone else and pretend I'm swimming in potential male suitors the way Molly Kennedy does every damn Monday after a weekend spent in debauchery."

I scooted close and lowered my voice. "Molly Kennedy might have a mess of male suitors, but they're only in it for one thing."

Quinn nudged me. "Sex?"

My head shook solemnly. "No-commitment-required sex," I said just as gravely. "And that, my friend, is not the kind of male suitor we're looking for."

I dropped my hand on the conference room door handle as Quinn mumbled, "No-commitment-required sex is better than no sex at all." Before I could say anything back, she lifted her finger at me. "And before you go all preachy on me, you're the one who hooked up with a total stranger last month."

"He wasn't a *total* stranger."

Quinn huffed so loudly it stretched all through cubicle land. "Please. You knew him for a few hours before you let him do the kind of filthy things I'm afraid to repeat out loud for fear of being smote where I stand."

My cheeks flamed instantly. "We had sex. It's not like we dog-earred every other page of the *Kama Sutra*."

"From the details you gave me, you two dog-eared *every* page of the *Kama Sutra*." Quinn tugged at the ends of my nonconformist red hair. "Hussy."

"Jealous hag."

"Shameless harlot," she crowed as she turned to leave.

"Bitter wench." I stuck my tongue out at her before opening the conference room door.

Promotion. Dreams coming true. It was all waiting for me on the other side of that door.

"Good morning, Mr. Conrad," I greeted as I stepped inside.

Mr. Conrad was sitting at the head of the conference table, waiting, but he wasn't alone. My feet stopped moving before my eyes landed on the unexpected third party. A small gasp spilled from me when I saw him.

"You," I said, my hand forming around the edge of the nearest chair to keep me steady.

Momentary surprise filtered from his face. "You," he echoed, his address sounding like less of an accusation than mine had. His jaw moved as he appraised me, blinking a couple of times as though he were questioning his vision. I wasn't sure if what I was seeing was real either.

"You two know each other?" Mr. Conrad's voice broke through my haze of disbelief.

My mind went blank, unsure how to answer that. Not even sure why this person was sitting at the conference table of the company I worked for in New York City. Had he tracked me down? Figured a phone call was too prosaic for the connection we'd shared that one night?

But why at my office? And why would Mr. Conrad's presence be required?

The questions would not end, the answers remaining far out of reach.

The room started to revolve.

"Arden, are you okay?" Mr. Conrad asked, his voice sounding muffled and far-off, like it was coming through a dream.

Snap out of it.

I managed to crack out of it a fraction, just enough to clear my throat and work up some kind of semi-coherent reply. "I'm confused."

"That makes two of us." Mr. Conrad waved his fountain pen between us. "Do you two know each other or not?"

"A little." His voice filled the room as his head turned away from me.

A little? There is no other man on the planet who has more cardinal knowledge of my body than him and we know each other a little*?* Not the word choice I would have gone for.

"And you two are on friendly terms?" Mr. Conrad asked, the slant of his brow doubtful.

"Friendly enough terms, yes," he answered again.

Friendly enough terms? Is that what you call it? I decided taking a seat was a good idea, but I selected the one a couple down from him and on the other side.

"Well now I've seen everything." Mr. Conrad chuckled.

"What are you doing here?" I smiled tightly across the table at him, reeling to catch up.

He clicked his expensive-looking silver pen, his gaze aimed away from me. "I'm guessing for the same reason you are."

The head of the Life and Style department position. That was the whole reason for my meeting with Mr. Conrad this morning.

"I'm here to talk about the Life and Style position opening soon," I said.

One slow pen click. "Me too."

The room went from revolving to spinning like one of those damn Tilt-A-Whirl rides I'd yacked on.

"You're a journalist?" I asked. "With what paper?"

Mr. Conrad cleared his throat. "I thought you two knew each other."

"Not in the professional capacity, Mr. Conrad," the pen-clicker announced, the corner of his mouth twitching.

My eyes narrowed at him, not that he was looking at me to notice. "Not in an unprofessional one either."

"Hannah, this is Brooks North," Mr. Conrad continued, not hearing—or ignoring—my comment.

"I get a name." My head tipped across the table at "Brooks North." "Thirty days later."

His gaze floated to me for a fleeting moment. "And do I get one as well?"

"Not until I figure out what you're doing here, at *my* place of employment, sitting at the same table as *my* boss, looking at me like I'm the only one in this room who doesn't know what's going on." I shifted in my chair, holding myself back from tugging at the waist of my pantyhose. The chocolate croissant was not settling well.

"Your guess is as good as mine." Brooks took a drink from the mug resting in front of him—from the looks of it, I guessed it was green tea. He was a tea drinker. One of *those* people. The kind fanatical coffee drinkers like myself did not consort with. I should have known.

"You might know Brooks better by his *nom de plume*." Mr. Conrad cleared his throat, the kind that was a stall, not caused from a tickle in his throat. "Mr. Reality."

My fingers squeezed the underside of my forearm, followed by a twist when I didn't jolt awake. Nothing was happening.

I wasn't dreaming.

This person, the man I'd slept with, was *the* Mr. Reality? Surely the fates couldn't have been such cruel bitches.

Brooks's brows were drawn together as he stared at me pinching my arm. "What are you doing?"

"I have an itch."

A slow smile crept into place. "One you couldn't help scratch?"

My fingers curled. He was screwing with me. No wait, not screw . . . *messing* with me. For being all amazing and wonderful that one night, he sure was letting his jerk flag fly today.

Too good to be true: the words I'd used to describe him to my friends that next day. How tragically prophetic those words had been.

"Hannah here is a bit of your professional nemesis, Brooks." Mr. Conrad cut through our verbal volley, seemingly clueless to the tension rising to a head down the table from him. "She writes under the alias of Ms. Romance."

Brooks's throat moved. When his gaze traveled back to me, there was a new glint in those pale blue spheres.

"Excuse me, Mr. Conrad?" The speaker on the conference room phone crackled to life with Mr. Conrad's receptionist, Shelly. "It's Mr. Davenport on the other line. He has a quick question for you."

Mr. Conrad's eyes lifted to the ceiling, no stranger to the innumerable "quick" questions that the *World Times*'s CEO had for him. "Patch him through." He lifted his index finger at the two of us. "This will just take a minute."

Mr. Conrad had no more than picked up the phone before Brooks popped off a chuckle. "You? Ms. Romance?"

It didn't really look like he was waiting for a confirmation, but I still gave him one in the form of sliding a business card from my purse. If I'd left one of those on the nightstand early that morning—instead of where I'd actually left my number—he would have known thirty days earlier that I was *the* Ms. Romance. But in my experience, there was no better way to exterminate the chance of a second date than by mentioning I was one of the most well-read romance journalists in the country. It was the equivalent of hinting at engagement ring preferences.

Brooks glanced at the card, turning it over before slipping it into the pocket of that pristine suit jacket. Today's was slate in color. That night I was fast coming to regret, the suit had been granite.

"How's that for irony?" he announced at last, going back to clicking his pen.

I had to unlatch my jaw before I could muster up a response. "Irony? Not the word I'd use." Leaning into the table, I checked Mr. Conrad to make sure he was still indisposed with his call. "Did you know?"

Brooks's forehead creased. "Of course I didn't know. Did you?"

"Do you really think what ensued would have happened if I did?"

The corner of his mouth tugged up. "With the amount of gin in your system, I could have proclaimed I was Hitler incarnate and that wouldn't have stopped you."

My eyes narrowed as I put a stranglehold on that Irish temper that had gotten me into plenty of trouble in the past. This man sitting across from me was nothing like the one who'd slid onto the barstool next to me last month. In fact, the two couldn't have been any more different.

Mr. Conrad plunked the phone onto the receiver before I could fire off a response. "Sorry about the interruption. Let's get back to discussing both of your applications for the head of the Life and Style position."

For the second time that morning, my eyes felt as though they were about to burst from their sockets. My finger stabbed in Brook's direction. "You're actually considering him for that position?"

A huff resonated across from me.

"I wouldn't have flown him all the way from San Francisco if I wasn't 'actually considering' him." Mr. Conrad gave me one of those looks I was familiar with—they usually followed one of my far-fetched article pitches, like "duck falls in love with fish."

"He doesn't even work for the *World Times*. He's a freelancer." Based on my tone, that was an offense as grave as clubbing seal pups in front of preschoolers.

"That's because no one can afford to keep me on staff full-time," Brooks interjected. "That's what happens when you build a following like mine. More readers means more money."

I ignored the coat-tail rider. "He has no idea what the culture is like here. You can't put an outsider into a role like this, Mr. Conrad."

"Go ahead. Keep talking about me like I'm not in the room. I'll just sit here, waiting, while you argue with your boss, who holds the decision as to who will get the job." Brooks clasped his hands behind his head and leaned back in his chair. "You can just keep paving the way for me to land the position we're both here for."

My tongue worked into my cheek to keep from shouting something childish at him. I couldn't believe I'd actually found him attractive. Sure, he might have been hard all over and built like an Olympic swimmer, with dark hair that contrasted against light eyes and a face that could make a nun blush, but he was *the* Mr. Reality. Which translated to him possessing a soul that could put Satan out of a job.

I forced myself to take a breath before speaking. "Mr. Conrad, you can't be serious."

"He applied for the job and is just as qualified." Mr. Conrad pulled at his checked bowtie before continuing. "And he has more readers than your column."

There it was. The sore spot. Ever since Mr. Reality pounced into the editorial world—hot on my heels after Ms. Romance's column started taking off, I might add— he'd been gaining a loyal, bordering on cult-like, following. Just a few months ago, his column had tipped more online reads, comments, shares, and likes than mine. Because he wasn't riding in on my coat tails or anything.

Sore. Subject.

Once I was mostly certain I wouldn't breathe fire when my mouth opened, I said, "That's because it's human nature to latch onto something negative over something positive."

Across the table, a sharp grunt sounded. "It's also human nature to prefer to be told the truth rather than fed a spoonful of lies."

"You're an asshole." *Temper alert. This is not a drill.*

In the face of my ire, Brooks remained completely chill as he glanced at the sleek watch on his wrist. "Eight twenty a.m." He shook his head. "Sorry, you don't hold the record."

"What record?" I asked, pulling at my grandma's pearls as though they were strangling me.

"Calling me an asshole earliest in the morning. That honor belongs to someone else."

"I'm sure plenty of women call you asshole in the morning." My arms crossed as I twisted in my chair a little more away from the steaming pile of cocky across from me. "When they roll out of bed once the alcohol's worn off."

Mr. Conrad was looking between the two of us, his expression drawn in a way that suggested he'd consumed too much cheese the night before.

"Ms. Bitter might be a better title for you," Brooks quipped, accompanied by another damn pen click.

"And Mr. Delusional might be more fitting for you," I replied, pulling out my own preference when it came to writing implements. And it wasn't a fancy silver fountain pen that had likely cost as much as my first month's paycheck working at the *World Times* almost eight years ago.

Brooks leaned into the table, one dark brow carving high into his forehead. "And what's your relationship status? Ms. *Romance*?"

I felt heat seeping into my face as I squished the urge to shift in my chair.

"That's what I thought," he continued. "Might want to take some of that relationship advice you deal to your junkies."

At the end of the table, I didn't miss Mr. Conrad covering his mouth. What was the level beyond wrath? I was a writer and couldn't find the right emotion to describe what I was feeling. A word had yet to be invented for the surge of fury jolting through me.

"Now that we've gotten the pleasantries out of the way, let's cut to the chase of why we're all here." Mr.

Conrad planted his hands on the table as he rose from his chair. "Readership is down across the board. Physical papers are becoming obsolete. In fifty years, they'll be displayed in museums as antiques."

My expression pinched together.

"There's no shortage of competitors out there, and we're all fighting for the same scraps. We need something fresh, different. We need to do something no one else has done. Something that will grip the nation like an addiction, readers refreshing browsers and dashing toward inboxes for the latest update."

This was the point in Mr. Conrad's spiel when Brooks's face showed uncertainty.

"We need 'Man Walks on the Moon' and 'America Enters World War II' and 'Women Win the Right to Vote.' We need something big—*massive*—and we need it now."

While Mr. Conrad paused to catch his breath, I jumped in. "I thought we were here to talk about the job position."

"That's precisely what we're talking about," Mr. Conrad replied.

"I'm afraid I don't follow." Brooks cleared his throat. "I write an advice column. I'm not a big headline journalist."

"You write an *anti*-advice column," I mumbled.

"Coming from the person who penned the dribble entitled 'We Can Have it All'? I'm good with you thinking I'm wrong because our definition of right could not be more different."

"Are you two going to sit here and argue all day? Or

would you like to act your ages and confirm I wasn't wrong in believing either of you would make a fine department head here at the *World Times*?" For being a short man, Mr. Conrad had a way of making me feel small based off his tone alone.

Both Brooks and I clamped our mouths closed and let him continue.

"I've hatched an idea, our Hail Mary, our 'headline' that will go down in history. Except it won't be just one article readers can't help but fawn over every word—it will be numerous. So many it will put us back on top and secure our future in these unsure times."

I uncrossed and recrossed my legs. I didn't have a clue what Mr. Conrad had come up with, but that wild glow in his eye told me enough. This was the man who'd rose to his height after pitching the idea that the *World Times* should charge an online subscription price for people to read our articles while every other paper was peddling their online goods for free. From the stories I'd been told by some of the employees who'd been around back then, the company knew it would either sink them faster than the *Titanic* or be the one thing that managed to keep the *World Times* solvent. Lucky for me, Charles Conrad's wild idea had panned out.

Mr. Conrad remained quiet, looking between Brooks and me like he was waiting for our own excitement to bubble up from within.

"What, exactly, is this idea?" I could almost make out the note of uncertainty in Brooks's voice, but it could have just been a bout of indigestion.

"It's a kind of social experiment." Mr. Conrad's stubby finger waved between Brooks and me. "And you two will facilitate it."

The gnawed-to-bits yellow number two pencil dropped from my hand. I didn't know where Mr. Conrad was going with this, but I could sense the direction was concerning.

"What kind of social experiment?" Brooks asked the question on my mind as well.

"The kind two journalists like yourselves should find enticing."

That was the point my throat started to take on that cottony feeling.

"An experiment that will prove, once and for all"— Mr. Conrad's thick, silver brows peaked—"which school of mind is correct where love is concerned."

Across the table, the villain chuckled, while I struggled to catch up to what had been said.

"And how do we do that beyond what we've already been doing to prove our own opinions on that topic?" The words kind of tumbled from my mouth like candy from a machine. "He believes there's no such thing as true love, that it's all some farce we've conjured up out of thin air, while I clearly believe there is very much a phenomenon known as true love."

"Key word being 'phenomenon.'"

I fired a glare at him, but he'd moved on to twirling his precious pen between his fingers. Mr. Conrad's shoulders raised as if I was backing up his idea.

"What do you need us to do, Charles?" Brooks asked, all calm and collected, as though his blood pressure wasn't charging into dangerous territory as I guessed mine was.

And . . .

Had he called him Charles? No one in the office called Mr. Conrad by his first name. Not that it was a spoken rule or anything, but it was definitely an unspoken one.

Mr. Conrad—*Charles*—drummed his fingers on the conference room table. "I need you two to put the *World Times* back on top."

"And we do that by . . .?" My hand twirled.

"By setting your laptops aside, and putting your money where your mouth is."

Brooks took a sip of his tea, his eyes giving away the same confusion I felt. "I think we're both going to need you to spell it out for us, play by play."

Mr. Conrad leaned more into the table, his round face practically rosy. "I want the two of you to start dating. I want to see who comes out the victor. Love or logic. Romance or reality."

I blinked a few times, wondering if Justin the Jacked had pumped a squirt of peyote into my coffee.

"If Hannah winds up falling for you by the end of it because of your so-called tricks and tools of the trade, your point will have been proven. Love can be manufactured with just about any eligible individual out there." Mr. Conrad was nearly bouncing now, as though he'd devised a surefire plan to save the world from imminent destruction. "If she doesn't fall for you, then Hannah proves her point —that there is one person for everyone, and love can't just be pulled out of thin air."

After a few moments' pause, Mr. Conrad continued. "So? What do you think?"

Silence. The kind that strained my eardrums and made me feel as if I'd taken a hard hit to the head.

Brooks was the first of us to find his voice. "Barring the obvious contempt Ms. Arden bears for me, I see one rather large problem with this 'social experiment.'"

Mr. Conrad's lips pursed. "What's that?"

"She knows of the wager. I can bring my A-game to every date, but she knows all she has to do is resist my attempts for her to come out the winner. That's along the lines of telling a chess player they might lose the game, then giving them their opponent's every move in advance. There's no possible way to contend with that kind of advantage."

"You're Brooks North. Look at you. I'm sure you, if anyone, could find a way to woo one biased woman with a slight advantage in this setup."

Brooks gave a huff at the "slight" part.

"Besides, Hannah will play fair. She'll make sure she stays as impartial and objective as possible, right? In the name of research?" When Mr. Conrad looked at me, whatever he read on my face must have been taken as a confirmation instead of a *What the hell?* "You on board, Hannah?"

"No." As my head shook, tangles of red hair whipped across my face. "I am not. In fact, I couldn't be any more 'off board' with this."

Mr. Conrad harrumphed. "Please. It'll be great. Your readers vying for you. His readers rooting for him. It will be the dating equivalent of Ali versus Foreman."

"Foreman almost had to leave the ring on a stretcher. And this analogy is supposed to comfort me how?" My nails scraped across my freckled wrist, feeling itchy from more than just the angora.

"You'd get to date him." Mr. Conrad thrust his arm Brooks's direction as though he were Aries incarnate. "Not exactly a consolation prize."

"What does that mean?"

Brooks cupped his hand over his mouth as though he were whispering, "Pretty sure it means we don't swim in the same social pools and you'd be trading up."

What. The.

Exhaling through my nose, *slowly*, I unclenched my fists. Then I leveled him with a look. "Sure. Trading up in the douchecanoe category."

"Douchecanoe? Really?" Brooks chuckled. "Now *that's* a first."

"Sure it won't be a last," I muttered before turning toward Mr. Conrad. "I can't do this." I noted the pleading tone in my voice. "It isn't fair to ask this of us, and you're overestimating how many people would actually find the two of us dating interesting. It's immoral and shallow and no. Just no."

Mr. Conrad's mouth did the pursing thing again. "Then fine. He gets the job." He dusted off his hands as he reclaimed his seat.

"That's not fair," I exclaimed. "I've put in eight years here and my column gets the most reads every week."

"Not counting my freelance column," Brooks added, grinning at me.

Mr. Conrad shrugged. "That's life."

"Yeah"—Brooks leaned in, pale blue eyes gleaming —"it's not so romantic."

"Mr. Conrad, I can't do this. Truly, anyone else. *Anyone.*"

"What? Because you two have differing opinions? Hannah, everyone in this room knows what a thick skin a journalist has to develop in order to survive." Mr. Conrad gave me a look, a closer one, almost like he was starting to see through what was really going on.

"It's not like you can't say there isn't a certain kind of chemistry you feel for me." Brooks rubbed his mouth while I focused on not wanting to punch him in it.

"That's true. The two of you, based on the topics you write, have a sort of professional chemistry that readers will love to watch on screen."

My hands flattened on the table. "On screen?"

Mr. Conrad brushed his face, avoiding eye contact. "That's a component to these dates you two will go on. We'll have cameras going throughout, live streaming for the world to tune into."

My heart was thundering; the fastest it had pumped since that one night . . .

I would never again be able to think about that night without burning sage and creating a salt ring after.

"I'm a writer. I *write*. I don't do cameras and live streams. Uh-uh. No way." My head whipped again as I pulled at the collar of my sweater.

"You are a *journalist,* thereby opening yourself to the public eye and their scrutiny. If you wanted to be one of those anonymous writer types, you should have gone into regency romance."

My mouth opened but clamped right after, hating that he had a point.

"How long do you see this social experiment running?" Brooks asked.

"Six months," Mr. Conrad responded, the answer on the tip of his tongue.

"Six months?!" My eyes went round. "I thought you wanted to get the position filled as soon as possible." It hadn't been this hard to breathe since I was a kid and glued to my inhaler.

"I did." Mr. Conrad poured himself a cup of coffee from the tray that had been set out for the meeting. Alongside the coffee and hot water carafes was a stack of pastries I would have normally dove into by now. "Until this idea hit me one night last week."

My butt shifted in the chair again, as though I were sitting on needles instead of upholstery. "You expect me to date *him* for six months, all while being live-streamed for anyone on the planet to watch?"

Mr. Conrad blinked at me. "Isn't that what I just said?"

"When do we get started?" Brooks set down his empty cup and scrolled through the calendar on his phone. I couldn't help but sneak a peek, noticing his daily schedule was fuller than my monthly one.

"Right now." Mr. Conrad tapped his watch. "I've assigned a videographer to the project, and I'll have him swing by to meet you both today."

My head was pulsing, along with the rest of my malfunctioning organs. "Wait. He lives in San Francisco. How are we going to 'date' when he lives on the other side of the country?"

Brooks pulled up a contact in his phone and punched

in a text. "Thanks for the concern, sweetheart." From his voice, it was a term of anti-endearment. "But I'll have my real estate agent find me a temporary apartment here for the duration of our courtship. Although I might want to make sure there's a potential for ownership once I get the job."

The arrogance projecting off of him was nauseating. To think I'd spent the past thirty days staring at my phone, trying to will it to ring . . .

"Three months. I'll do it for three months."

I was as surprised by my acquiescence as they were, based on the looks on their faces.

Mr. Conrad tore off a piece of bear claw he'd swiped from the top of the pastry pile. "Three months isn't long enough for a person to fall in love. It wouldn't be fair to Brooks."

"Three months is plenty of time to fall in love with someone. If they're the right one." I smiled innocently between the two of them and waited.

"Three months is long enough to convince a person to *think* they're in love." Brooks set down his phone, twisting in his chair so he was facing me dead-on. "That's more than enough time for you to fall for me."

Revolt stirred inside me. Along with something else I was not as keen to assign a name to. Especially with the precarious situation I was about to be thrust into with him.

"I'd really rather it be six months," Mr. Conrad said. "To drag out the ratings as long as possible."

"Drag it out too long, and you'll lose your following. Three months is the perfect amount of time." Brooks glanced at Mr. Conrad. "Trust me."

Debating it for all of two seconds, Mr. Conrad nodded. "Three months it is."

I about snapped my poor pencil again. What the hell was this? Some kind of boys' club? That might have been the case in the news world an eon ago, but it was not the way the game was played now.

I was going to show him. Both of them. I was going to prove that I was right and that a woman could believe in romance and true love and still be a powerful force in her chosen career field.

It was open season on the douchecanoes of the world, and Brooks North was the first target in my crosshairs.

Shoving out of my chair, I tucked my pencil into my purse and started to leave the conference room. But not before snagging one of the cherry strudels from the pastry pile. For later. When my chocolate croissant wasn't staging a revolt and the reality of what I'd agreed to set in and I required the comfort that only a doughy, sugary edible could provide. "I've got an article on deadline. If there are any more details I need to be aware of, I can be reached by email."

Brooks rose from his chair, buttoning his jacket. For a moment, I thought he was doing so in the old-fashioned way a gentleman would rise whenever a woman in the room did. Then I reminded myself who I was dealing with.

The antithesis of the gentleman.

He clasped hands with Mr. Conrad as he headed for the door behind me. "Charles, always a pleasure."

"I have them preparing an office for you as we speak. As soon as it's ready, I'll let you know."

I froze with my hand on the doorknob. "He gets an

office? A freelancer?"

Space in Manhattan came at a premium, and private offices were more coveted than personal drivers these days. Not even I got an office.

"A cubicle will be fine. Wouldn't want anyone to get the impression I'm being given special favors." Brooks slid his phone into his pants pocket, moving closer in the kind of way that made my heart skip a beat too many given my disdain for the specimen creeping closer.

"You've got a long road ahead of you, Brooks. I don't envy you." Mr. Conrad wagged his finger between the two of us. "Might want to put a florist on speed dial and keep the ego in check. Don't let her articles and outlook on love fool you. Hannah doesn't let just any guy into her life."

A low-timbered chuckle vibrated in Brook's chest. "Oh no. I'm sure she's very discerning."

Biting my tongue, I threw open the door and left the conference room.

From cubicle city, Quinn's head peeked over the top of hers, a phone tucked to her ear. When she saw the look on my face, her smile fell.

"What's wrong?" she mouthed.

I answered with a quick shake of my head. This wasn't the time. I could tell her tonight with she stopped by my place for movie night. Right now, I needed to focus on not flinging my laptop through the nearest window.

When I reached my cubicle, I ducked inside, more collapsing than sitting into my chair. What had happened to my life? Running into One-Night Stand in my workplace was enough to ruffle a girl's feathers, but realizing I was going up against him for my dream job? And, no big deal, we were going to be the stars in some dating show, broadcast to the world, that ended with whoever proved their love theory being the winner of said dream job?

I knew now I wasn't dreaming. Only because my dreams were never this unbelievable.

"Question? What type of flowers do you like?"

I jolted so hard, the strudel went flying from my hand. Into the garbage can. Dieting by accident.

Trying to ignore the dark suit hovering beside my cubicle, I busied myself with powering up my laptop.

"Never mind. Your eyes say it all."

"If you read in my eyes that the only kind of flowers between the two of us will be the ones I drop on the grave of your career, then you'd be correct." My eyes narrowed at the computer screen.

"Boxers or briefs?"

He was looking for a reaction. I would give him one.

"I know you're just trying to get under my skin. It won't work." I wasn't looking at him, but I could feel his stare.

"I already got into your pants. I think I'm up to the task of getting into or under just about anything of yours."

My head whipped in his direction, checking to make sure no was passing by who might have heard that. "Fine. Briefs. Tight ones." My words were acid in verbal form. "Dusted with itching powder."

Brooks leaned into the wall of my cubicle, his gaze scanning the contents inside. When he spotted my embroidered frame picture that read, "You Can't Please Everyone. You're Not Pizza," he lifted his brow at me.

"I'll stick with what I wore last time. You seemed to

be a fan of ripping those off of me." He grinned like a demon as he turned to walk away.

Bursting up from my chair, my fists balled together, "I'm getting that job, you know that?"

One dark brow carved into his forehead before he disappeared from sight. "But first, you've got to get through me."

CHAPTER
Two

"**W**ould you please stop staring at me as if I'm about to start sobbing like Mrs. Bennett when she finds out Mr. Bingley isn't going to marry Jane?" I hissed at Quinn as she helped me pour butter over the six bowls of popcorn. I glanced into the living area to make sure no one was paying attention to us.

Not even. Mr. Darcy had just entered the scene in all his Firth goodness.

"I'm not staring. I'm aiming occasional glances. Concerned peeps." Quinn's eyes dodged me as soon as I looked at her.

She was staring at me, and had been ever since I'd dished all the dirty deets before lunch in the women's bathroom. She'd listed off the same dozen explanations I had in my head: that Brooks had an identical twin brother, that he'd been lobotomized, a poltergeist had infiltrated him, he was a secret government spy who had to act cold and callous in order to protect me from the Illuminati . . .

If only it was that easy to explain the sudden one-eighty from my dream man to the devil himself.

"I can't believe you're actually going to go through with it though. I mean, that's three months of your life that could seriously eff up the entire rest of your existence. You know this, right?" Quinn set the pan of melted butter aside once all of the bowls had been adequately drenched.

"He already screwed me. I'm not going to let him fuck me over too." Remembering what was playing in the background, I crossed myself. "Pardon my French, Mr. Darcy."

"I can't believe Conrad would even propose such a sexist, moronic idea. I mean, who does that? It's like settling a bet in the gladiator ring or something—let's see who proves their theories on love to secure one of the most prestigious positions at the *World Times*." Quinn pulled at her bra strap for the thousandth time that day; poor girl could not get used to an actual bra. "Actually, I still can't believe *you* agreed to something so sexist and moronic."

Grabbing a few bowls, I shuffled toward the cluster of women buttressed around the television. "I can't believe *he* agreed to it. The odds are stacked against him, not me. All I have to do is not fall for him over the course of three months and I get the job. I might as well start packing up my cubicle now."

Quinn sniffed, following me. "This is the very same guy who had you spending the past thirty days staring at your phone, waiting for him to call you. Are you sure it's going to be such a slam dunk?"

"That was before I discovered he is a Grade-A Ass-hole." I huffed. "The only way I could ever fall for that turd is if I got a brain transplant."

Quinn paused a few feet from the sofa four of our friends were squished together on. "I don't want to see you get hurt."

"I won't. I'm going to get even," I said. "By getting the job he has the audacity to think he can just slide into as a freelancer who pretty much owes his rise to Ms. Romance's column."

"Trying on a new look? Because humble wasn't working for you?"

"I'm just saying, he emerged out of nowhere a few months after my column took off. For a while, it felt like every article of his was playing devil's advocate to whatever article I'd recently published. He's an unoriginal, opportunist hack." I handed off the bowls before heading back to the kitchen for the rest. "I am not letting a slimeball like that skate into my dream job."

I caught Quinn shaking her head at Sybill when she opened her mouth, probably to ask which slimeball was being talked about this time. In this large of a group of single women knocking on thirty's cryptic door, the list wasn't short.

The others didn't know about the arrangement yet. Per Mr. Conrad's instructions, I wasn't supposed to tell anyone, but Quinn was the person to go to if I had something to get off of my chest. She guarded secrets like a Rottweiler protecting its turf.

"I want you to remember the way you're feeling right this minute when you two are out on a date and he's giving you that look while smelling all good and telling you how your eyes remind him of the ocean at sunset." Quinn nudged me as we grabbed the last of the popcorn. "Deal?"

I'd fallen for his act once—no way in hell was it happening twice. "Deal."

After handing out the last few bowls, I'd just plopped into the oversized chair with Riley to drown my worries in *Pride and Prejudice*, when the doorbell rang.

"You expecting anyone else?" Riley asked, glancing around the room as if checking to make sure everyone was accounted for.

"Nope," I responded, wiggling out of the chair. Most of us were old college friends, but a couple were fellow employees from the *World Times*. The original group had started out larger, but one by one, Misses had become Mrses and Thursday Night Chick Flick had turned into couple's yoga or staying in or whatever the happily married people of the world did.

When I checked the peephole, I exhaled.

"Who is it?" Quinn called from the living area.

"A male specimen," I answered as I debated opening the door.

"What? Really?" It sounded like Annie was half a note away from a shriek. "What are you waiting for? Let him in."

After unlocking the door, I swung it open. I felt the air stir behind me from the five heads that whipped toward the door.

"Oh. It's just Martin." Sybill's voice was the equivalent of a shrug. "Back to the movie. No offense, Martin!" she shouted a moment later, as an afterthought.

"None taken," Martin called into the apartment, switching the bag he was holding from one arm to the other. "How's it going, Hannah?"

I worked up a smile, reminding myself he was the neighbor who never called in a complaint when Thursday nights got out of hand. "I'm fine. Thanks." Uncomfortable silence. "How are you?"

Martin was a nice guy, but kinda odd. The odd that made one wonder if he led some kind of secret life that could have been as unexpected as being a Dom or more likely was being the president of the Ragdoll Cat association of the North-East.

"I was walking by Sucre on my way home and noticed they'd just put out a fresh batch of croissants. I picked up a dozen since I knew it was Thursday night." Martin pulled out a light pink box that had Sucre stamped across the top in elegant lettering.

Sucre was one of the more trendy, expensive patisseries in the city, and a dozen croissants from there had probably cost way more than my budget would have allowed without some creative scrimping for the rest of the month.

"Thank you. How thoughtful," I said as he handed me the box. "We'll put them to good use."

Martin smiled as he pushed his glasses farther up on his nose. He was a computer engineer at one of the bigger finance companies in Manhattan, and even though I guessed his salary could have warranted a much larger, more posh apartment on the Eastside, he stayed here with the rest of us paycheck-to-paycheckers.

"Anyway, I just wanted to drop those off. I didn't want to keep you from . . ." He listened to the dialogue in the background. "*Pride and Prejudice*." His brows lifted. "Didn't you all watch this a few weeks ago?"

"You can never watch *Pride and Prejudice* too much in a lifetime, Martin. Get with the program."

I didn't miss Quinn's sigh in response to Annie's proclamation.

"Do you want to join us? The more men exposed to Mr. Darcy's ways, the better off this world will be," Annie continued.

"I guarantee that if you model half of his ways, you can woo any woman you want," Sybill chimed in, not seeming to blink as she gazed at the television screen. "You're single, right, Martin?"

"Single." He lifted his left hand as though that were a confirmation. "The very epitome." Then he shifted his weight. "What about you, Hannah? Still a card-bearing member of the singles club?"

I was about to confirm my membership, albeit grudgingly, when Quinn gave a purposeful clearing of her throat. "Actually . . . I think my card's in the process of being suspended."

The skin between Martin's brows creased. "That sounds ambiguous."

"More like convoluted." I started to close the door, but Martin had never been good at taking a hint.

"Doesn't the guy who dropped off a dozen Sucre croissants at your doorstep get any more details than that?" He pulled at the collar of his shirt.

Soon enough, the world would know the details of my

"relationship." Not that it was pathetic at all that the first one I'd had in four years was of the contrived variety and set up with my arch enemy.

As I was about to bid Martin adieu, the elevator doors down the hall chimed open and a heap of flowers paraded out. Someone was carrying the ginormous arrangement, but they were only visible from the knees down. They must have been going to the brunette siren at the end of the hall. From the revolving door of deliveries she received, it was as though she were dating the entire defensive team for the Giants.

When the flowers stopped beside my door, I was prepared to point down the hall toward apartment twenty-five.

"Miss Arden?" Whoever was holding the arrangement panted. "I've got a delivery for you."

My mouth fell open. "Miss Arden as in Hannah Arden? Apartment nineteen?"

From the living room, I could tell they'd paused the movie and were tiptoeing closer.

"That's correct, ma'am. Can I carry them inside for you?" When the delivery boy moved inside, Martin got whacked by a few sprigs of greenery. "It's pretty heavy, so if you just point me where you want it, I'll get it situated."

I turned toward the interior of my apartment, experiencing a head-scratching moment. I didn't have a lot of experience with where in my apartment to place obscene bouquets of flowers.

My friends helped, waving at my small round dining table.

"Right over here will be great," I said, staying beside the young man to guide him in the right direction. It was a miracle he'd made it up here without running into or over something.

Five female whispering voices were not so quiet. Or discreet. I shot a warning glare back at them as I signed for the flowers.

"Here's the card to go with them." The boy pulled a small envelope from his pocket before ambling toward the door, shaking out his arms as he did. "The next time I make a delivery that size though, I'm going to request a dolly."

"Thanks," I mumbled, my fingers turning into thumbs as I struggled to pull the card from the envelope.

Since you didn't want to tell, I took a guess. Every flower you can find in a floral shop is included, so in a way, I picked your favorite. Well, all except for the rose, because even you in all your romance blindness aren't so cliché to favor a rose the best.

Yours (for the next three months at least)
BN

"Who are they from? What does it say?" Sybill moved closer, going between gaping at the flowers and card in my hand.

When my eyes connected with Quinn's, I saw she already knew. Her arms were crossed and she was fuming in silence, her eyes moving toward the flowers like she was trying to set them on fire.

Still perched in the doorway, Martin gave a whistle. "I don't want to imagine the payment plan that guy had to take out to buy those. I once ordered a Mother's Day bouquet for my mom back in Milwaukee, and it cost me over a hundred bucks and the flowers came out looking like a preschool class had assembled them." He shot me a smile before starting to close the door. "Doesn't look like that relationship is so convoluted after all, Hannah."

Standing there for another minute, blinking at the note while my friends pawed the flowers like they'd been plucked from the Garden of Eden, I warred with dueling emotions. One part of me was touched and moved by, quite frankly, the most elaborate gift I'd ever been given by a man who was not my father. The other part was outraged that he was pulling out shots like this so early in the game. He was in this to win it. He wanted that job; he wanted to prove to the world that love could be molded and formed the way a potter worked a lump of clay on a wheel.

He wanted to beat me.

But I wanted to beat him *more*. Crumpling the note, I tossed it in the general direction of the garbage can. It landed about five feet short.

"This is war."

CHAPTER
Three

Friday mornings I got into work early, usually so early Flour Power wasn't even open yet to let me snag my standard breakfast. I liked to get in and finish my article, which printed every Sunday, free of distractions and noise. I spent the first part of the week collecting research, brainstorming, and outlining, but I wrote the article on Friday. By that point, I was itching to get my thoughts down on paper, and the words flowed. Typically, I was done with the first draft before anyone else even made it into the office. I spent the rest of the morning editing and revising before handing it over to copy edit.

However, *this* morning, words were in short supply and creativity was coming up empty. Not even the fresh splash of inspiration from P&P last night had conjured up my writing muse. As I rubbed my eyes and contemplated taking a coffee break, the floor creaked behind me.

When I whipped around in my chair, I found the other early bird at work at six on a Friday morning. Brooks's eyes narrowed on my laptop screen.

"'Flowers are a relationship enhancer—not a relationship fixer. And they're not a substitute for bad behavior. Buy them because you want to make her happy, not because you've done something to make her sad.'" After reading the last part of my first paragraph, Brooks chuckled. "This wouldn't be inspired by a certain bouquet of flowers that showed up at your place, would it?"

I closed my laptop screen and scooted away from him. "Only a narcissist would assume that."

Another chuckle. God, I really hated that laugh. Two notes, deep in the chest, oozing condescension.

"I've got a deadline looming. Why don't you scurry off to your office hole and pretend you have something to do other than annoy me?"

"By the way. You're welcome. For the flowers." Brooks inspected my outfit, grinning when he noticed the broach pinned to my fuchsia cashmere cardigan. It was old-fashioned and kind of gaudy, but it had been my grandma's, and therefore, it was timeless.

When I refused to offer any kind of response, especially gratitude, he continued. "I declined the offer of the office in favor of a cubicle, remember? Didn't want anyone thinking I had any unfair advantages when I get the job."

I worked to unclench my fists. "Yet another thing a narcissist would say."

"Oo. Two for two." Brooks checked his watch; this one was different than yesterday's, but somehow looked even more expensive. "But sadly, not a new record for being called a narcissist twice this early in the morning."

I needed a distraction. A cup of coffee to sip from. A newspaper to skim through. A damn article to finish writing—except I didn't need King Chauvinist reading every syllable over my shoulder.

"Electing to sit in one of these cubicles like the rest of us minions? How big of you," I muttered.

"It's only for three months. I can manage." Brooks was lingering, holding a tray with a few coffee cups.

I waited for him to move on and let me get back to work.

Any time now . . .

"Any chance you'll be heading to that lowly cubicle of yours any time soon?" I asked when another minute ticked by with him standing there with that gorgeous smile and stare that somehow managed to make me violent.

"Since it appears I won't be receiving a thanks for that monstrosity I sent you last night . . ." He made it all of one and a half steps before stopping. "By the way, what time should I pick you up tonight?"

My head tipped. "Excuse me?"

"For our date." He was looking at me like I was missing something.

"*What* date?"

He rubbed his mouth. "Our first date."

"That's not happening tonight. I didn't agree to that. And you don't ask a girl on a date by asking what time you should pick her up." My arms crossed. "Only a narcissist would pose a date that way."

"Three times." Brooks checked his watch again. "Now that *is* a record."

"I'm sure it won't hold long."

46

"My god, woman. Can you cram any more pluck into that petite frame?"

Glancing down at myself, I wondered what petite frame he was talking about. My height was on the petite-ish side, but my frame was very un-petite.

"About that first date."

"Again. Not a way to ask a woman on one."

His phone buzzed in his pocket, but he didn't check it. "I already know where you live, so let's say I show up around nine?"

"Nine? That's a person's bedtime, not the ideal hour to head out for a date."

"A nine o'clock bedtime? I remember those days." He leaned in a little, his eyes flashing with amusement. "Then I graduated the first grade."

Grumbling, I twisted back around in my swivel chair, only to catch the ankle of my pantyhose on one of the wheels. I'd snagged them already, and it wasn't yet seven in the morning.

"Charles already informed the camera guy and scheduled the first official live feed for tonight. So if you want to go tell him you're not going to go through with it . . ." Brooks motioned down the hall toward Mr. Conrad's office. It was dark and empty this early, but it wouldn't stay that way.

"He already scheduled the first date?" Whipping open my laptop, I pulled up the *World Times'* homepage, and sure enough, the top article read *Ms. Romance vs Mr. Reality. Who will win the battle of love? Find out tonight at 9pm EST.*

My throat did that cotton thing again—a common re-action to Brooks's presence.

He nudged my shoulder with his hand. "It's a date."

My eyes narrowed on the screen. "It's a cheap trick."

"Are you saying I'm cheap? Or you are?" Brooks leaned back out of arm's reach, having at least some sur-vival instincts. "Because I recall the bar tab that night and you were *not* cheap. At all."

"You were the one who ordered the drinks. I didn't know what I was drinking."

"So you're saying you *are* cheap?" That amused tone of his was going to be responsible for me committing vio-lent acts. "That I should scratch the reservations I have at the five-star and go with a curb seating by the local hotdog vendor?"

My fingers drilled into my temples. I needed to stock up on Tylenol for the next three months. "I've got an arti-cle to write. Will you *please* leave me alone?"

"Do you want me to leave you alone before or after I drop off the coffee I got you?" Sliding one of the cups from the tray he was holding, he held it out.

When I examined the label, I found he'd ordered it exactly how I took my coffee. Extra cream and sugar. Not that that was an exceptionally unique order, but still, it wasn't exactly the single Manhattan woman preference of black coffee, no sugar or cream because lord forbid a calo-rie come in liquid form.

Instead of waiting for me to answer, he set the cup down beside my laptop. As he did, his eyes fell on one of the framed photos I had sprawled along my desk. "Mom and Dad?"

My eyes moved to the same photo, one taken almost twenty years ago, of them standing beside the small prop plane Dad had learned to fly in college. People said I looked like my mom, but I didn't see it. She was a rare beauty, vintage Hollywood like. They looked so happy—the kind a person didn't believe was real—but growing up with them for eight years of my life, I knew it was. Maybe not easily attainable or accessible, but achievable with the right life recipe.

"Yeah," I answered at last, looking away.

"Let me guess. High school sweethearts, married after graduation, go on evening walks together after dinner, still fall asleep in each other's arms—"

"You're not going away!" Pretty sure my voice just echoed down the hall, it was that loud.

"There's my exit cue." Brooks turned and left. But he didn't go far.

Only as far as the cubicle across from mine.

Rolling my neck, I took a breath. "What are you doing?"

"Scampering off to my cubicle. Isn't that what you wanted?" The wall between us made it hard to see more than the top of his head, but I could imagine the expression on his face based off his tone alone.

"And is there a reason your cube is directly across from mine?" My fingers hovered above my keyboard, writer's block burrowing deeper with every passing second.

"There's a reason for everything, Arden."

Packing up my things to find some quiet corner, I replied, "That doesn't mean that reason is a good one."

"See you tonight. And don't worry. I'm not expecting you to put out on the first date or anything." Brooks's voice followed me down the hallway. "Oh wait."

CHAPTER
Four

My article was in the copy-editor's hands with thirty-six seconds to spare before deadline. I'd never cut it so close before. I hated that I'd almost missed a deadline, and I hated even more that the article I'd written was lacking the usual Ms. Romance polish and finesse. It read more like a college humanities paper some frat guy had written twenty minutes before class, still burping up last night's tequila and Taquito fumes.

"When Flowers Aren't Romantic" would be published this Sunday, and as I left the office that night, I realized why the article was so flat—because I'd let my emotions cloud my judgment. I'd spent the week researching the correlation between decreased anxiety and being in a committed relationship, and I had thrown that all aside because some dick had mailed me flowers in a pathetic attempt to woo me to the dark side of coupling. The side that viewed love and romance as nothing more than scratching an itch that had been birthed from early man's need to procreate.

There was this big thing known as evolution. It happened. Over the course of thousands or millions of years, depending on what school of thought you subscribed to. Our ancestors might have thought of nothing but survival and procreation, but times had changed. Literally.

"Do you know where you guys are going tonight?" Quinn called from my closet, still digging through my clothes for what I should wear.

"Don't know. Don't care," I answered from the bathroom, where I'd already changed into my outfit for tonight's fake date.

When I walked back into my bedroom, Quinn stopped pawing through my heap of dresses. Her forehead creased as she inspected what I was wearing. "Okay, I've never even seen you in jeans, and the first time you decide to put a pair on is the same night you're going to a five-star restaurant with Brooks North?" The lines on Quinn's forehead carved deeper when she inspected the emblem on my T-shirt. "It's like you raided my closet or something."

My shoulders lifted beneath the worn heather-gray shirt. "You were my inspiration when I swung into Lady Sport at the mall earlier. I never knew I was a fan of the Mets until I put this on." I pulled on a pair of granny loafers to complete the look.

"Conrad is going to be pissed, Hannah. He's expecting a spectacle, and if you show up looking like a homeless person while Brooks is all dappered out in a suit that cost more than what I could get for selling one of my kidneys on the black market, you're going to hear about it."

"Exactly, he wants a spectacle." Flipping my head

upside down, I raked the red tangles into a ponytail. "I'm going to give him one. Both of them. The whole damn world."

Marching over to the mirror settled above my vanity, I checked my reflection. Makeup had been removed, hair was in a messy pony circa lazy, pajama Sunday, and I'd thrown on one of those sports bras Quinn was such a fan of. It didn't so much seem to make my boobs smaller as it turned two boobs into a uni-boob. Meh, that worked.

"What is the world going to think when they see Ms. Romance arrive to a first date in a pair of mom jeans?" Quinn asked.

"They're going to think exactly what I've been telling the world for years—love cannot be conjured, created, or coerced with just anyone. Brooks is not the one. Actually, it's hard to imagine a man like that could be anyone's 'the one.'" My nose curled as I considered it.

"Rewind forty-eight hours ago and I remember a starry-eyed girl who almost had me convinced her solo one-night-stand mystery man could have been 'the one.'"

"That's what too much gin and not enough consciousness will do to a person. I probably could have looked Mussolini's ghost in the eye that night and been convinced the specter was my one true love."

Quinn checked her sporty rubber watch after rehanging the fancy black dress I'd picked up a while ago. It still had the tags on it, thanks to my lack of actual formal events to wear it to and not wanting to look like a sausage in casing when I squirmed into it.

"It's almost nine." Quinn snagged my favorite cardigan from my closet and followed me.

"I hope he's late. That will be exactly the kind of first impression I need him to make to the world." I detoured into the kitchen to pour some orange juice. All this stress was making me thirsty, and it wasn't good for the immune system either.

"Is the camera guy going to meet you here or what?"

I poured Quinn a glass too, because we all needed our Vitamin C. "Don't know. Don't care."

"And you're really going to wear that for your debut to the planet?" Quinn took a sip of her juice.

"I really am. I don't care what the planet thinks of my wardrobe choice."

"And what if your 'one' is watching? Would you care then?" she asked.

"If my one is watching, he won't care what I wear. Because love is blind, in case you forgot." I shot her a tight smile and poured myself one more glass.

Quinn shot me a sideways look. "Well, let's hope it's far-sighted, at least."

My foot was tapping as I checked the time on my phone—five minutes to nine. If he'd do the douchy thing Brooks North excelled at and arrive a good thirty minutes late, that would be a great way to kick off the next three months with the odds in my favor. How many people could really get behind a guy who showed up late to a first date? Especially when it was being streamed across the planet?

Right then, my phone pinged with a text.

"Your chariot awaits."

Then, right after.

"That's what you people who believe in fairy tales

want to hear, right?"

My teeth ground together as I stuffed my phone into my purse and started for the door.

"He's here?" Quinn jogged after me, slipping the cardigan between my purse straps.

"Unfortunately."

"I'm a phone call away. Anytime you need a pep talk or to rant or cry or whatever, I'm your woman." Quinn unlocked the door and pulled it open for me. "I'll be waiting here for you when you get back so we can recap the night."

"And craft a voodoo doll with his likeness?"

Quinn waved as I headed for the elevator. "What do you think I've got planned for right now?"

"Don't forget that chin dimple. I'd like to stab him in it as many times as he smirks at me tonight."

She flagged a salute before I jumped onto the elevator. It wasn't until the doors closed that the moment caught up to me.

Holy crap.

I was about to go on a date with Brooks North, Mr. Reality, my first ever one-night-stand.

With the world watching.

The stakes being my dream job.

My hand curled around the rail in the elevator to keep me from wavering.

When the doors pinged open on the first floor, I almost ran into Jimmy, the cameraman.

"Shit. Sorry." He grabbed my arms to keep me steady. "I didn't expect you to come barreling out of there like a bull in Barcelona, you know?" He had this ridiculous-looking camera strapped to his forehead and was wearing an oversized Metallica shirt and a pair of black Converse that looked so worn they could have been first generation.

"My fault," I said, fixated on the small camera that would be the window into my private world for the next ninety days.

"I just wanted to prep you real quick before I start rolling." Jimmy tapped at the headpiece and continued. "I'll be with you and Brooks on the date the whole time, but we don't want it to feel like I'm there. It's just you and him and whatever chemistry will or won't be drudged up."

"Won't be," I interjected.

"I'll be panning between the two of you, but be natural. Don't talk to the camera or anything. Just pretend it's like any other date." He clapped like he was eager to get this thing started. "Any questions?"

"Any other date that's been set up with my arch nemesis, on camera, being streamed to the world?"

He clucked his tongue and shoved the door open.

The moment I saw the scene waiting for me curbside, expletives popped off in my mind. In part because Brooks had pulled out all the stops, and in part because my first date fantasies were before me, like he'd crept inside my brain and highlighted that section.

"And three . . . two . . . one . . ." Jimmy gave a thumbs-up after pressing a button on that camera of his.

A green light flashed on it while I stood there, frozen and gaping. Hello, World. Behind me, I heard a car door open, and that was enough to snap me out of my temporary paralysis.

"Miss Arden." Brooks's voice, all deep and slow, was the first to greet the world. Plus, he was on time for our date and dressed like cardiac arrest, holding open the door of an extremely nice sedan.

Like, so nice, I didn't recognize the make.

He'd probably already won the majority of viewers' hearts in the first few seconds of these few months. That didn't matter though, I reminded myself. In the end—the job, the truth—was decided by my heart.

And he was not winning that. Not in three months. Not if he had three lifetimes.

"Mr. North." I peaked my brow as I started for the car, feigning confidence.

Jimmy came up behind to get the side view as I approached. I didn't make eye contact with Brooks, despite his eyes drilling holes through me.

"You look beautiful," he said, that half smile detectable in his tone.

I pinched my Mets shirt before climbing into the backseat of the car. "Why thank you." Since the camera wasn't on me, I took the opportunity to roll my eyes.

There was a driver in the front seat, and Jimmy crawled into the passenger seat and twisted around so the camera was facing the back, while Brooks glided in beside me.

Three men, mostly strangers, a camera filming the whole thing, and the viewers of the world. My skin itched.

"The natural look suits you." His eyes met mine, a flash captured in the light orbs.

He was teasing me. That was obvious to yours truly, but it wouldn't be so obvious to the viewers who had yet to become acquainted with the man who'd written the SmartAss Almanac.

"The stiff, formal one suits you," I replied, working my most convincing smile into place.

The car pulled away from the curb, ducking into traffic seamlessly. I stared out the window, letting the blur of city lights calm me, but it was impossible to ignore the camera rolling from the front seat.

Worst case of stage fright ever.

"Where are we going?" I asked as I forced myself to turn my attention back inside the car.

"It's a surprise," Brooks said, his eyes on me like they were trained to drift nowhere else.

"I don't like surprises."

"Everyone likes surprises."

I shifted in my seat, unable to get comfortable on the plush leather. "People who haven't been surprised think they like surprises."

"What kind of surprise have you been disappointed by?" His voice was different, though his expression remained unchanged.

"All of them."

The car continued maneuvering in and out of traffic, while I kept my gaze aimed out the window. This was the single most uncomfortable position I'd ever been in, and I wasn't good at pretending.

"How was your day?" Brooks asked, clearly trying to keep some semblance of conversation rolling.

"Fine," I said, going with the standard teenage response.

A moment's pause; that damn camera focused on the

two of us in the backseat.

"Did you finish your article?"

The reminder of how hard it had been to write made my neck stiffen. "Finished."

"I finished mine too. It's titled, 'They Want Flowers. Except When They Don't.'" Brooks leaned over to nudge me. "You know, in case you want to check it out in this Sunday's paper."

My nails dug into my palms as I felt steam about to spout from my ears. He'd written his article in direct opposition to mine. What. A. Turd. Not that this was anything new for Mr. Reality. He'd been feeding off my feast for years, but his articles of differing opinions usually came a week or two after mine had been published, rather than printed in the same day's edition.

That was the last time I let him anywhere near my laptop when I was writing.

"I might skip it. In favor of a root canal without Novocain."

A puff of air burst out of his nose. Glad he found my every comment so amusing.

I found his every comment the very opposite of amusing.

"Tell me about your very first date." He read the confused look on my face. "The first date you ever went on with a boy. What did you do?"

He was really pulling at threads in an attempt to keep an audience captive. An actor on stage. A manipulator playing his game.

"We met at an arcade, where he used most of my quarters to play some car racing game, then I found him making out with a different girl by the soda machine." I looked him in the eye, blinking innocently. "It was the worst. But even as bad as that date was, I know it won't hold a candle to this one."

His initial reaction was surprise—I caught that in his eyes—but it was almost immediately concealed by that nauseating bravado. A slow, rolling chuckle. "From reading your articles, I didn't realize you had such a good sense of humor."

My fake smile fell. "I don't." Then I twisted around in my seat as much as I could and stay belted in, effectively putting my back to him.

After a silent minute, the tension became so stifling, the driver cracked his window an inch. Even Jimmy shifted in his seat.

Mercifully, the car edged to the curb right after that, sliding into a tight space in front of a restaurant I'd never been to. Only because it had a three-month waiting list and a meal cost almost as much as my annual subway pass.

When Brooks opened his door and slid out, I gaped at the people filing in and out of the glass doors. They were dressed as though they were attending dinner with foreign dignitaries—while I was dressed like I was about to play beer pong in the garage with the football team.

When my door opened, I found Brooks standing outside, his hand reaching toward me. Jimmy had come around the front of the car and was filming the exchange, causing several people to stop and watch.

I hadn't considered that yet. The attention we'd garner wherever we went, having some dude with a camera strapped to his forehead documenting our every move. Not to mention if this whole concept took off and droves of people tuned in the way Mr. Conrad was hoping/pleading/sacrificing for, our faces would become recognizable wherever we went. Privacy would be a once-upon-a-time luxury.

From out of nowhere, I felt the stirrings of a panic attack climbing to the surface.

Brooks must have noticed something was wrong, because his brows drew together. Then he angled himself so his back was blocking Jimmy's view, and he lowered his head. "Are you all right?"

Focus on your breath. In to ten. Out to ten.

It took me that long before I could manage a reply. "I'm okay," I whispered.

Brooks didn't move, angling yet again when Jimmy tried to get in the fray. "You don't look fine."

The measure of gratitude I felt for the arrogant ass shielding my near-miss from the world buffered what could have been a scathing response. "I'm about to go into the nicest restaurant in the city dressed like a scrub. Of course I don't look fine. I look homeless."

Could that have been a real smile? Not one of those summoned from some ulterior motive?

Looked convincing enough.

"I told you, if anyone can make the natural look work, it's you." Brooks extended his hand again, and before I knew what I was doing, I took it. Hell was freezing over as we spoke.

By the time I'd climbed out of the car, I'd cleared my face. Jimmy's jaw was tense with what I guessed was frustration, since Brooks had been intentionally blocking his shot. Brooks kept my hand in his as we started for the door, but I slid it out. He was still Enemy #1, despite that moment of mercy or weakness, whatever it was.

When he swung the door open for me, I was confident I experienced what it would have felt like to actually show up to school naked in real life instead of through the haze of a dream. It felt like every eye in that waiting area latched onto me, and even though I had clothes on, I felt naked. I might have caused less of a scene if I had arrived sans clothing.

Brooks acted like nothing was out of the ordinary, strolling up to the reception desk with an enviable degree of confidence while mine withered.

My wardrobe choice, which had seemed like a great idea an hour ago, was trending in the other direction.

Brooks was talking with the hostess, but it seemed like an in-depth conversation for a simple reservation. As I approached, I detected words like dress code and inflexible.

I went to tuck in my shirt . . . before I realized that wasn't the solution that would take me from sloppy to swanky.

Brooks whispered a few more things to the hostess before her shoulders relaxed and her face softened. "Amanda will show you to your table, Mr. North."

Brooks stepped aside, waving me past. I didn't miss the way he scanned the waiting area in such a way that stares diverted instantly.

"What did you say to her?" I whispered to him as we were led through the dining room. Perhaps the long way around it, but still, we were inside. "She went from looking like she was about to have security throw me out on my ass, to tossing petals along my path."

Brooks slid one hand into his pants pocket, channeling Rat Pack cool. "I told her you had one month to live and eating dinner here was your dying wish."

My mouth dropped open. "You did not tell her that."

"Of course I did. She wasn't going to let us eat here if I didn't come up with something creative."

"You lied."

"You showed up to a five-star restaurant dressed like a member of a Nirvana tribute band." He was fighting another smile. "Call us even."

"Excuse me? I don't dress for the purpose of impressing others. I don't care what everyone thinks about me."

"Obviously."

Before I could remark, we were at our table. I didn't miss how it was one of the tables tucked into the shadowy corners of the restaurant.

Brooks swept behind me to pull out my chair before I could do it myself. Jimmy caught the whole thing, of course. I could just imagine the dreamy sighs coming from the girls watching. Brooks North was hitting every play in the Gentlemen Handbook, but his intentions were anything but gallant.

"Should I grab another chair?" The hostess shot an unsure look at Jimmy, who was hovering at the table, panning between Brooks and me.

Jimmy shook his finger because I guess he couldn't exactly shake his head without causing a serious hiccup in production value.

"Well, okay. Have a nice dinner." Shooting one last

look our way, she bolted off.

"She didn't leave a menu. Do you think the server will bring one?" I checked the table to see if menus were tucked between the salt and pepper shakers, like the diners I frequented. No dice.

"They don't have menus here." Brooks glanced around as though he were as comfortable here as he was in his own living room. "Every night the chef puts together an eight-course menu, and that's what every guest is served. No choices. Everything's delicious. Simple."

Jimmy was crawling around the table, trying to find a good angle I guessed. It was unnerving. Along with everything else pertaining to this whole situation.

"But what if someone doesn't like what's being served?" I asked.

"What if *you* don't like what's being served?" Brooks cocked a dark brow at me. "Are you a picky eater, Miss Arden?"

My eyes circled the restaurant. "If by picky you mean eating snails, duck liver, and caviar, then yes, I am picky."

"You're a cheeseburger and fries kind of girl then?"

I folded my napkin into my lap. It was the nicest article of fabric I had on. "Along with fried chicken and mashed potatoes."

He smiled at that as a server approached the table, giving Jimmy the same look the hostess had. In his hands was a silver bucket and a couple of fancy glasses.

"The champagne you requested, sir." The server presented the label to Brooks who, after giving it a check, gave a wave, at which the server tore off the foil wrapper.

When he set the champagne glass in front of me, I

shook my head. "No, thank you. I won't be drinking any."

"This is good stuff. You're going to want to have some." Brooks motioned for the server to pour me a glass first.

I covered the glass with my hand. "I don't want any," I said slowly, more to Brooks than the server.

"Then what are you going to drink all night? Ice water?"

"Coffee." I removed my hand once the server had moved to pour into Brooks's glass. "It's late, and I need to stay alert."

His head tipped. "Alert?"

"Awake." I cleared my throat, although I knew I needed to stay both awake and alert around him. Sleep with me once and turn out to be a dick, shame on you. Sleep with me twice as a known leader of the dicks, shame on me. Or something like that.

"And ice water," I added as the server left to go find me a cup of coffee.

Brooks lifted his glass at me. "To uncovering the truth, once and for all."

I cheered with my empty glass, knowing exactly what truth would be uncovered when this whole thing was said and done.

"Did your real estate agent find you a temporary place yet?" I asked, putting an emphasis on a certain word.

His mouth quirked, his eyes expressing he knew how much I hated this whole arrangement. And that he didn't care. "My luggage's already moved in, and my agent assures me it can turn into a long-term contract if need be."

"Need won't be," I said, picking at my nails. Might as

well continue chronicling what not to do on a date.

He ignored my quip, his gaze wandering the restaurant aimlessly. "So. Ms. Romance. How does a person get into writing a weekly romance column?" He didn't miss the way my head tipped. "One of the most read columns published in the most prestigious paper in the country?"

Better. I had a sore spot where my writing was concerned—more specifically, the topic it addressed. My high-brow colleagues considered romance a tasteless topic meant for a writer who couldn't hack it in the real world of journalism. Covering wars and politics was what they were getting at.

"Well, let's see . . ." I lifted one of the five forks in front of me. It had been polished to such a high sheen, I could probably blind someone with it if I wanted. "She starts out as an avid reader early in life, moves on to reading the Sunday newspaper with her dad during breakfast in kindergarten, and after that becomes the editor in chief of her high school's newspaper. As a sophomore." I paused for emphasis. "From there, she gets accepted into five Ivy Leagues."

"How many did you apply to?"

"Five." The corner of my mouth quivered when that smirk of his was cracked by a seam of surprise. "She graduates magna cum laude from *the* top Ivy League in the nation, and pretty much has her choice of offers from any paper in the country." When the server arrived with my coffee, I leaned back into my seat. "That's how a person gets into writing a romance column."

For half a second, he was speechless. It wasn't a record, but it was something. "All of those . . . gold stars, and you *choose* to write a column on romance?" He watched me stir a heap of cream and sugar into my coffee. "Why?"

"Because it's what I like. And romance has gotten an unfair reputation. It's not fluff."

"No. It's fiction."

Keep cool. You're on camera. I'm not going to win anyone to my side by throwing coffee in the face of the door-opening, chair-sliding-out slice of man pie.

"So, Mr. Brooks? How does a person get into writing an anti-romance column?"

"It's not anti-romance. It's reality."

Jimmy shot us a thumbs-up, whatever that meant. We were communicating at least, though I wasn't sure how constructively.

"And it's *the* top read opinion column in the country, so I can't be alone in my thinking."

Another server appeared tableside, going from looking at me to Jimmy, and then repeating before managing to set down the plates he held. The first course, I presumed. Although what it consisted of, I couldn't say. I couldn't even take an educated guess.

"You peddle fairy tales and false hopes. I sell things the way they really are, with a side of snark." Brooks was already getting after the first course, failing to acknowledge the grenade about to go off across the table from him. "Happily ever after, soul mates, meant to be, 'til death do us part. The only place a person can find that kind of stuff is in the pages of a picture book, not in real life. And when a person gets that image in their head of the way relationships should be, they'll never be happy. No matter who they wind up with."

Inhale. Exhale. Repeat just to be safe. "By your argument, you could pair that guy with that girl"—my finger pointed between two individuals at different tables—"and they could be happy together just like that."

"Not just like that." He finished his bite, shaking his head. "But if that guy and that girl were both heterosexual, emotionally available, and willing to let go of the romance dribble society has infected us with, then yeah, it could happen. In the right situation."

"The right situation?" I took a sip of my coffee and was surprised to find it was pretty damn good. Not Flour Power good, but close enough for an honorable mention.

"One like this." Brooks waved between him and me. "Two single people giving each other a chance, being as objective about one another as possible." He glanced at me in a way that suggested he questioned just how objective I was about this setup. "Add time, patience, mutual respect and affection . . ." His shoulders moved beneath his dark jacket. "Then yeah, the odds are quite good any two people could fall in love. Love isn't some magic spell. It's a detailed recipe."

"So you *do* believe in love?"

Brooks set down his fork. "I believe in tolerance. And being able to tolerate certain people more than others. Love? We can just lump that in with the soul mate shit."

A clearing of a throat sounded beside us, followed by Jimmy slicing his finger across his throat.

"Stuff," Brook's edited. "Soul mate stuff."

"You aren't right, you know?"

He slid his plate aside, half finished. His eyes found mine. "And you can't prove me wrong either."

The remaining seven courses followed, and I managed to take a bite of all but one of them. Snails. I knew some kind of crustacean would make an appearance. The conversation stagnated after our romance versus reality feud, and Brooks seemed to relax as much as I did when the bill finally arrived.

I already had my card out, but when I went to slide mine in with his, he swung the envelope out of reach.

"It's on me," he said. "This is a first date."

"We're splitting the bill," I said, setting my credit card on the edge of the table. "And this is a *pretend* first date."

Beside us, Jimmy shifted. Damn that camera. It had been rolling for barely two hours and I already wanted to drive my butter knife through the lens.

"Pretend?" Brooks's head tipped. "This might be the most real first date ever. You know my thoughts on relationships, and I most certainly know yours. We don't have to go through a decade of dating, engagement, and marriage before the curtain falls and who and what we really are is revealed. You see the real me." He leaned slightly across the table toward me. "And I see the real you."

I glanced at my garish outfit, resisting the urge to roll my eyes at his shameless soliloquy. "And what is it exactly you think you see?"

Brooks had his credit card in the waiter's hand before I'd noticed him approaching. Brooks shot a smug look my way, one that read that I was cute for trying. "I see someone who's believed something for so long, it's become a part of her. The guiding part. Maybe even the defining part. To admit to herself it's all been a lie would be like confessing her whole life has been one, and that's too steep a price to pay. So you hold on to your belief, clinging to it as a child to a security blanket. You've gotten to a point in life where you're no longer determined to prove yourself right, but are terrified of the cost of being wrong." Brooks paused, unblinking. "That's who I see in front of me."

The waiter had just returned with the credit card slip to sign as I shoved out of my seat. "For your information, you can't see anyone, or anything, when you're blind, Mr. North."

I made a beeline for the exit, weaving in and out of tables of people who seemed as enthralled by my wardrobe choice as they did the man following me with a camera strapped to his head.

How dare Brooks say that, as though he could sum up the entirety of who I was in a handful of words after spending a few hours with me.

How dare Mr. Conrad set this whole thing into motion, as though he could slap two journalists together at his whim to star as actors in some reality soap opera.

By the time I charged through the door, I was fuming. The driver was waiting and when he saw me coming, he started to open the back door. I turned down the sidewalk in the opposite direction. I was done with this "date."

Jimmy was following me as I hailed the first available cab I saw. I could almost see him flying into the back of the cab with me, so I sprinted the last few feet toward it. As I did, one of my granny loafers fell off, but I didn't stop to collect it. When the driver asked me where I was head-

ing, I froze for a moment. The question took on a complicated meaning.

"Just. Go."

CHAPTER
Five

"**H**e does a lot of these triathlon thingys." Quinn's voice was muffled thanks to the pizza she was chewing on. After a Sunday's worth of digging up intel, a large supreme from Gianni's was in order.

"What's a triathlon?" I asked, glancing up from my laptop as I did my own research.

"It's one of those events where you swim, bike, and run."

My nose curled. "Why would anyone want to do that? It sounds like a form of torture."

"Not only does he do them, he's even done the long ones."

"What's a long one?" I asked, separating a fresh slice of pizza from the box.

Quinn's eyes narrowed at her own laptop screen. "Try a couple mile swim, over a hundred-mile bike ride, and then just top it all off, a marathon."

My mouth fell open. "That's an actual event that people *choose* to participate in?"

"Against all reason, yes."

My head shook. "Well that explains a lot. Anyone who volunteers for something like that has to be void of any and all joy."

Quinn reached for her bottle of water. "And from the places he's come in at these joyless people's sport, he's pretty damn good too."

"Of course he is. Brooks North is positively the most joyless person on the planet. It gives him an edge in the sport of masochists."

I clicked around his dad's architectural firm's website, based out in Arizona. From what I'd gathered, it was a successful corporation that employed hundreds of people with offices around the nation. Being the only child of Xander North, Brooks would have had an easy in with the millionaires' club if he'd followed in his dad's footsteps.

Yet instead, Brook's had gone to one of the top universities in the nation to major in journalism, a far cry from architecture. Going into freelance work straight out of school, he had to have known lean months. God knew I had, even as a staff writer straight out of school. Those last couple of days before paydays, I'd sustained on tap water and cup o' noodles.

"I bet he's a trust fund kid," I stated, scanning Xander's bio and portrait. There was a serious resemblance between him and his son. "His paychecks are probably less than he spends at the country club pro shop before tee time on Sundays."

Quinn shot me a look above her laptop. "I don't think so. From what I've been reading, his dad didn't make it big until Brooks was in high school, after the divorce. Brooks lived with his mom until he left for college, and I can't seem to dig up any photos of him and his dad following the divorce."

I wiped my greasy fingers on my napkin. "Falling out?"

"Looking that way. Especially when you see a picture of the new Mrs. North and discover they married less than six months after the divorce was final." Quinn spun her laptop around. A large picture took up most of the screen.

I blinked a few times. "He married someone the same age as his son pretty much." I scanned the photo of Mrs. Brooks—former name Heather Divine, according to the caption below the photo. "Who looks like she could have been the leading lady in a mess of adult films." Because really, who needed an augmented chest that large if it wasn't porn related?

"Correction." Quinn lifted her finger. "She *did* star in a handful of adult films."

"Of course she did." I blew out a breath.

"Okay, so here's a guy whose parents divorced when he was fifteen after Mom supported the family while Dad was going to school and building his career. Months after the divorce, Dad finally makes it big and marries a semi-retired porn star who was 'twenty-one.'" Quinn flipped the screen around and clicked to something else. "No wonder the guy's a little cynical when it comes to love."

"Cynical? He wrote an article titled 'Love is Dead. Get Over it Already.'"

Quinn bobbed her head from side to side. "I don't know a more extreme version of cynical. Sorry."

"I do," I muttered. "Brooks North."

"Oh no." Quinn set down her water. "I just found an obituary for Janice North." Her eyes scanned the screen. "His mom died two years ago. Of cancer."

That little ache in my chest was not supposed to be felt where Brooks was concerned.

"He doesn't have any siblings, doesn't seem to have a relationship with his dad anymore, and has never been married." Quinn frowned. "Talk about a lonely life."

"I'm sure he's not that lonely."

Quinn exhaled sharply. "Why? Just because he hooked up with you means he's hooking up with everyone else?"

"Pretty much."

Her shoulders fell. "Maybe he assumes the exact same thing about you."

"That was my first time ever doing something like that," I said, tossing an uneaten scrap of pizza crust at her.

I didn't come anywhere close to hitting her.

"And what if that was his first time doing something like that too? And here you are, making assumptions that he's scoring more than Shaq during his golden era."

I got back to my "research." "Who's Shaq?"

Quinn threw her head back. "I can't even."

"Come on, Quinn. Let's jump on the expressway back to reality. Brooks North is about as selective and monogamous as a bonobo. You've read his articles. He believes in the total opposite of what we do."

"Of what *you* do," she muttered, fingers clacking

75

against her keyboard.

My expression flattened as I wondered if I'd heard her right. Sliding my laptop aside, I directed a pointed look at the person I thought I knew inside and out. "What *I* do?" I said slowly, not missing her unwillingness to make eye contact. "But not what you do?"

She pretended to be enthralled by whatever was on her laptop screen. "Let's just say, for argument's sake, that maybe relationships aren't so cut and dry. You have some valid points . . . and so does he." With that, Quinn looked like she was bracing for me to toss a carton of eggs at her.

"He basically believes love is the byproduct of two individuals' needs to satisfy an innate sexual demand, as well as humanity's desire for companionship. Which translates to two people being drawn together because they want to hump and don't want to be alone." Just saying that put a bitter taste in my mouth.

Instead of looking like she was about to take back what she'd said, Quinn lifted her hands. "What's so wrong with that? *I* don't want to be alone forever. *I* want to have sex."

"But not with any random schmuck who puts the offer on the table," I argued, feeling the teensiest bit betrayed. "I mean, Brooks is the guy who penned a full two-thousand-word article about the scientific reasons men gravitate toward an hourglass figure."

Quinn raised her hand at me. "And when you look at it from an evolutionary perspective, that article made sense."

Yet again, she'd managed to render me speechless.

"I can't believe this. My best friend. Taking that Neanderthal's side."

"I'm not taking his side. All I'm saying is that I think you both have valid points . . . and not-so-valid ones." Quinn blew a chunk of hair out of her face. "What's so wrong with finding some middle ground and, I don't know, compromising?"

"What's wrong with that, friend, is that you can't compromise with a man who believes that marriage is a death sentence."

CHAPTER
Six

"**C**inderella, you dropped something the other night."

My abandoned granny loafer dropped at my feet Monday morning, making me flinch.

"Don't feel bad. I have that effect on a lot of women." Brooks winked at me from where he was leaning into the side of my cubicle, looking like he'd spent his weekend at a spa for deities.

"I'm sure you do. Right as they bolt the opposite direction." I got back to replying to emails, breathing through my mouth so I didn't have to smell his cologne. Which I was reminding myself smelled like sulfurous eggs.

"Kinda like what you did that night in Chicago? Oh wait . . ."

My fingers fumbled over the keys, successfully typing *shit* instead of *shot*. If that wasn't foreshadowing for the direction this Monday was taking . . .

"Could you just die of ego-poisoning already?" I muttered, deleting my typo.

"Ah, but then who would you get to spend your Friday nights with?" Brooks dropped a cup of coffee on my desk before going. All ten feet away to his own cubicle. "Your cats?"

"I don't have any cats, thank you very much."

His mouth worked as he settled into his chair. "You manage to drive them away too?"

Breathe. Just breathe. Don't let him drag you down to his level. "I've got work to do."

"So do I."

From out of nowhere, a chocolate croissant from Flour Power appeared on the ledge between our two cubicles. My traitor stomach grumbled, since I'd had to forgo my morning ritual thanks to staying up late last night digging up dirt on the man sitting across from me.

Brooks grinned across the divide at me. "Getting you to fall in love with me."

Chocolate croissant or not, I was about to send it toppling over his cube when a voice boomed through the entire office. "Arden! North! My office! Now!"

I'd only heard Mr. Conrad use that tone a few times, but never directed toward me.

Brooks grabbed his coffee and paused beside my cubicle. "Wonder what this could be about," he said, his face indicating he knew exactly what it was about.

"What did you do now?" After a brief internal debate, I grabbed the coffee he'd left for me. I could ignore who it was from if I tried really hard.

"I think this has more to do with what *you* did."

As we wove through the office, I felt like everyone was watching us. Quinn was on the phone, but even she was staring at us like we were marching toward our doom.

"I didn't do anything," I replied as we approached Mr. Conrad's office.

"Exactly. Dead fish have more panache than you did Friday night."

Before I could fire something back, Brooks stepped into the office where Mr. Conrad was pacing behind his desk, his face a rare shade of red.

"What the bloody hell was that?" he said before I'd moved past the threshold. "In what world, by whose definition, was that charade of a snoozer considered a date?"

Mr. Conrad didn't ask me to close the door, but I went ahead and sealed it anyway. Not that it mattered; everyone could probably hear each word being thundered in these four walls anyway.

"This is a totally new, dare I say wild concept, Charles." Brooks set his coffee down in order to roll up his sleeves. Hello, forearms. How nice to see you again. "Taking into consideration it was our first ever airing, the ratings were solid from what you told me."

Mr. Conrad snorted. "Sure, they started out solid. Until minute by dull minute, those numbers went down instead of up."

Brooks's head rolled. "We tried."

"No, *you* tried." Mr. Conrad stopped behind his chair and pointed a stubby finger my way. "She sabotaged—"

As I was preparing to defend myself, things took an unexpected turn. Brooks powered a few paces toward Mr. Conrad, leveling him with a look. "It was our first time.

Given everything, I'd say we did a damn decent job of selling the circus you dropped in our laps."

My head swiveled toward Brooks. I'd expected him to defend himself, but I hadn't been anticipating him defending me as well. There was truth in what Mr. Conrad was saying—I had done most everything I could to sabotage that setup of a date. Brooks had gone with the opposite, pulling out all the showy stops to really sell it.

Mr. Conrad exhaled, his gaze landing on me. "You stormed out on a date that was being filmed."

My arms crossed. "You wanted it to be believable."

Beside me, a rumble echoed in Brooks's chest.

"You dressed like you were going to hit the buffet line before playing bingo with your knitting club," Mr. Conrad continued, the red draining from his face. Slowly.

"And all of that—running out on a date, dressing like some teenage punk rocker—every bit of it was fresh and different from what viewers might have expected of this kind of dating experiment." Brooks ran his hand through his hair, moving his other hand animatedly. "The canned responses, the black dress, the fake laugh, the batting eyelashes . . . all of that was what viewers expected. *That's* boring. Hannah gave them a show they couldn't keep up with and, mark my word, you'll see your viewership jump on date two."

The way he said it, was more like Date Two, as though it were an event about to go down in the history annals.

For some reason, I couldn't think of anything to say. I was too shell-shocked by Mr. Conrad's sneak attack, and dumbfounded by Brooks seeming to be . . . *defending* me?

Mr. Conrad licked his lips. "You better be right about that, North, because so help me God, I will drop another couple into your spots if you don't start giving us a show actually worth tuning into."

My arms crossed a little tighter, wondering how a department head position had turned into this experiment in humiliation.

"Trust me. You'll have more viewers than you know what to do with," Brooks assured him.

"Good." Mr. Conrad nodded once. "You'll have a chance to prove that tonight."

My eyebrows pulled together. "Excuse me? What's going on tonight?"

"Date number two, that's what." Mr. Conrad cracked open his first can of diet soda of the day and gulped down half of it in one swig.

"It's a Monday night." I glanced at Brooks for back up, but he didn't notice.

Mr. Conrad finished the rest of his soda before dropping it in the garbage can. He plastered on a big smile. "The quest to prove love true or false never rests, Ms. Arden."

"Did you see his article?" I paused on the sidewalk to tuck the newspaper into my purse, managing not to drop my phone tucked between my ear and shoulder as I did.

"You mean the 'What Not to do on a First Date' article published in yesterday's paper?" From her voice, I could imagine Quinn's face. When I made an mm-hmm sound, she continued. "Didn't read it. Scanned the title and kept flipping."

"You know how I can tell when you're lying?" I glanced up ahead where I was supposed to be meeting him for Date Two, my posture falling. The Darwin Club couldn't have been any further from my scene. "Your voice gets all high and you start speaking a million words a minute."

On the other end, Quinn grumbled, "Okay. Fine. I read it. Every word was an insult to the English language." She paused to take a breath. "Happy now?"

"No. Considering he pretty much wrote it as a direct reflection of what happened on our first date."

"Wait. Your real first date or your fake first date?"

My head fell back. "Our fake one."

"I don't think it was directed at you specifically. I think it was more a newsflash to the world kind of thing. A PSA to all the single people on the planet." Quinn's voice was still high, and she was speaking like a turbo booster had been planted in her windpipe.

"I'm going to write my own article on what not to do on a first date. I'll need twice the word count to finish, but I'll show him exactly who needs pointers when it comes to dating." Checking the time, I saw I was already running late . . . which made me want to linger a few more minutes.

"That'll show him."

I leaned into the building behind me. "I gotta go. I've got a second date with an asshole at The Darwin Club."

"And here I was about to feel sorry for myself for spending tonight cuddled up to a box of Lucky Charms and NBA highlights." On cue, what sounded like cereal being poured into a bowl rattled on the other end. "Good luck. Give me a ring if you need moral, mental, or physical support."

"Thanks. I'll check in with you in the morning."

Adjusting my jacket, I started toward the club's entrance. I was wearing heels—not my typical granny wedge kind—and I felt like a noob circus performer trying to balance on stilts for the first time.

Eight on a Monday night, and a crowd had already gathered outside, if that was any indication of how popular this place was. It was where people came to be seen, which was just perfect for someone who preferred to navigate life free of attention-seeking behavior.

From the look on the face of the guy guarding the entrance, hell would have to freeze before he let me in, but then a familiar face waved at me from behind the velvet rope.

"Arden!" Jimmy shouted above the din.

The bouncer already had the rope unclipped, stepping aside to let me pass.

"Hey, wow, look at you." Jimmy waved at me. "You kind of went the opposite direction of Friday night."

My gaze followed his as I second-guessed my wardrobe selection. "Is that the Jimmy way of saying I look like a five-dollar hooker?"

Jimmy barked out a laugh, steering me aside before we moved through the doors. "Fifty-dollar one at least." That earned him an elbow into his side while he wrestled with the machinery on his head. "Okay, so Conrad wants us to start doing mini interviews before each date. Just a few questions I ask each of you before the date begins. So we get to hear, in your words, how things are progressing." Jimmy turned to me, adjusting my positioning just so. "I'll record each of your interviews, then dub them into the end of the date for viewers to check out."

"Did you already do Brooks's?"

"Done and done." Jimmy started counting down with his fingers, giving no other warning.

My eyes did the saucer-blinky thing before I composed myself as he gave the recording signal.

"Okay, Hannah, alias Ms. Romance, we're one date into this social experiment to prove which school of thought is correct when it comes to love and relationships." Jimmy was holding a cue card, his voice sounding exactly like he was reading from one. "Has your opinion, in any way, been changed after spending some time with Mr. Reality?"

I gave a little smile. "Not at all. If anything, it's only further secured my belief that love is very much a real, indisputable entity."

Jimmy shot a thumbs-up and continued with the next question. "Have your feelings for Brooks changed at all?"

I had to bite the inside of my cheek to keep from popping off the first words that came to mind. Mr. Conrad had come up with these questions, just as he'd come up with this idea. If I wanted to become a dating reality television star, I would have signed up for the *Bachelorette*.

Holding my tight smile, I replied, "I feel the same way about Brooks now as I did before."

Jimmy glanced at the notecard in his hands. "What's one quality you admire about Brooks?"

My face fell. I had not been expecting that kind of a question—saving the worst for last. As I chewed my response out on my lip, my mind vetoed every potential response. Taken from a stance of objectivity, Brooks had a laundry list of admirable qualities . . . but I was the last person to be in a position to view him from an objective standpoint.

Jimmy circled his hand as my silence continued. There I was, a person who made her living as a writer, and I couldn't come up with a few-word response to a basic question.

My armpits were damp by the time something rolled past my lips. "He's got nice forearms."

Jimmy covered his mouth to keep from laughing, while I sweltered under the humiliation of what I'd said. *He's got nice forearms?* Good god. I couldn't say anything right. Even if he did have the most notable forearms in existence, who listed that as quality they admired in another human being?

Oh yeah, that would be me, the woman driving her career into the ground.

Jimmy pressed the record button and the green light stopped flashing.

"That was a disaster." I wiped my palms on my dress. "Can you please ask me that third question again?"

"Sorry." Jimmy started for the entrance. "Conrad said no editing or re-shoots. He wants the answers to be unrehearsed and raw."

"I just said forearms on film." I had to rush to catch up to him, which made me teeter like a newborn horse

86

thanks to the heels I had on. "I can't let the world hear that."

"Why not? He does have beefy forearms." Jimmy swung the door open for me, the rumble of music breaking over my body as I stepped inside. "Don't give me that look. Just because I noticed they're solid doesn't mean I was the one to admit it to the planet."

I didn't miss how he was careful to move aside a couple extra feet, just out of arm's reach.

"Jimmy—"

"Sorry. I can't help you. I need this job, and I wouldn't put it past Conrad to fire my ass if he found out I did any editing." Jimmy held up his hands as we wandered inside. "Trust me, as far as answers you could have given, it wasn't that bad."

"No. It was worse," I mumbled.

The club was busy, though it wasn't one of those places that packed bodies in until it was standing room only. In the upscale venue, white leather furniture and tile floors glowed in the soft purple light. Men were dressed in suits, women in clingy dresses, and even the employees were dressed to the nines, although their suits and dresses were alabaster.

I felt so out of my element, Conrad might as well have suggested an underwater venue for our second date. "Is it just me, or might this place be the root of pretention?"

Jimmy made a clucking sound. "Not just you."

As I scanned the vast space for Brooks, a question popped into my head. "What did he say when you asked him that last question?"

Jimmy rubbed his mouth. "You're going to have to ask him."

"A hint?"

"Let's just say it was a legion deeper than your answer."

My shoulders fell, and as I was about to ask him to expand on that, Jimmy started doing his finger countdown. When he was down to one finger, that's when I saw Brooks. On the dance floor, drink in one hand, the bend of a brunette's waist in his other.

Where in the dating handbooks did it say it was okay to dance with a woman when you were supposed to be on date two with another woman? Beside me, I was aware of Jimmy panning between my face and Brooks out there, moving with a woman who made me look like a negative two.

Making sure I didn't let my annoyance show, I searched the room for an empty table. When I found one, I zipped straight to it, trying to ignore Brooks and his partner. It was a task I couldn't accomplish though. Especially when watching him move the way he was had me thinking back to that night his body had moved with mine.

A shockwave bolted down my spine as I tried to flush those memories from my mind. For someone as uptight and obnoxious as he was, the man could move. His mind was rigid, his body loose.

When I slid into the booth buttressed behind the small white table, I glanced everywhere but Brooks's direction. Jimmy shifted the camera between the dancing couple talking and laughing, and me, alone and waiting.

I swear this social experiment had turned into a quest

to make me look as pathetic as possible.

Brooks must have noticed Jimmy, because he managed to peel himself away from the femme fatale to grace us with his presence. Again, I tried to make my expression as unreadable as possible, because I didn't want him to know I cared who he did what with. Because I didn't.

"And here I was thinking I was being stood up." Brooks adjusted his jacket as he approached.

"Sorry I was late. But it looks like you found a way to pass the time." My gaze shifted to the brunette still standing there, attempting to will him back with the look in her eyes.

"What's that?" Brooks tapped his ear as he slid beside me. "Is that a note of jealousy I detect?"

"Ha," I huffed, scooting aside. "That's the note of indifference. You can dance with whomever you want. I couldn't care less."

The strange coloring and shadows in the room drew odd patterns across his face. "And what if I want to dance with you?"

Flip. Flop.

Went my stomach.

I excused it as indigestion from the chips and queso earlier. "I would say I don't dance."

He gave me a look that hinted at exactly what he was thinking. "And I would call bullshit."

Jimmy drew a finger across his neck, but I didn't think Brooks noticed. Or cared.

"Come on. It's a club. There's music. Dance with me." In his eyes, there was a challenge. "It wouldn't be the first time."

My back stiffened as I reminded myself yet again to keep my emotions off my face. "The first time was the last time."

Brooks didn't acknowledge my response, instead lifting his hand at a server scanning the club. "I ordered you a drink."

"And I told you I don't drink alcoholic beverages on a date."

"Which is exactly why I ordered you H20"—Brooks took the tall glass from the tray after the server stopped at our table—"with a twist of lime."

I eyed him suspiciously as he set the glass in front of me while the server set a tumbler of gin by him. Before taking a drink, I sniffed it, just to make sure it really was water.

"Why with lime? Most people do lemon in their water," I asked as I squeezed the green wedge into my drink.

"Too sour."

My forehead creased. "Limes are sour."

"No, limes are tart."

"There's a difference?"

Brooks took a sip of his drink, no longer staring at the lime wedge. "Sour is unbearable. Tart is irresistible."

I held his stare too long.

"So?" He took another sip of his drink, shifting closer. "Are you any closer to falling in love with me?"

Even Jimmy's eyes widened.

Stalling by taking a drink of water, I composed an answer appropriate given the question. "No. But it's not your fault you're an asshole, so don't be too hard on yourself."

Again, Jimmy sliced his finger across his neck, but it

was a half-hearted one, like he was resigned to the fact we weren't going to edit ourselves anytime soon.

"If you don't fall in love with me, it will have more to do with you being an invertible shrew than me being an insufferable ass." He nudged me, which made me flinch. "It wouldn't matter who the man was, Satan or Adonis, it would still take months to crack through that ironclad, man-hating crust."

I really should have been more disciplined when it came to my New Year's resolution of daily meditation. "I don't hate men."

Brooks's head fell back, a chuckle following. "Oh, that's right. You just expect us to be perfect all the time. If we're not, then you hate us."

Breathe in peace. Exhale anger. I thought that was what that meditation book had suggested. All three pages I'd gotten through.

"I do not hate men," I enunciated.

He leaned in as though to tell me a secret. "You hate me."

"I have a very good reason for hating you."

Brooks faked an injured expression. "What reason is that? Because from what I recall, you have *three* very good reasons for not hating me."

It took me a moment to realize what he was getting at. Those three reasons from the night I'd made the biggest mistake of my life.

"There are three million reasons for—"

"For you to love me," he interrupted.

My fingers wound tighter around my glass. "Oh, and by the way, you are an egotistical, arrogant, cocky—"

"Asshole?" Brooks clinked his glass against mine, the gleam in his eyes telling he was loving every second of this diatribe. "All the same meaning by the way. Kind of redundant for a journalist who knows the price of every word."

For a few minutes, I'd forgotten about Jimmy and the camera and the viewers. That changed when a server rolled up to our table and brought me back to reality.

"This is from the woman at the bar," she said as she set a drink in front of Brooks. It was wrong; he didn't drink whatever dark alcohol was swishing inside.

"Which one?" he asked, his eyes roaming the line of women sidled up to the bar as though he were ranking their screwability.

The server had already left when he asked his question, but I guessed it was more voiced to rile me up than to actually satisfy a curiosity.

"I know what you're doing," I said before faking a yawn.

Brooks turned toward me. "What am I doing?"

I ignored him, twirling my straw around in my water. "Trying to make me jealous in some desperate hope I'll throw myself at you when I learn how in demand you are. But let me tell you something—dating has nothing to do with supply and demand."

Brooks slid aside the fresh drink. "Of course it does. The fewer men, or women, that are available, the higher demand drives."

I couldn't help the face I made from his response. "Of course you would look at relationships like an Economics 101 class."

"That's because most everything in this life is tied to economics, whether it's energy prices or potential suitors." Brooks motioned at me. "And you *are* jealous. Or else you wouldn't have brought the topic up in the first place."

How that man had a talent for bringing my blood to an instant boil. I bit my tongue for a moment. "The only thing I'm jealous of is that those women aren't sitting beside you instead of me right now."

A noise emanated from his chest. "You know, they say disdain is veiled love in its infancy. Just like one day love becomes masked disdain." He lifted his gin glass as though he were making a toast. "It's the circle of life."

My body angled away from him as I calculated how many more minutes I'd have to stay for this to count as a date. "Who says that? Adam Smith the father of modern economics?"

Before Brooks could reply, my phone pinged with a text. A moment later, so did Brooks's. Mine was from Mr. Conrad and brief, albeit to the point. Judging from the sigh that came from Brooks, his message was identical to mine.

Slipping his phone into his pocket, he held out his hand. "What do you say about that dance?"

My hands remained folded in my lap. "I say it's a bad idea," I said as I stood, Conrad's message ringing in my ears like he'd screamed it instead.

"And plenty of bad ideas have been the catalyst for something great."

When I met him around the front of our table, I didn't miss the way he was staring at me. Appraising me in a way I hadn't felt in a while.

"I can't think of one real-life example of that being

true," I said, smoothing my hands down my dress.

"And I can think of endless ones. That's the difference between you and me. You think there's only one path to a destination, whereas I see hundreds. You see life as one big search to find it, while I say you already have."

His words were making my head hurt as we moved toward the dance floor, Jimmy floating in front of us. For a barbarian, Brooks had surprising depth. It was too bad that depth was totally flawed in its logic, but it showed he'd actually spent some time reflecting on life instead of gallivanting through it.

"Have I managed the impossible and potentially silenced *the* Ms. Romance?" Brooks's arm nudged mine.

Maybe he had. But he definitely did not need to know that.

My head tipped as I turned to face him. "I thought we were supposed to be dancing, not debating."

"I thought you could do both." As he turned toward me, one of his hands slipped around my waist.

The air felt as though it were being siphoned from my lungs.

"Could is different than should," I said, hearing my voice wobble a little when his other hand found its way around my back. "And if you don't want to get kneed in an area responsible for your future offspring, let's keep our debates to an arm's-length distance."

His chest rocked against mine from his muted chuckle. "Fair enough."

As Brooks stepped into me, his feet staggering between mine, I froze, feeling like I'd lost all function in my limbs. *Dance,* I instructed myself, but I couldn't recall the last time I'd danced. At least not when I wasn't locked in my bathroom while Prince got me through my morning routine.

Even in high school, the one formal dance I'd attended, I'd gone with friends, not a date. The way one moved with friends was totally different than the way one danced with a man.

Seeming to pick up on my uncertainty, Brooks moved in a bit closer, leading, slowly guiding my body. The music and other people faded away until all I could make out was the dull beat of the drums.

"Not a big dancer?" he said, quietly enough I guessed Jimmy's mic wouldn't have picked up on it.

"Dance or the dentist. It's a toss-up for which I'd rather do." My hands fumbled to find a place to drop. They wound up draped over his shoulders, which seemed like a reasonable place.

"You're keeping up just fine," he said as he managed to manipulate my body just enough I didn't look like I was having a seizure.

"Yeah right." I glanced over at Jimmy a few feet away. With all of the noise and bodies, it was unlikely he could pick up any of our conversation, but I still found myself lowering my voice.

Brooks's shoulders lifted beneath my hands. "Dancing is exactly like having sex, except you're vertical and have clothes on."

My spine tingled from the image that jumped into my head. "So you have a lot of experience having sex?"

"When it comes to experience, it's about quality, not quantity."

His hips swayed against mine, responsible for making my nails dig into his shirt harder than I'd intended. "So you've had quality sex?"

His blue eyes darkened a few shades. "What's your opinion on that? Given your personal experience."

My eyes cut to Jimmy. All of those people watching . . . even though they couldn't hear what we were saying, expressions could hint at the tenor of our conversation.

"Don't worry." Brooks's mouth lowered to my ear. "I'm not going to tell the world you fell into bed with some guy whose first name you didn't know. That would be too easy."

My knee actually twitched from holding back. "And don't worry, I'm not going to tell the world the size of your—"

"Wouldn't exactly hurt my case, would it?" His brows lifted as he smirked at me.

I exhaled, knowing arguing was pointless. In Brooks's case, his ego actually did match the appendage hanging between his legs.

My eyes met his, the challenge in them mirrored in Brooks's. "You're never going to prove your point, you know?"

Brooks pulled me closer abruptly, sending the slightest of shivers down my back. He didn't miss it. "I've already proven it." He grinned. "Now I just have to prove it to the world."

CHAPTER
Seven

Viewership was up. Date Two had lured in more viewers than even Conrad had hoped for so early on. He was practically frothing at the mouth waiting for what Date Three's numbers would garner.

I, on the other hand, was dreading it. Partly because of the number of viewers . . . and partly because of Brooks. At the end of our second date, Brooks offered to drive me home, but I'd decided to take a taxi instead. I needed to keep my time with him as minimal as possible because, as hard as it was to admit this to myself, I felt something stirring inside. The same stirrings I'd felt that night we spent together. I was certain it was nothing more than a carnal craving, but *any* urge where Mr. Reality was concerned had to be concealed until it was extinguished.

"If we head back now, you'll make it in time for rummy club," I said as I maneuvered Mrs. Norton's wheelchair on the path.

"Are you going to join us this time, honey?" Mrs. Norton tightened the knot on the scarf wound around her hair. The breeze had a bite to it today.

"I'm still recovering from my last loss playing with you card sharks, so probably not."

"When you live at an old folks' home and all you have is time on your hands, you become proficient at cards, puzzles, and gossip." She smiled back at me. "Quite the glamorous life."

"You staying warm enough?" I asked as a rush of wind cut across the park. She was bundled up in a big coat and a blanket cinched around her lap, but I remembered how my grandma could never seem to stay warm those last years of her life. I'd find her in a sweater and slippers on a July afternoon, nursing a cup of Earl Gray.

"The cold is worth the fresh air." Mrs. Norton inhaled, taking in the sights. "You're a darling for spending your Sundays with us, when there's only about a million other things a person your age could and *should* be doing."

I had to grit my jaw as we approached a hill. Even though it was slight and the path was paved, my endurance was on par with a couch potato's. "There's nowhere else I'd rather spend my Sundays than here."

"Even with your grandma having passed?"

"Especially now." We slowed to a snail's pace as my heart hammered from the exertion. I hated this damn hill. "You all remind me of her. Part of her still feels alive here."

"Your grandma would not shut up about you. She was so proud of you." Mrs. Norton glanced back at me, concern exaggerating her wrinkles. She was probably worried I was about to pass out and send us both rolling down the hill. "But she had every right to be proud of you. You turned into one of those people who're going to change the world, instead of the other type intent on destroying it." One of her hands dropped to her wheelchair wheel, trying to give me a little help up the hill. "Like that insufferable Mr. Reality. What a heinous human being, and now with you being forced to date him . . ." Mrs. Norton pffted, shaking her head. "If he ever crosses my path, I'm going to give him a piece of my mind. The piece I've held back for ninety-five years."

Pausing to catch my breath, I made sure to set the brakes on the wheelchair. Mrs. Norton hadn't survived a great depression, one world war, and giving birth to six children to see her last moments on this earth bouncing backward down a nature trail.

"If your grandma were around to hear about all of this . . . she'd have something to say about it. Something that would burn a sailor's ears."

Blowing my hair out of my face, I shoved my sweater sleeves up past my elbows. "If Grandma were still around, she'd remind me not to let anyone or anything get in the way of what I want. And I want that job as the head of the Life and Style department. If dating a heinous human being is attached to that, I can manage."

"Heinous human being, eh?" A new voice surprised me from behind. "I thought I detected my ears ringing a half mile back."

I placed the voice an instant before my head whipped around. My eyes bulged when I saw who was standing beside me, wearing nothing but a pair of shorts and running shoes.

"What . . . ?" I started, sounding as confused as I felt.

"What are you . . . ?" Words got stuck in my throat again.

"What am I doing here?" Brooks filled in, giving me a half smile when he caught me checking out his chest. "Stalking you. Obviously."

My eyebrows pulled together. "Why—"

"Hannah, that was a joke." He motioned at himself, yanking free the shirt dangling from his shorts to wipe his sweaty face. "I'm out for a run." He noted my expression. "You know, a run. Physical exertion. Heartrate elevated. That kind of thing?"

Mrs. Norton's head was whipping from him to me, almost gaping between us the way she did when one of her favorite soaps was on.

"I thought you found an apartment close to the office."

"I did." He shrugged as he moved on to wiping off his neck.

"That's got to be at least ten miles from here," I said.

Checking his watch, he tipped his hand. "More like eleven and a half. Sunday's are my long run days."

I must have been making a face, because it made him laugh. "A long run is a mile," I said.

"A mile's a warm-up."

Then I remembered some of the dirt Quinn and I had dug up on him last weekend. "You're one of those exercise fanatics, aren't you?"

"I'm one of those fanatics who like to stay healthy."

"You could run two miles and be healthy," I said.

"I like a challenge."

That was when Mrs. Norton reminded me of her presence with a clearing of her throat.

"Oh, sorry. Susan Norton, meet Brooks North." I motioned between them, not missing the way Mrs. Norton was looking at Brooks like he was an ice cream cone melting under the summer sun. "Brooks, meet Mrs. Norton."

"A pleasure." Brooks slipped on that rogue-ish smile as he held out his hand.

"Indeed." Mrs. Norton was blushing like a schoolgirl. Dear god, did this man's effect on women have no bounds, age included? "Why didn't you tell me your boyfriend was so easy on the eyes, Hannah?"

I shot her a look. Wasn't she the woman who'd just been bad-mouthing the "heinous human" I was forced to endure?

"Yeah, why didn't you tell her I was so good-looking?" Brooks crossed his arms, which made it all the more difficult to keep from staring at his chest.

"Because there's little, if not nothing, to tell." Undoing the wheelchair's brakes, I braced myself before attempting to heave Mrs. Norton the rest of the way up the hill.

"I already told you I can tell when you're lying."

"No, you've deluded yourself into believing I'm lying whenever I say something that doesn't correspond with your worldview that you are flawless."

Brooks fell in beside me, looking like he was ready to jump in if I gave myself a heart attack. "I've got a flaw or two," he said, pulling his shirt over his head. Mrs. Norton expressed what she thought about that in a long sigh. "But those have nothing to do with my looks. Or my forearms, isn't that right?"

My face heated when I realized he'd heard my humiliating answer from the other night. "Your degree of arrogance is repugnant."

"It's not arrogance if it's the truth, honey." Mrs. Norton waved her finger at me, shooting another smile in Brooks's direction.

Can you say traitor?

"Would you please let me help you?" Brooks actually butted in, grabbing one of the wheelchair handles I was holding. "It looks like that vein in your forehead's about to burst."

"If it bursts, it's because you are annoying me with your presence, not because of the physical exertion." I swatted his hand away and kept pushing at a tick above a snail's pace.

"Why don't you let him help? You sound like you're going to have an asthma attack back there." Mrs. Norton twisted around in her chair, her eyes filled with concern. "Tell me you have your inhaler."

"Wait. You've got asthma?" Brooks paused before rushing back up beside me. "Then I'm not asking anymore. I'm telling." His shoulder bumped into mine as he tried maneuvering me out of the way. "Step aside."

The surge of anger I felt over being told what to do gave me a fresh burst of energy. "No. You don't get to 'tell' me anything." I pushed against him, my hold on the handles edging into death grip territory. "And I walk this hill all the time."

"Pushing a wheelchair?"

"Yes," I grunted as the top of the hill came into view.

"Last time she did it, she gave herself an attack," Mrs.

Norton added.

"It wasn't an attack." I fired another glare at Brooks when he looked like he was about to step in again. "It was an episode."

"One that took you ten minutes of lying on the ground to get over." Mrs. Norton waved at a patch of grass as if that was the very place I'd collapsed last month during my "episode."

When we finally crested the top of the hill, I exhaled with relief, feeling as though I'd just won Olympic Gold.

"You don't look so good." Brooks studied me as I kept walking down the level pathway.

"Coming from you? I'll take that as a compliment." I kept my gaze forward and tried to ignore the way my limbs felt like putty and my chest was tightening in a familiar way.

"No, really. You're white as a sheet." When Brooks's face lowered to mine, there was actual concern on his face. Not the manufactured kind.

"I'm fine." I wheezed, eyeing the bench up ahead and wondering if I could make it.

"Of course you're fine. If by that you mean you are not at all fine." Brooks didn't play around this time when he moved in behind Mrs. Norton's wheelchair, wrangling me aside in one lithe movement. "Can you make it to that bench?"

"Of course I can," I answered, though I wasn't half as certain as I sounded.

"You have your inhaler, right?" Mrs. Norton eyed my purse slung across my body.

I nodded because I'd sound like a dying frog if I

opened my mouth to answer.

"Hannah, for Christ's sakes. I'm going to throw you over my shoulder and run to the first emergency room I can find if you don't sit down and catch your breath." Brooks stopped pushing Mrs. Norton, eyeing the patch of grass next to us.

"The camera isn't rolling. You don't have to pretend you care." I managed to make it to the bench and pawed through my purse once I collapsed into it.

"I'm not pretending." He fixed the brakes on the wheelchair and crouched beside me still struggling to un-earth my inhaler. He stuck one hand in and pulled it right out. When I grabbed it from him and took my first puff, he let out a long exhale. "If you die, I get the job, and then I'll always be known as the guy who got the job by default. When I get it, I want to be because I earned that title."

As I leaned forward and continued to focus on my breathing, I bumped my knee against his. "*If.* Not when."

"You poor thing." Mrs. Norton rubbed my back. "Let's get you inside once you feel ready to move."

"I'm fine," I said, shoving off the bench, embarrassed Brooks had witnessed what he had. I didn't want him to know I possessed any sort of weakness.

"Give yourself a minute," Brooks said, rising with me.

"I don't need a minute. I'm *fine.*" No sooner had the words snapped out of my mouth than my legs crumbled beneath me.

Brooks's arms flew around me before I made it far. "Why do you make it your mission to do the opposite of what I ask?" He adjusted his hold around me right before heaving me into his arms entirely.

I gasped with surprise. I wasn't used to being thrown into a man's arms against my will—especially a man moving with the kind of ease that suggested I was packed with feathers. "Put. Me. Down."

Brooks ignored my death stare, glancing at Mrs. Norton. "Will you be okay here for a few minutes on your own while I take her inside?" He tipped his head at Glendale Assisted Living facility.

"No, she will not be okay. And neither will you if you don't set me down before you finish taking that breath." I wiggled against him, but all that did was cause his arms to tighten.

Mrs. Norton waved us off. "I'll be just fine. I'd love a few more minutes of fresh air anyway. Take your time, handsome." The way she winked at him made me wonder if there was some kind of hidden message behind it. "Just inside the doors, there's a sitting area, or you're welcome to my room if you'd like some privacy."

"We don't want privacy," I said as Mrs. Norton dug around in her purse for her keys.

"I'll be right back," Brooks told her before turning up the walkway that led to Glendale's entrance.

"Put me down," I repeated, trying on my most no-nonsense look.

"No."

My nostrils flared. "*Please* put me down."

His pace picked up. "No."

My hand whacked his chest. "You're a cretin."

"And you're no princess either."

An annoyed grumble spilled from me as we

whooshed through the sliding glass doors. Under other circumstances, being carried by a strapping young man wouldn't have been so infuriating. In fact, this was Ms. Romance gold if I could have traded out the man, but instead, I found myself mired in Ms. Romance sludge.

Thankfully, the sitting area was empty and, other than a few residents staggered around the hallway waiting for afternoon coffee service, no one was present to witness the spectacle.

"Would you put me down already?" My voice echoed in the empty room as I slugged him one more time in the chest.

"Fine," he snapped, dropping me.

Onto the couch. Whether or not he knew it was there, I couldn't say.

Not saying anything else, he marched out of the building, presumably to retrieve Mrs. Norton. That gave me a few minutes to collect myself and decide how I would greet him when he reappeared: with gratitude or contempt.

"Miss me?" His voice echoed through the room a few minutes later.

"Like a leech pried off of my ass," I muttered.

"A blood-sucking hermaphrodite." He rested one hand over his chest. "Again, one of the nicer things I've been called."

"Where's Mrs. Norton?" I asked, tucking my inhaler in my purse.

"Making her move on the single males club circled around the coffee station." He hitched his thumb over his shoulder where the lobby was. "What are you doing hanging around with people four times your age anyways?"

The high from my attack was draining away, leaving me tired and woozy. "My grandma lived here for about five years before she died last year. I can't seem to kick the habit of hanging around a happening place like this."

Brooks slowed his pace as he approached me. "You two were close?"

"She raised me from the time I was eight, so yeah, we were close." My throat moved as I wondered why I was telling him this.

Brooks settled onto the edge of the chair beside me. "You didn't live with your parents?"

"I did." My tongue worked into my cheek. "Until they passed." When I chanced a look at Brooks, I found nothing distinguishable on his face. No pity. No judgment. Just . . . recognition. "After that, I moved in with Grandma until I left for college."

Brooks was quiet for a moment, but it was a relief to have someone not feel the need to fill the silence when they found out about my parents.

"How did they die?" he asked.

"In an airplane crash," I said, surprised he'd been so direct. People never asked *me* how they died; they found out through a friend. His honesty was as refreshing as it was unexpected. "Dad had his private pilot's license, and one of their favorite things to do was spend an afternoon flying. They flew hundreds of times, without so much as an emergency landing, until that day . . ." Images of my parents flooded my mind. "They died doing what they loved, together."

Brooks shifted, the scent of sweat and man hitting me. "That's why you believe what you do, isn't it? Because of them?"

"I suppose so." I stared at my clasped hands. "Because they were a real life example. They proved that love and commitment and romance are real. I believe what I do —I write what I do—because of them."

Had that inhaler come laced with truth serum or something? I didn't usually open up like that, and certainly not to a brigand like Brooks.

"I believe what I do because of my parents as well. At least part of it." The chair whined as he moved, his voice sounding a key deeper. "My parents married straight out of high school, and I came along a few years later. Dad was working construction while Mom stayed home, until he got the grand idea that he was going to go to college and make something of himself. Mom supported the idea . . . by working two jobs and still keeping up with the house-hold chores while he 'chased his dream.'" From the corner of my eyes, I could see him staring out the window, his expression vacant. "Once he graduated, Mom exchanged two jobs for three so he could start his own architectural company. It was years before he was able to turn a profit, and a few more before it was a considerable one. A few months after finally 'arriving,' he served her with divorce papers as a thank you for years of hard work and commit-ment." Brooks cracked his neck, his posture stiff. "Even after the divorce, she never gave up hope that he'd come back to her. That they were 'soul mates.' She never stopped believing that, even when he married a woman half her age who looked like she'd been sprung from a life-size Barbie box."

I found myself scooting down the couch toward him, unsure why. My body seemed to be making the decision for me.

"Mom was diagnosed with cancer a couple years after the divorce. She died still loving the man who likely hadn't spared a single thought for her since walking out." Brooks shook his head, still staring out the window. "That's the tragedy. That's why I refuse to lie to my readers about what is and isn't real. A harsh truth is more merciful than a pretty lie."

My teeth worked at my lip, not sure if I should say something or stay quiet. "You don't believe your mom actually loved your dad?" I asked softly, scooting to the very end of the couch.

Brooks didn't seem to notice I'd closed the gap between us. "Mom loved the idea of him. The version of him she'd built up in her head. She didn't love the real him, because there was nothing there to love."

When I found my hand moving toward his, I pulled it back. "Just because it didn't work out for your parents doesn't mean it isn't real."

"Real?" Brooks snorted. "Love is about as real as my stepmom's lips."

I covered my mouth to hide my smile. "I guess that's what we're going to prove, one way or another."

"More than half of marriages that vow 'til death do us part wind up in divorce. You've got your work cut out for you."

"Yet when polled, three-quarters of the population believe in true love." I shrugged. "You're the one who's got work to do."

CHAPTER
Eight

"**Y**our life is going down in the annals of weird." Quinn shook her head as we moved up in line at our morning haunt, both of us eyeing the stock of chocolate croissants.

"It's not that weird," I replied, second-guessing myself for detailing yesterday's events to her.

"You spent your morning chilling with people who were alive when Babe Ruth was playing, proceeded to have an asthma attack pushing a ninety-pound woman up a five-percent-grade hill, had to be carried to safety by the —"

My hand flew up. "I did *not* need to be carried anywhere."

"Fine. You were *swept off your feet* by the very guy you're pretending to date on live television for some job you're both vying for. Then you wind up heaving a dizzying amount of dirty laundry on each other in the brunch room of an old folks' home." Quinn shared a wince with me when the lady in front of us ordered a couple of our standard breakfast. Nothing like kicking off a Monday with a boring old regular croissant instead of one stuffed with chocolate goodness. "Then to finish off your Sabbath, you head to a Renaissance festival with Martin, your neighbor one floor up."

I rubbed my temples as I remembered last night. "I felt bad. The girl he was supposed to go with canceled at the last minute."

"You can feel bad for him without sacrificing yourself on the altar of knights and damsels, you know."

The moment we made it to the counter, a familiar face emerged from the kitchen.

"Justin the Jacked is looking extra jacked this fine Monday morning," I whispered to Quinn, who had been hit with a sudden attack of attention deficit disorder. She was looking everywhere but forward as she pulled out her phone and punched random apps.

"Good morning, ladies." Justin beamed that glorious smile of his, dimples and all. "The usual?"

I waited for Quinn to say something, but she'd been struck with an acute case of mute as well.

"One of these days we're going to surprise you and order something different," I said, tapping the case. "But that day is not this one."

Justin held that glorious smile as he reached for a set of tongs to bag our breakfasts. With his attention on the pastry case, I elbowed Quinn.

"Ow. What?" she hissed, rubbing her arm.

"Say something," I whispered.

"No."

"Why not?"

"Because I don't want to."

"You want to have his children. You might have to actually open your mouth and say something to him."

Quinn's mouth fell open as she checked the line behind us. If anyone was listening to our conversation, they were doing a good job pretending to be otherwise occupied.

"Okay, two chocolate croissants, two coffees. Anything else?" The way he said it, I could just pick up on the undercurrent. Quinn was immune to it though.

As I dug in my wallet to pay—Quinn and I traded off on footing the breakfast tab—I tried to think of any excuse I could to stall. "How was that basketball game you had tickets to?"

Justin seemed to be making change at an especially slow pace. "It was good. The Knicks won."

"Did you ever find anyone to take that extra ticket off of your hands?" I made it a point to nudge Quinn as I asked him.

"Nah. I just went by myself."

As he handed me my change, I went with tapping my foot against Quinn's. She wasn't taking any of the hints I was throwing at her.

"That's too bad. I bet that was boring."

One of Justin's massive shoulders lifted. "It was okay. I'm used to it," he said as he handed us our coffee cups. "I think I'm going to get the hook-up on a couple more tickets for a game later this month. You know, in case you hear of anyone else who likes the Knicks." He might have been talking to me, but he was looking at Quinn.

Who was staring at her feet like her sneakers were the Mona Lisa in shoe form.

"I'll keep my ears peeled. I'm sure I can find some-one." I lingered at the counter, blinking at Quinn, who had a barely visible blush bleeding through that bronze skin of hers.

She'd gone from awkward to a stage-ten disaster around Justin. At least she used to be able to carry on something of a conversation with him, but now, she couldn't even look in his direction, let alone open her mouth to say something. I didn't miss the annoyed looks we received as we navigated down the line of customers toward the door—like the pastries, Justin was a hot com-modity.

"What was that back there?" I asked Quinn after we started down the sidewalk.

She let out a rush of air as though she'd been holding her breath. "I don't know. I just froze. I couldn't think of a single thing to say to him."

"Hello or good morning are nice options."

"Ugh, I know. That was pathetic. He probably thinks I'm some kind of freakazoid now." Quinn's posture slack-ened. "I'm going to die alone."

"Would you stop that? You are not going to die alone. You just need to figure out a way to read between the lines when a guy like Justin is asking you out. Also, speaking is something you might want to work on."

She grimaced as she looked to be reliving the play-by-play in the café. "That's easy for you to say, Ms. Ro-mance. Especially when you've never come close to feel-ing so flustered over a guy because you have yet to find one perfect enough to fit your standards." Quinn's eyes got big after that, immediately followed by her hand covering her mouth.

Swallowing my bite of croissant, I blinked at her. "Excuse me?"

"Just forget it, Hannah. My brain's only firing at ten percent this morning."

"No, please. Explain." I took a sip of my coffee and braced myself. Quinn was known for her honesty—the brutal variety.

She let out a heavy sigh. "All I'm saying is that it's easy to see what everyone else is doing wrong when it comes to the cut-throat world of dating, but for all the advice you give, you never actually take any of it." Quinn glanced my way, and whatever she saw didn't stop her from continuing. "You seem to hold all potential suitors to this level of perfection no human could achieve, and I'm not sure if it's because you're afraid of being hurt, scared of opening yourself up to someone, or actually believe someone with perfect flowing in his veins is waiting for you. You're a romance professional without any real life experience."

My feet had stopped moving a few steps back. "Next time you're being honest with me, try to keep in mind I have these delicate things called emotions." I caught back up to her and chugged a solid drink of coffee. "And I'm not scared or biding my time for perfection. I'm just waiting for that feeling, you know? The one that can't be explained, but we know it when we feel it."

Quinn plucked her coat collar up around her neck. "What feeling is that?"

"The *feeling*," I said, sweeping my arm in front of me.

"In quantitative terms please."

"You can't quantify feelings," I said around a groan. "Especially *the* feeling."

"If you can't measure it, then it isn't real."

My eyes rolled. "Says the sports writer who only deals in scores and stats."

"But, really. What if this feeling you and the rest of your cronies are waiting for isn't real? What if it's more of an instinct that, over time, grows into something bigger?"

I tucked what was left of my croissant into my purse because my appetite was waning. "You sound just like him."

"Who?"

"Brooks. Public Enemy Number One."

Quinn waved her finger at me. "No, he's Hannah Arden Enemy Number One."

"Whose best friend are you? His or mine?" I slid away from her, but she gave me a look and scooted back up to me.

"Yours. And as your best friend, I have your best interests in mind and would rather see you happy with a great guy who possesses some flaws then holding out for some perfect dude who isn't out there."

My heels clacked against the pavement as I finished speeding the last block toward the *World Times*. Why did it feel like the whole world was turning on me? Brooks and his philosophies were poisoning the population.

"Thank you for your concern, I know it comes from a good place. But I'm not sure I should take relationship advice from someone whose response to being asked on a date by her dream guy is that she'll let him know if she hears of anyone who might be interested."

Quinn tipped her head at me. "And yet you haven't had a relationship that lasted longer than six months and you feel qualified to write an advice column on romance and relationships."

"Okay, okay," I groaned, lifting my hand at her face. "Enough tough love for one morning."

She made a zipping motion across her lips.

"It's you, isn't it?" A woman walking the opposite direction as us stopped, waving her finger at me.

My readers didn't recognize me as I never published my articles with a photo of myself. This was the first time I'd ever been stopped because of my column. "That's right. I'm Ms. Romance."

The woman shook her head. "You're that woman who's been set up with that hottie in the online dating social experiment."

Quinn covered her mouth when she laughed.

I frowned. "In the flesh and blood."

"Oh, honey. That last date at the club?" She rested her leather-gloved hand on my arm. "I had to go find the box fan to keep from overheating."

My forehead creased.

"The chemistry between you two." She made a sound people make when enjoying a good meal. "I had to turn that old fan all the way up."

When Quinn got out her phone, no doubt to record this display, I swiped it out of her hands. "That wasn't chemistry. That was me experiencing copious amounts of physical and psychological trauma having to be so close to that man."

Her hand wasn't moving. It stayed planted on my arm, making me all kinds of uncomfortable. "Well, where do I sign up for that kind of trauma? That's just the kind I need in my life."

I glanced at Quinn, hinting that I was drowning and needed a life ring, but she was no help. Working up a smile, I stepped aside and moved toward the building doors. "So nice of you to say hi. Thanks for your support."

"Oh no, honey. I'm supporting him." She folded her fur coat tighter around her when the breeze picked up. "I've seen enough of life and relationships to accept that love is a bunch of malarkey doused in perfume. It might smell nice, but it's still just a load of shit."

My mouth fell open as Quinn's arm rung through mine and she steered me through the doors. I found myself digging for the remnants of my croissant, needing something to comfort me.

"Can you believe her?" I said, punching the up button at the elevators. "Oh wait, never mind. Of course you can believe you. You're on the same side."

She gave me a look that suggested I was acting like a child. Which might have been warranted to some degree. "I'm not on her side. I'm not on his side. I'm on *your* side because we are the kind of friends that would bleed for each other. However"—she ignored my little huff—"I don't think either of you have it totally right. When it comes to all of that love stuff, I think you both have your points and the truth lies somewhere in the middle."

One side of my face pulled up. "Where is the middle

between soul mates and fuck buddies?"

Of course, the elevator doors had chimed open as I was talking, so I received some interesting looks from the people inside as they climbed off.

"Um, I don't know. Best friends who are attracted to each other, whose relationship is built on trust and respect?"

I'd been so ready to argue with her, her answer stopped me short.

"Let me guess. You think that's a steaming pile of horse crap?" she added when I didn't reply.

"No. I don't think that," I said as a fresh wave of bodies filed onto the elevator. "I'm not sure I agree with you one hundred percent, but I'm not sure I disagree either."

Quinn's arm bumped mine. "Kind of like a happy medium?"

"I'm not sure I want a happy medium where love is concerned. It sounds so . . . mediocre. Boring."

When the doors opened on our floor, we had to shimmy out of the packed elevator. "Ordinary doesn't have to be boring. Ordinary can be kind of . . . comforting."

"Comforting?" I felt my nose wrinkle as we powered toward our cubicles. "I want adventure, a pounding heart and a tingling stomach. I want epic, not ordinary."

Quinn swept her dark hair behind her ear. "Epic is short-lived. Ordinary stands the test of time."

"Yeah, only because it feels like forever." I held my arms out as I backed away from her cube toward my space. "You enjoy that basic, boring future you have planned for yourself."

Quinn tore off a Post-it note, crumpled it, and sent it flying in my direction. "At least I've got a future. One that isn't lived one delusional daydream to the next."

"Oh yeah," I said, yawning with exaggeration. "With the progress you're making with Justin, you two should finally go on that first date by the time you qualify for the senior discount at Perkins."

Her comeback was sticking out her tongue. Real mature, I thought, even as I stuck out my own tongue at her.

After making it to my cubicle—I hated getting in this late—I noticed something out of place on my tidy desk. A newspaper had been spread out in front of my chair, and I didn't miss the byline of the article that sat front and center.

"True Love? Of Course it's Not. Settle Already."

That was the title of his article, and I only made it to the second sentence before I folded it up and flung the paper into my trashcan. No need to guess who had left it for me; the smirk on the face across from me solved that mystery.

"What do you think?" Brooks's blue eyes shone above the partition between us. "I think it might be my best work yet."

"I think very little of your articles and your opinions actually," I replied, even as I scratched down the title for an article that had just sprung to mind. *We Can Have it All. Stop Settling."*

"For such an angelic face, you have one devil of a smile." Brooks leaned over the partition to see what I was up to.

My hand slammed down on my sticky note. He'd

built his career by playing devil's advocate to just about every article I'd ever published—I could hedge some of mine on doing the same to him. "For someone who touts playing the field, your pick-up lines need some work."

"That wasn't a pick-up line."

"Then what was it?"

"An observation." He reclined back into his seat, disappearing from view. "I wasn't trying to pick you up. If I was, you'd know it and wouldn't stand a chance in hell."

My eyes lifted as I scribbled some bullet points I wanted to hit in my article. "How does that morning bowl of ego poured over arrogance taste going down?"

His chair whined from the way he was rocking in it. "Not nearly as good as it feels coming out."

"You're repulsive."

"Yeah, the way you were gaping at me yesterday when I stepped in to save the day really gave off the repulsive vibe."

My pencil lead broke as heat burst into my veins. "For calling yourself Mr. Reality, you sure have a difficult time staying grounded in it."

"Arden! North! My office!" Mr. Conrad's voice burst through my phone intercom, about tossing me out of my seat.

My back slumped as I went to stand. Mr. Conrad's office felt like the principal's office lately.

"What do you suppose we did this time?" Brooks whispered as he fell in beside me.

Across the office, I caught someone seemingly taking a picture of us. Kinda creepy. Especially since I had no idea who the person was.

"He's probably pissed you were dancing with another woman when I showed up for our date," I said.

"Don't think so. That's the kind of drama that drives ratings through the roof. If anything, he's going to congratulate me for it."

I gave an overdone shiver. "It's like we've become some evening soap opera. I feel dirty."

"Making progress," he said under his breath right before ducking inside Conrad's office.

"Close the door," Conrad called from behind his desk when I filed in.

Brooks gave me a look that hinted at doom.

"Well?" Mr. Conrad folded his hands over his desk, looking between Brooks and me as we dropped into chairs across from him.

He waited for one of us to say something, but Brooks was a rare quiet, as was I.

"Did you see the number of views you two brought in?" A smile stretched across Conrad's face as he thumped his desk. "I knew this idea was genius. Publicity gold. And you two really sold it on that last date of yours." He leaned across the desk, tipping his hand by his mouth like he was about to tell a secret. "You almost had me fooled."

"That she's falling for me?" Brooks leaned forward. "Mission accomplished?"

A sharp sound came from me.

Conrad waved his stout finger at him. "That you maybe were doing some falling of your own." Conrad chuckled, his eyes almost twinkling he was so giddy. "Now that was a turn I wasn't expecting."

"I thought you wanted it to look like I was falling for her." Brooks glanced at me from the corner of his eyes, something I couldn't quite decipher in them.

"I did. I do." Conrad gave a silent clap. "I just didn't expect it to be so convincing."

"He sells snake oil for a living. He's made convincing an art form."

Conrad's head turned toward me. "Still haven't warmed up to Mr. North?"

I feigned a smile. "As warm as the Arctic Circle."

"If that's what you want to call it," Brooks said under his breath.

For all of the apparent progress we'd made yesterday, we were going backward at warp speed today.

"Was there anything else you wanted to talk with us about, Mr. Conrad?" I asked, glancing at the door.

"I just wanted to congratulate you both on such an early success. Even in my wilder dreams, I never envisioned hitting so many views this early on." Conrad glanced at his phone. "And I also wanted to schedule out the next month's worth of dates. With the way things are going, we won't be able to keep flying by the seat of our pants. I'm thinking of staging dates, hiring more camera crew, hell, maybe even bringing in a lighting team to really give viewers a show."

For the second time that morning, my head throbbed. "I thought the point was to make this a real-life social experiment. You start adding all the frills and extras and it's nothing more than a staged reality show."

Brooks nodded. "I'm with Hannah on this one, Charles. We should keep this as simple as possible. We want it to have a raw feel—that's what's drawing viewers in."

My stomach twisted. How had I become a pawn in this game? My goal was to protect romance, not peddle a designer imposter to the masses.

"While you two work out the details, I'm going to head back to my desk and write an article like we journalists do." I shoved out of my chair and marched for the door.

"How about tomorrow?" Brooks called after me.

"For what?" I asked, thought I already knew.

"Date Three." Again, the way he said it led a person to believe it was an event that would go down in the history books.

"It's a work day."

"This *is* your work, Arden," Conrad threw out.

"Fine," I said at the same time I threw open the door. "But I get to pick the location."

The weather foiled my plans for a rainy picnic. I'd never been so annoyed to see clear blue skies and sixty-degree temps. After unpacking my rain jacket and umbrella, I loaded up my bags and picnic basket and left my apartment.

I'd told Brooks to meet me at the Sheep Meadow around noon for Date Three. He'd sounded unsure about the whole park-and-picnic idea, but didn't put up any kind of formal objection.

As I was about to push open the outside door, someone coming in, saved me the effort.

"Hannah. Fancy meeting you here." Martin stepped aside and held the door for me, waving me through and reaching for my bags. "Can I help you?"

"I'm good, but thanks." I moved down the first stair to put some space between us.

After that renaissance festival, he'd been calling or texting me daily, wanting to know when we could get together again. For all of Martin's old-fashioned chivalry and all-around decency, I could not conjure up an ounce of attraction for him. That feeling . . . wasn't there. In fact, I wasn't sure I could feel any less for a man than I did for Martin.

"Good day for a picnic," he said, noting the basket tucked into my elbow. "I'm off work for the rest of the day. I decided to live dangerously and take a half day with it being so beautiful out."

My throat cleared when I realized what he was hinting. "That's what I thought too. That's why I'm heading to the park to meet someone."

Martin's eyes drooped the teensiest bit. "That Brooks guy? The one you're pretending to date?"

I moved down another step. "The very one."

"I can't believe the paper put that together. Forcing you into something like that. It's sad to think with as far as our society's evolved, women are still being subjected to that kind of treatment."

My invisible hackles rose. "I *made* the choice to be a part of this. No one forced me into it." I left out that the job I wanted might have been jeopardized if I didn't agree to it.

"Yeah, but still. It seems like something straight from the ninety-fifties."

My fingers tightened around the picnic basket. "I've got to get going. You enjoy your day."

"You don't have feelings for him? It's all just an act, right?" Martin moved his briefcase from one hand to the other, swallowing.

"I couldn't have any less feelings for that man if I was a sociopath." Hurrying down the last few steps, I flagged down the first taxi I saw.

I felt like I'd barely had a chance to catch my breath before the driver was pulling up to Central Park. After paying my fare and climbing out, I prepared myself for Brooks and the camera and an experience that vacillated from feeling real to fake.

Just inside the park, as promised, Jimmy was waiting for me to ask me whatever new questions Conrad had devised. Brooks wasn't anywhere to be seen.

"Another dress that scores a ten." Jimmy gave a small whistle as he waved at my white linen dress. "Great cinematic value, by the way."

"I don't know why I wore this. White might be the worst color for my pale skin, not to mention a picnic in a park is a rainbow of stains waiting to happen." I brushed at the skirt, wondering what link to reality had come undone when I'd reached into my closet this morning.

"You look great, trust me." Jimmy slipped the camera over his head. "Maybe just pass on ketchup . . . or any condiment for that matter." He scooted me around so the park was in the background, then started his countdown.

"Can't I have, like, one minute with the questions before I answer them on film?"

"Too rehearsed," he said before his last finger lowered.

"And we're back to *Romance Versus Reality*, here with the lovely Hannah Arden, on date number three, and we have a couple of questions for you." Jimmy wasn't reading from a note card anymore. "How have your feelings for Brooks changed from the first date to now?"

Feelings. Why was everyone so concerned about my feelings where Brooks was involved?

"I'd say they haven't changed at all." I smiled at the camera, and my expression felt about as fake as my senior photo smile. "I feel the same way about him now as I did then."

Jimmy fanned his hand over his mouth in a silent yawn. I ignored him and waited for the next question.

"How do you think Brooks's feelings for you have changed from the beginning to now?"

That question made me pause. Adjusting the picnic basket to my other arm, I went with the first thing that came to my mind. "I'm sure Brooks's feelings are the same as mine. Unchanged."

Jimmy pressed something on the camera, the filming coming to an end. For now. Soon we'd be live for the hundreds of thousands of viewers that had tuned in last time, although with this being in the middle of a workday, I was hoping the numbers would reflect that difference. Not that the actual filming time mattered when anyone could watch the videos at their leisure since Conrad had created a *Romance Versus Reality* website, where fans could watch past episodes, read Brooks's and my bios, and even weigh in with their thoughts on the love topic.

Jimmy followed me toward the open field, my heart floating higher into my throat with every step. What was this? Nervousness? Anxiousness?

Heartburn?

It was a strange sensation I wasn't used to feeling and thus couldn't accurately identify. My limbs felt all jelly-like, while my stomach felt like a boulder had been dropped into it.

"There he is." Jimmy's arm lifted toward the trees lining one side of the clearing.

A shadow leaned against one of them, staring at the open field like it was laced with land mines. As I approached, his head shifted my direction. He lowered his sunglasses over his eyes.

"You look like you're in pain over here," I called, realizing the smile on my face had formed of its own accord. That probably had to do with him looking like we were about to jump into a pool full of hungry sharks.

"That's because I am in pain." He pushed away from the tree and moved toward me, still staying in the shadows. "Who picks a picnic in a park for a date?"

Holding up the basket, I shrugged. "Me."

Jimmy glided up behind me, getting into a neutral position between Brooks and me. And the cameras were rolling.

"Come on. No one ever died from spending an afternoon relaxing in a park." I set down my bags and basket, then dug out the blanket.

"I find that hard to believe." Brooks shifted, the shine

of his dress shoes flashing from the tree line.

"You're dressed like you're either going to a wedding or a funeral." I eyed his dark suit, complete with white button-down shirt and a leather belt that matched his shoes.

"What is the standard outfit one should wear to a picnic?"

The way picnic rolled off his tongue had me biting my lip to keep from laughing.

"I don't know. Jeans, T-shirt, sneakers?" I watched him inch closer as I finished smoothing out the blanket on the ground.

"I wear sneakers and T-shirts to run in. And I haven't owned a pair of jeans since college." When I kicked off my shoes to let my feet feel the grass, his brows lifted into his hairline.

"You're a big runner, right? Surely you run in parks some of the time."

"That's right. I run *through* them. As fast as I can. I don't loiter to eat lunch and 'relax.'" He paused at the edge of the blanket, watching me dig through the picnic basket to get everything laid out.

"If I'd realized how much you hated communal outdoor settings, I would have proposed this idea from the start." After setting out the plates and silverware, I glanced up at him. Even through his sunglasses, I could make out his eyes; they were focused on me in the kind of way that made something in my stomach compress.

I made myself look away.

"You actually made lunch?" Brooks stepped closer. "You didn't pick something up from a restaurant or store?"

"Well, everything came from the store, but I had to do some peeling, mixing, and cooking to make it resemble a meal."

Brooks crouched beside me, his presence rolling over me like an invisible wave. Jimmy floated around the blanket, making sure he had a good view of the two of us.

"You cook?" he asked, sounding astounded, like I'd just admitted I was a cliff jumper or something.

"I also eat," I said, lifting out the stack of picnic fare I'd made for today. "Unlike the women you're likely used to."

"The women I've been with eat."

"Yep," I said with a smack of my lips. "They order a side of kale with their ice water."

Brooks sighed, reaching into the basket to help me unload the rest. He studied the sealed glass bowl of potato salad I'd made last night. "I'm impressed."

"I'm a real oddity. I cook *and* I eat."

"More like a rarity."

"Just because I can cook doesn't mean I'm going to stand for someone expecting me to cook. I'm not down with that domestic detail as an expectation when it comes to a relationship." Finally, I unpacked the bottle of sparkling cider and plastic wine glasses.

Brooks's mouth worked when he saw the beverage I'd chosen. "Your grandma taught you?"

"She was the kind of cook who won blue ribbons at any fair she entered a dish into. She never used a recipe, did it all by memory or instinct." I peeled off the foil wrapper on the bottle before prying the metal cap off with my bottle opener.

Brooks held out the two glasses for me to pour into. "My grandma was a great cook too. Used to do Sunday dinners with ten times more food than all of us could eat." He let himself settle onto the edge of the blanket. "It's too bad all of that talent is disappearing."

When my gaze cut to him, he lifted his hands. "I mean that in the least chauvinist way possible. Good food . . . I don't know, it brings people together. It's a bandage for a whole slew of family tensions and problems. It makes a bad day better with just one bite."

I made myself take a breath before firing my initial response at him. He wasn't saying it was a woman's job to live in the kitchen; he was merely lamenting the loss of home-cooked meals that brought people together.

"What was your favorite dish she made?" I asked as I popped open the container of roasted chicken segments.

"Cheese manicotti," he answered instantly. "My grandma was Italian, so she made everything from scratch. The noodles, sauce, sausage, everything. She made some complicated, beautiful dishes, but the simplicity of cheese manicotti was perfection." He was starting to relax, no longer looking like he was about to be drawn and quartered.

"My grandma was Irish, and she made this stew that was out of this world. Carrots, potatoes, onions, beef— some of the most boring, basic ingredients out there, but somehow she turned it into magic. Anytime I was sick or having a rough day, a bowl of stew would find its way onto the dinner table and I'd walk away feeling better."

Brooks was watching me, his expression almost peaceful. His sunglasses were still in place, but his stare was penetrating. I could almost feel it moving inside me, searching deep.

My head felt woozy, probably from skipping breakfast. "Do you like the breast, leg, or wing?"

Brooks smirked. "Take a guess."

I refused to give him the response he was hoping for. "Here. Have a wing." I smirked right back.

"Did it hurt when they ripped off your wings and sent you down to earth?"

Brooks laughed when I chucked a napkin at him. "How immature are you?"

"I'm a guy. We die with a little boy still living inside us."

I made a face as I scooped some potato salad onto our plates. "More like a horny, hormonal teenager."

My lips clamped shut as soon as I remembered Jimmy's presence.

"Don't give away all of my secrets to the world." Brooks tipped his head toward Jimmy and the camera. "You might play a role in one or two of them."

My cheeks heated, knowing what he was hinting at.

"So?" His head lowered toward mine. "Have you fallen in love with me yet?"

A single-noted laugh escaped from me. "No. Sorry to burst your bubble."

"You know it's only a matter of time."

"Before our three months are up and, lo and behold, I haven't fallen madly in love with you?" I plopped one more scoop of potato salad onto our plates. "Yeah, I know that."

He held out my glass of cider, scooting closer. "Am I

really that offensive?"

"Taken as a whole, no, you're not." I moved on to the macaroni salad, happy to be kept busy by any distraction, given the topic. "But taking this whole set-up into account, along with your beliefs that love is for weak-minded ninnies, then yes. You really are so offensive."

A half smile emerged as Brooks stabbed his fork into the potato salad. "What do your readers think about this whole thing?"

"My readers definitely don't want me falling for you," I answered, glancing at Jimmy. I wondered if I should make him a plate too.

"But your readers love romance, and some handsome, roguish fellow taking your hand in a park while you're dressed in a white dress is the definition of romance." Right then, Brooks's hand covered mine where it was resting on the blanket.

Instead of stiffening or whipping away, I found myself relaxing under his touch. The camera's presence screamed at me from the corner of my eye.

"My readers believe in finding the one." My hand slipped from beneath his, reaching for my fork. "Not the one who takes your hand and pretends to like you so he gets the promotion."

"Who says I couldn't be your one?"

I laughed. "Even I don't need to run the numbers to know that has about a one-in-an-impossible chance of happening."

Brooks slid his glasses onto his head, his eyes unapologetic in their stare. "You and me? You couldn't see it?"

I had to look away. "Not even a little." Tearing off a chunk of my chicken, I popped it into my mouth and plotted how to change the topic. "When it's right, you know it. You feel it."

Brooks's head shook before he took a drink of his cider. "I admit, it's a nice idea. But don't you feel it inside? The realization that it's just not true?" He stared out at the park and the people in it.

I gazed with him, trying to ignore that pit opening up in my stomach. "I'd rather spend my life chasing a dream than swallowing a cruel reality."

"You'd rather spend your life lying to yourself than being honest?" Brooks asked after taking a bite of the potato salad. "Side note? This is quite possibly the best thing I've eaten in months. Maybe even years."

I fought a smile as I took my own bite. Just the right balance of spices and tang. "I don't think any of what I believe is a lie. Soul mates, unconditional love, happy endings—it's all real."

"Fairy tales," he muttered before taking another large bite of salad. "So explain why a marriage dissolves after twenty years because of fifteen minutes of indiscretion."

Reaching for my glass, I answered, "It wouldn't have if he kept it in his pants."

He blew out a sharp breath. "No, that's like saying twenty years, our kids, our house, our finances, everything is worth less than that fifteen minutes of fucking." His arms threw out, his tone rather impassioned. "That's not unconditional love. That's the very conditional kind."

"You're right. It is the conditional kind. On the part of the one who engaged in the fifteen minutes of extra marital . . ." I just caught Jimmy's hands flailing before I said, "*Screwing*. That was one-sided unconditional love, and that never works in a relationship."

One of his brows rose. "That's a convenient explanation. But I'll stick to my beliefs that all of that unconditional love junk is worth its weight in bullshit."

I shot Jimmy an apologetic look. "Then how do you explain the couples it has worked for? The ones who live a long, happy, committed relationship together." Pulling my floppy sunhat from my bag, I dropped it on my head to cut the sun.

Brooks appeared amused by my hat, but he kept his thoughts on it to himself. "I call it a case of two determined people willing to overlook each other's weaknesses and not be hell-bent on changing or fixing the other, who've figured out a way to laugh at themselves, forgive easily—not to mention often—perfect the fine balance of selflessness and selfish, and on top of that, won the relationship lottery." Brooks clinked his glass against mine before finishing what was left of his cider. "That's how I explain that."

I blinked at him. "Wow. Don't hold back or anything."

"That's just half of it." Brooks refilled my glass, then his before taking a swig as though he'd forgotten it was cider, not gin.

"And how 'bout that picnic lunch?" I shifted so my feet were touching the grass. It had been a long winter of close-toed shoes and pantyhose; I was going to soak up this perfect spring day.

Brooks picked up his wing and tore off a bite. As he

chewed, his eyes landed on me. "Damn, woman."

I pulled another bite of chicken free. "Good?"

"If you define good as being life-defining, then yes, this is 'good.'" He licked his fingers. Like really got in there and sucked off the juices. I didn't think Brooks North was capable of a proper finger lick. "No matter the outcome of this little experiment, can we schedule a standing monthly meeting like this?"

"Only if you're cooking every other time."

"Cooking?" Brooks cringed. "I'm better at swiping my credit card at the local deli."

We made some more small talk as we finished our lunches, Brooks managing to down a breast, leg, and another wing. It was nice sharing a meal with someone else, and I felt an odd thrill that Brooks was enjoying the food I'd made. No way in hell I would ever speak that out loud, but it was there, that swell of pride that I'd managed to take a bundle of raw ingredients and turn them into something that had an uptight man like Brooks practically moaning out loud. That must have been Grandma in me—she'd always said good food had magic powers.

"Where do you put all of that?" I asked when he went in for one more scoop of macaroni salad. My gaze wandered to his belt, where not a pinch of stomach was folding over. Even with the fraction of lunch I'd eaten in comparison, I was thankful I'd worn a loose dress.

"I don't need to put it anywhere. I burn it off before it gets stuck to my gut."

"How many miles did you put in today? Twenty?" I said sarcastically as I packed away the remnants of lunch.

"This morning was a swim practice. Five thousands meters."

My nose wrinkled as I roughly calculated how many miles that was. "What time do you have to get up to finish that kind of a workout?"

"Five a.m. Every morning, swim practice or not."

My throat cleared as I recalled one morning he'd slept in past five o'clock.

"Tonight, I have a forty-mile bike ride to squeeze in." As I was about to snap the seal closed on the chicken, he snagged one last leg. "The challenge is to eat enough to keep up with my energy requirements."

I let out a grumble. "My problem has been the total opposite."

Brooks shot me a funny look. "Okay. Crazy."

"So where does one get the insane idea to compete in triathlons?" I asked.

He set the leg on his plate. "I didn't say I competed in triathlons."

My heart stopped when I realized my error. He hadn't mentioned that—Quinn's and my research had dug up that fact. "Don't you? I can't imagine anyone spending that much time running, swimming, and biking if they didn't compete."

Brooks watched me for a moment, searching. Then he leaned back. "I guess I like the feeling of challenging myself, my body. I like the high that comes with pushing myself for hours on end, riding the line between conscious and unconscious."

I tipped my sunhat a bit back since the sun was higher in the sky. "Sounds fun. Said no one on the planet besides you."

Brooks laughed, shrugging like he wasn't disagreeing.

"Why can't you be like everyone else and go to the gym a few days a week and lift weights or something?"

"For a hundred different reasons. And even though those meatheads might look good, welcome to the stamina party. VO2 max." Brooks bobbed his brows at me. "It's a thing. Especially when it comes to sex."

"If you do say so yourself," I said as I pulled a couple bottles of water from the basket. It was getting warmer, and he was still dressed like he was attending a semi-formal gala.

"So what now?" he asked, glancing around. "What else is there to a picnic?"

"I don't know. You take off your shoes and jacket. You relax."

"You relax?" Brooks repeated.

"Yeah, you read a book or take a nap or maybe play a little Frisbee if you feel like moving."

"Did you bring a Frisbee?"

"I don't even own a Frisbee. I prefer the as-little-movement-as-possible picnics over the ones where you jump from one activity to the next." After clearing the blanket, I lounged back. "Just lie down and try to take a nap. You might find you actually enjoy the art of relaxing."

"I don't relax," he replied even as he lay back beside me.

"I said *try*."

After a few seconds, he exhaled. "Did you at least bring a book?"

"Nope." I adjusted my sunhat so the sun could hit all of my face. "Not really a fan of those reading marathon picnics either."

"You're a fan of the eating and napping ones?"

I made a clucking sound to answer him.

He managed to be quiet for a stretch. For all of thirty seconds. He sat up with an exasperated sigh. "I've got to do something."

My nose wrinkled. "Ugh. You're one of those people who can't relax, aren't you?"

"Isn't that what I just said?"

"You sleep, don't you?"

Brooks peeled off his jacket and rolled up the sleeves of his shirt. I guessed it had more to do with the heat than getting comfortable. "Sleep is not the same thing as relaxing. It's the opposite."

"They don't seem so different to me."

"For starters, one is done consciously, the other is unconscious. One is recuperative, the other is idleness."

My eyes snapped open. "Idleness?"

Brooks shook his head as he rose.

"What are you doing?" I asked.

"I recognize an argument when I see one coming." He indicated the direction of an ice cream vendor across the park. "I'm practicing losing-argument avoidance."

As he backed away, Jimmy got up to follow him. I guessed going with Brooks was more exciting than my relaxing.

"What do you want?" Brooks asked.

"You're judging me for relaxing while going for ice cream ten minutes after inhaling six pounds of food?"

"You want something or not?"

I folded my hands over my stomach and closed my eyes. "Or not."

As Brooks and Jimmy wandered to the ice cream vendor, I tried to relax. It wasn't happening. Inside, I felt fidgety. All of Brooks's restless energy must have rubbed off on me, I thought, as I sat up with a grumble.

Since Jimmy and that confounded camera were with Brooks, I let myself watch him for a minute. Even from a distance, he was easy to look at, that aura of confidence almost visible to the naked eye. My eyes narrowed as I really focused, attempting to look hard or long enough to extinguish that unsettling clench in my midsection I felt whenever I looked at him.

In fact, it only seemed to get worse the longer I watched him.

Rolling onto my stomach, I picked at the grass and attempted to outline my thoughts on the article I was working on, but I could not distract myself from the man who'd just been suckered into an impromptu soccer game by a group of preschoolers. One of the girls had accidently kicked the ball into his back, but instead of reacting the way I'd assumed Brooks would—an inconvenienced sneer —he gave a theatrical performance of acting as though he'd nearly been dropped from the power of her kick.

Jimmy, not missing the opportunity, panned along with Brooks as he volleyed with the kids. Their teachers were paying more attention to him than they were the four-

and five-year-olds. At least I wasn't the only one with Brooks North fever.

After passing the ball to a boy who was practically half the size of the others so he could score the goal, Brooks high-fived some of them before he stepped back in line at the ice cream truck. Was that a genuine smile on his face? Had I just heard an honest-to-goodness laugh?

The kids got back to playing their game while Brooks gave his order. Never had I imagined Brooks might have been a fatherly type.

Until now.

Plucking at the grass, I conjured up all of the instances when Brooks North had been an ass. The list wasn't short. Still, I could not get rid of the tightness in my stomach, the sensation that seemed like a warning or a precursor or something important. I'd never felt it before, and now that I finally had that *feeling*, I wanted it to go away. To go into hibernation until another man entered the scene and my life hadn't been reduced to a damn circus.

When Brooks started to head back, I laid my head on my arms and tipped my sunhat just enough to shade my eyes from him. For all he knew, I was taking a nap and not having an internal panic attack that the first man I'd felt the *je ne sais quoi* for was the last person on the planet I could let myself feel anything for.

Behind him, a chorus of cheers echoed where the kiddos had been playing, but Brooks and Jimmy were blocking my view to see what had elicited such a response.

"Miss me?"

Yawning, I pushed up on my forearms. "You keep asking me that question."

"I keep waiting for a different response."

The sun was right behind him and I couldn't look at him without being blinded, so I diverted my eyes across the field toward from where he'd just come. Then I saw the source of the cheering.

"You didn't have anything to do with that, did you?" I asked as the ice cream vendor handed a few more ice cream cones to the kids circled around the stand, their hands flailing.

"Don't know what you're talking about." The smirk in his tone gave him away.

"You bought ice cream for all of those kids?"

Brooks glanced over his shoulders, lifting his hand when the young women attempting to corral the pre-schoolers waved. "And their nice teachers."

I bit my tongue to keep from saying something snarky over the "nice" part. "You? The stoic, grumpy realist? Bought ice cream for a classroom of ankle biters?"

"What?" Brooks crouched beside me. Too close. But then his presence would be too close no matter where he was. "It's a beautiful day, and just because I'm a realist doesn't mean I don't believe in random acts of kindness."

I leaned away as discreetly as I could. "Sure. Like a stranger buying ice cream for a bunch of little kids in a park. The definition of a random act of kindness. Not at all creepy."

His face froze for a moment as he glanced back at the ice-cream-inhaling young'uns. Then he laughed. "Christ. I didn't think of it that way." He continued laughing. "No wonder the ice cream guy gave me a funny look when I said I wanted to buy ice cream cones for them all."

I found myself laughing with him. "You're going to wind up on an episode of *America's Most Wanted*."

Jimmy slid around beside us, kneeling a little too close for comfort.

"Here." Brooks held out a waffle cone towered with several flavors of ice cream. "I got this for you."

I blinked at the cone that probably weighed as much as I had when I'd been born. "I said I didn't want anything."

He gave me a look, moving the cone closer. "Whenever a guy asks a girl if she wants dessert and she says no, it always mean yes." He took a bite of his own massive waffle cone, practically setting mine into one of my hands.

"That doesn't apply to everything," I said, taking the ice cream. "No does not mean yes."

He winked at me when I took my first lick. "Only when it comes to dessert."

"I want to argue with you, but I'm not," I said as I took another lick of the top scoop—salted caramel.

"Because I'm right?"

I lifted my index finger. "This one time."

Taking a seat on the grass, he turned his face toward the sky. "Women might hate me for what I write, but I pay more attention than most guys. In fact, if you all could see past the pragmatic beliefs, there's a pretty solid life partner hiding behind all of this realism."

I stared at him for a while, wondering why I had to fight every instinct demanding I move closer. I should be leaning away, creating distance, wanting space. My mind dictated that. But my body told a different story. "Women don't want a life partner. They want a soul mate."

Brooks looked down at me. "What's the difference?"
"It's *all* the difference."

CHAPTER
Nine

My eyes were burning from staying awake so late. My stomach churned with nausea from going so long without sleep. But I couldn't go to bed until I'd finished this article. I had a deadline, and all of the time I'd been spending with Brooks on camera had taken a serious dip into my work time.

I was on the final paragraph, the grand finale that would wrap up all of my thoughts into a few poignant sentences. The last words I'd leave my readers with, the ones that would resonate with them for days to come if I'd done my job right.

If only those words would come already.

Letting out frustrated sigh number one thousand thirty-seven, I drilled my fingers into my temples as I closed my eyes. *Focus, Hannah. The article's already written, you just need to finish it. The final paragraph's done, you only need to get it down on paper.*

My typical pep talk was not working, and I couldn't help blaming my writer's block on one good-looking stiff in a suit.

Right then, I felt something totally unexpected, though it wasn't the stroke of genius I'd been hoping for.

Rain drops. Pattering on my head. Inside my apartment.

My eyes snapped open at the same time my head fell back to stare at the ceiling. No, the ceiling had not opened up to reveal a night sky bloated with rain clouds.

"What the . . . ?" I muttered, shielding my laptop with my body as drops of water rained down from the ceiling.

More drops fell as the wet spot on the ceiling spread. After tucking my laptop into my bag and hiding it below the table, I rushed to the kitchen to collect as many pots as I had stuffed in my cupboards. Which wasn't nearly enough given the amount of water falling from the ceiling.

Still, I scattered the pots around on the floor, hoping to catch at least some of the water, before rushing toward the bathroom to procure some towels. As I was rounding into the bathroom, there was a pounding on my door.

Scattered, I didn't think to check the peephole before whipping the door open. On the other side I found Martin, sporting a pair of plaid flannel pajamas and one of those nasal strips.

He looked surprised, his mouth opening but nothing coming out. I understood why when I realized where his gaze was aimed. It was almost two o'clock in the morning, and I'd ditched my bra and blouse in favor of a cozy camisole hours before.

"This isn't a good time. I've got a bit of a situation on my hands," I said as I ducked into the bathroom for towels *and* a bathrobe.

"That's why I'm here." He moved inside a step, cleaning his glasses off on his pajama shirt. "The apartment right next to me, the one directly above yours, is experiencing some issues." His face actually fell a little when I emerged from the bathroom with my holey old bathrobe cinched on.

"Some water issues?" I said as I hustled toward the table, but when I got there, the water had spread into the living room too, leaving dark spots on my light pink couch.

"She started a bath, then I guess walked away to pour herself a glass of wine and got distracted."

"By the whole bottle?" I muttered as I mopped up what I could on the floor. The water was dripping faster now, holes opening up in the ceiling as rivers of water burst out.

"The apartment manager is having everyone below her apartment evacuate until they can get everything cleaned up and fixed." Martin kept coming in, so I tossed him a towel.

"And where are we supposed to evacuate to? This is New York City. Space is a limited commodity." All of my towels were soaked through and the water wasn't easing up. I'd be lucky if anything was salvageable after this mess.

"I guess he's checking with some hotels to see if he can secure rooms for all of you. I told him I'd let you know and help with whatever you needed. Might want to pack a few bags because who knows how long it will take to clean this all up."

Giving up on my mopping up endeavors, I beelined

for my bedroom to put a few bags together. The moment might not have fully caught up to me yet, and I had no idea where I was going once those bags were packed, but I knew having some dry personal effects would be better than none if I waited any longer.

"You know, you could always stay at my place." Martin followed me into my bedroom, his eyes almost instantly moving toward my bed. The water hadn't made its way in there yet, but I guessed it was only a matter of time. "I'm only a floor above and my apartment's bigger than yours. There's plenty of room for one more person." His throat cleared as I threw clothes into a large duffel. "That's why I got it."

I made a face into my closet. I'd rather move into a run-down roadside motel with owners named Bates than into Martin's sweet pad. For a bunch of reasons, all of them starting and ending with me not wanting to wake up to the sound of heavy breathing in the middle of the night. "Thank you, that's a nice offer, but I've been living on my own for too long. I'm sure I'd drive a roommate, even a temporary one, crazy."

Martin's slippers squeaked across my floor. "You wouldn't drive me crazy."

I kept focused on my frantic packing, trying to think of a polite way to ask him to leave. "I'm going to look into a hotel. But thanks again."

My eyes cut toward the door, but he wasn't getting the hint. So as I stuffed another couple bags full of odds and ends and toiletries, I made use of Martin's lingering presence to carry a couple of them.

"Are you sure you don't want to spend the night at

my place tonight? It's practically morning." Martin dropped my bags in the hallway with a grunt, as though I'd stuffed them full of steel plates.

"I've got a good friend who lives close by."

"You've got a friend who lives one floor up too." He pointed above us.

"A *girl* friend," I added as I pulled out my phone and scrolled through my contacts.

"It's the twenty-first century. Nobody cares about that stuff anymore."

"Except God. And my priest."

Martin's forehead folded. "I didn't know you were religious."

"It's more of a newfound faith. A born-again type of thing." I chewed on the inside of my cheek before I said anything else and dug myself into an even deeper hole. Knowing Martin, he'd be waiting outside the building door on Sunday morning with his Bible in hand, waiting for me.

"It's not like we'd do anything inappropriate. We'd just sleep. You in one room. Me in another." Martin rubbed the back of his head, shifting in place.

I was damp. My apartment was a rain forest. And I was exhausted.

My patience ran out.

"Thank you again for the help, but if you could just give me some space to figure out my next steps, that would be much appreciated." I capped my request with a smile as he headed for the stairway.

"You've got my number?"

I shook my phone. "I've got it."

"You'll call if you need anything? At any hour?"

I made an X over my chest. "Cross my heart," I said, my fingers doing some crossing of their own behind my back.

He paused when he made it to the first step. "Can I help you carry your bags at least? That's quite the load—"

"*Goodnight*, Martin." I took a calming breath and held it while he climbed the stairs to his floor. Finally.

I heard some commotion coming from upstairs and heard the apartment manager's voice from down the stairs, but the rest of the building was quiet. Everyone was sound asleep while my apartment was filling with water.

Leaning into the wall behind me, I wrung out my hair with one hand as I scrolled through my contacts with my other. Quinn was the obvious choice, but thanks to her student loan payments, she lived with two roommates in an apartment half the size of mine. One bathroom and four women might not have qualified for third-world conditions, but it was a first-world problem for sure.

If I asked, she'd say yes and would give up her twin bed for me and sleep on the floor that should have been replaced two generations ago. She'd be pissed if she found out what had happened and I hadn't called her, but I couldn't take advantage of a friendship when I had the means to put myself up in a hotel.

Contact after contact I knew I could call and, without hesitating, would tell me to get my butt over to their place, but I couldn't force myself to ring a single one of them.

However, I found my finger twitching over one name. The last name I should have considered when it came to sharing a living—and sleeping—space.

Chiding myself for even considering it, I was about to

pull up a search engine to book a hotel, when my damn traitorous thumb slipped.

Right over Brooks North's phone number.

It had barely started ringing before I hit the end button, cursing as I did. It couldn't have gone through. I'd caught it and ended the call too soon. Brooks would never have to know about the time my finger had slipped at two in the morning, calling him.

Not even three seconds later, my phone rang. Guess who?

"No, no, no." My head thumped against the wall behind me in time to my words.

I wasn't sure what to do. If I didn't answer, it would be obvious I was ignoring him, especially since I was the one who'd just traitor-thumb-dialed him in the middle of the night.

If I did answer, what in the hell was I going to say? What legitimate reason, other than severe bodily trauma, could I have for calling Brooks at this time of night? I mean, other than the handful of texts we'd exchanged having to do with our dates, I'd had no talking interaction with him over the phone.

At the last minute, I made my decision and answered. "Hello?"

Another head thump when I realized how dumb that sounded.

"Hello? Hello yourself. You're the one calling me at two-oh-four on a Thursday night. Make that Friday morning." Brooks's voice didn't sound like he'd been rocked awake by my call. It sounded the same as any other time I talked with him.

"Sorry about that. I accidently butt-dialed you." I frowned at my apartment as more water poured inside.

"What are you doing still awake?"

"What are *you* doing still awake?" I echoed back.

"Finishing an article." The sound of ice clinking against a glass whispered through the phone.

"Me too," I said in a rush when I noticed the apartment manager marching up the stairway toward me. "I'm going to let you get back to your article. Sorry again about the butt-dial."

He gave a low rumbling chuckle. "Your butt can dial me anytime she wants."

"You're not funny."

"I've gotten you to laugh a few times. I have to be semi funny."

Andre, the apartment manager, didn't seem to notice I was on the phone. Before I could cover it or end the call, he started talking a mile a minute. "Miss Arden, we are so sorry for this significant inconvenience." When he got his first look inside my apartment, his face looked as though he'd witnessed a Great White flopping around in that spray of water. "I've called a dozen hotels already, all of them are full, but don't worry, I'll keep making calls until I find you a place, even if that means forfeiting my room for the remainder of the night."

When his phone rang, he lifted his finger at me and answered the call. Andre was wound tight on a standard summer Saturday, so tonight he looked as though he were clinging to the last thread of his sanity.

"What's the matter with your apartment?" Brooks's voice streamed through my phone.

I exhaled. "It's kinda flooding as we speak."

"Flooding?"

"Flooding." I motioned inside my apartment. "The lady above me forgot she was drawing a bath. From the looks of it, she forgot last month."

"What are you going to do?"

"The apartment manager's booking me a hotel," I said.

"He just said he couldn't find a vacancy."

"He *also* said he was going to keep checking."

Brooks exhaled. "Come to my place. It's not far from you, and it's big enough for the two of us."

The tightness had now wound its way around my throat instead of my stomach. What the heck was going on with me? "No, I couldn't do that."

"But you could shack up with your apartment manager, who sounds like he's this close to losing his grip on sanity?" Brooks gave me a few moments to process. "Really, just come over tonight and if it's so terrible being here, you can check into a hotel tomorrow night. No one needs to know."

A wave of exhaustion pulsed over me, and the lure of sleep became overpowering. "I'm not sure it's a good idea."

"Why not?"

I hadn't been prepared for him to ask that question. "Because. It just doesn't seem like it is."

"Are you afraid Conrad or Jimmy or the viewers are going to find out?"

I hadn't been, at least until now. "A little."

"Worried I'm going to sneak into your room at night?"

My arms crossed. "No."

"Worried *you're* going to sneak into my room at night?"

"No!" I hollered, louder than I'd intended. "I just don't think it's the best idea, okay?"

"It probably isn't the best idea." In the background, I made out a sound. Was that typing? "But it isn't the worst idea either, and quite frankly, it's your only option at this time of the night-slash-morning."

"I can call one of my friends," I said as I crouched to dig a pair of shoes from my bag. Wherever I was going, I couldn't get there barefoot.

"But that means you'd have to wake one of them, and I'm already awake." The typing came to a pause. "Just come over. You can figure something else out tomorrow."

I was preparing to stave him off when out from my mouth came, "Okay."

There was a long enough silence I could tell he was as surprised by my agreement as I was. "Can I come and get you? Do you need help with anything?"

I'd already stuffed my feet into my sneakers and shouldered my last few dry belongings in the world. "No, I'll catch a cab."

"You're sure?"

"You might ask that because you're trying to be helpful—maybe—but all I hear is you questioning my capability and competency to complete a basic task on my own." My feet squeaked in my shoes as I crept down the stairs.

Brooks made a sound of amusement. "I might question a lot, but not that. Never that."

After saying goodbye, I was almost to the doors when Andre caught me. He'd gone full-spectrum frantic. "Where are you going, Miss Arden? I'm still working on finding you a hotel room."

"I'm heading to a friend's place." The word felt wrong, but was it? "If you need to reach me, I'll have my phone."

Andre's shoulders relaxed some. "I've got an emergency cleaning crew en route, and they're going to get your apartment back to normal before you know it."

The last image of my apartment flashed through my head. "Could you let me know when they think I'll be able to move back in? I'll probably need to come back tomorrow to grab a few things I forgot."

Andre's head never stopped nodding. "I'll take care of everything," he said as he pulled the door open for me. "I am so very sorry for the inconvenience, Miss Arden."

I liked how he made it sound like I'd had to wait five minutes over my reservation time at dinner, instead of the neighbor above unleashing a torrential downpour on all of my worldly possessions.

Andre waited at the door as I flagged a cab, and he waved at me after I crawled inside, before whipping around and rushing god knows where.

What a mess.

My apartment.

Me.

The night.

My current situation.

For something that could be so peaceful and refreshing, water could really rip open a vortex of suck in a person's life under the right circumstances.

The drive to Brooks's apartment wasn't long, not even ten minutes. After paying the driver and climbing out, I stood on the sidewalk long enough to give myself an opportunity to change my mind.

My feet made the decision for me.

When I buzzed the apartment number he'd texted me, the doors unlocked instantly. This apartment building was nicer than mine—newer, but also colder. The designer had clearly forgotten to work in some warmth in the midst of all the sharp edges and cool colors.

In the elevator, I took a moment to tighten the belt on my bathrobe and comb my fingers through my damp hair in an attempt to make myself look like less like a drowned gerbil. When the doors opened on the seventeenth floor, I tiptoed out of the elevator like I was in a library. After finding my way to the door with number 123, my fist froze before knocking.

What was I doing?

I couldn't just spend the night with Brooks North in his apartment. If my readers found out . . . if Mr. Conrad did . . . if my inhibitions lowered for one fraction of a fraction of a second . . .

This really was the worst idea.

Just as I was about to whip around and leave, the door whispered open. Brooks had that smirky grin, his hair almost disheveled. "Looked like you were having a difficult time with the knocking part, so I thought I'd give you a hand." Tapping the peephole, he swung the door open all the way and stepped aside.

It took me a few moments before I moved inside, better judgment still warning I should turn and abort, but once I crossed the threshold, I was stuck. All resistance drained out of me as the night caught up to me all at once.

"Damn, you look rough, Arden," Brooks said after locking the door.

I shot him a look that didn't need any translation.

"You know what I mean." He waved at me. In my old bathrobe that no eyes other than mine should be expected to see. Wearing my sneakers that had been on trend last decade. Wrangling a hodgepodge of bags overflowing with the odds and ends of my life.

"Can you please be nice for a whole five-minute stretch?" I said, finally noticing what he was wearing. Or more like what he *wasn't* wearing. "And can you put on a shirt? This is already awkward enough without you running around half naked."

He gave a small laugh as he pointed at a room just off the hall. "That's the spare room. You can drop your stuff in there if you want. There's only one bathroom, but I cleared out my stuff to make room for yours."

Brooks disappeared into the kitchen, so I stuck my head inside the room he'd indicated. Flipping on the light, I was surprised by what I found. It was tidy, the blankets on the bed had been folded down, and there was a bottle of water on the nightstand.

I wasn't sure what to make of it all; if this was Brooks doing an honest-to-goodness decent thing or if this was some play to make me fall for him. It could have been either, and quite honestly, one felt as likely as the other at this stage. Whatever the reason, I didn't have the mind-power to stew on it, so after propping my bags against the wall and sliding out of my sneakers, I moved back into the hall.

"I boiled some water if you want a cup of tea." His voice streamed from the kitchen as I wandered into the living area.

"Do you have anything without caffeine?"

"Eh, yeah, I think so." The sound of shuffling through cupboards followed. "I've got chamomile or jasmine."

I wasn't a tea person, but if ever there was an occasion to sip a warm cup of steeped dried leaves, it was tonight. "Jasmine sounds good."

"Coming right up."

Padding around the room, I didn't find anything of a personal note. Except for the laptop sitting on the table like mine had been back in my apartment. It seemed both of us were having a difficult time meeting our deadlines while playing the modern version of *The Dating Game*.

"Working late?" I said when he wandered out of the kitchen with two cups.

"Always," he replied as he handed me my tea.

"What are you drinking?" I glanced at the dark liquid in his.

He lifted his chin at the laptop. "Darjeerling. I've still got an hour's worth of work before I can call it a night."

"I thought you get up at five in the morning."

"I do."

When I tried peering at what he was working on, he closed the laptop completely.

"That means you're going to get less than two hours of sleep," I said.

"And that's better than no hours of sleep." He lifted his cup before taking a sip.

"I didn't paint you as an optimist."

"I'm not. That's the realist in me talking."

Taking a sip of my tea, I felt a fresh nudge of heaviness push me. I was about to fall asleep standing up if I didn't get to bed soon. "Sounded pretty positive to me. Seeing the glass half full kind of thing."

His eyes lifted. "And yet it wasn't because, in fact, two hours of sleep is better than no sleep. That's just the truth." Moving toward my room, I didn't miss the way he was inspecting me. "Nice bathrobe."

My eyebrows lifted. "What's that supposed to mean?"

"It's supposed to mean . . ." He held out his arms. "Nice bathrobe."

"Yeah, but the way you said it—"

"It's nice, Hannah. That's what I said, and that's what I meant. No hidden agenda." His mouth moved before he could cover it, and that's when I knew he was messing with me. "It looks well-loved."

"Jerk." I slugged his arm, which was still bare, along with the rest of his upper half. "At least I have the decency to put on clothing when I'm in people's presences."

"Actually, I'd find it much more decent if you refrained from clothing." The corners of his eyes creased when he realized what he'd said. "When it comes to that antiquity," he added, pointing his cup at my robe.

"I'm going to bed now. Before you move on to insulting my sneakers."

He moved just out of arm's reach. "I don't need to insult them when their very existence is offensive enough."

When I lunged to land another thump, he laughed and managed not to spill a drop of his tea.

"I kinda hate you, you know that?" I said as I backed into the bedroom.

"Yeah. I know that." With a wink, he wandered to his laptop. "If you need anything, just ask or help yourself."

Before I closed the door, I stopped. My attention was fixed on him focusing on his laptop. The pale light coming in from the window behind him cast highlights along his back, drawing lines eyes and fingers were made to follow.

"Hey, Brooks?" My throat moved as his gaze flitted my way. "Thank you."

His face changed, relaxing under the constant restraint he maintained. In that moment, I caught a glimpse of the man I'd so quickly and carelessly fallen for that night in Chicago.

"Hey, Hannah?" he replied with a slow smile. "You're welcome."

CHAPTER Ten

Sleeping with the enemy. I'd done it.

Maybe not in the way I had that winter night a couple of months ago, but I'd slept under his roof, in his bed—*one* of them—and was waking to the smell of fresh coffee.

It wasn't such an awful thing. Especially since Brooks had nice sheets on his bed—the ones that had a two million thread count and probably cost as much as the mattress, which was lavish in its own right.

My alarm had gone off at six, but given the night I'd had, I snoozed until seven fifteen. As I rolled out of bed, I felt like I could have slept another ten hours no problem.

"Brooks?" I called after peeking out the bedroom door.

He was probably still out biking five gazillion miles and had left the coffee pot on for me, guessing I turned into a troll if I didn't get some caffeine in my system a few minutes after rising. He would have been partially right.

When I got no response, I padded toward the kitchen.

With sun spilling in through the windows, it cast his whole apartment in a different light. The place was still as impersonal as the lobby of a dentist's office, but the grays in the décor didn't come across so monochromatic. There were more shades than I'd guessed—too many to count.

On the counter, I found a clean cup by the coffee pot, along with a note letting me know creamer was in the fridge. He'd set out a mess of sugar packets and a spoon beside the cup, because I guessed he thought I was practicing for diabetes.

After making my coffee, which might have required three . . . and a half . . . packets of sugar to make it taste right, I was about to duck into the bathroom for a shower when the front door thundered open.

"Sweet baby Buddha!" I exclaimed when Brooks barged inside looking like he'd just come from a shower himself. A sweat shower.

"Sorry. Didn't mean to startle you." As he hung up his keys, he stopped. His eyes traveled my way. They went wide.

That was when I remembered I wasn't wearing my bathrobe, instead sporting nothing besides cotton shorts and that same cami Martin had had a tough time ignoring.

"And you have the gall to accuse me of running around half naked?" He motioned at me as though I were streaking down Lexington Avenue in nothing more than boobie tassels.

"I thought you were gone or I would have put on that robe you're such a fan of," I gritted out as my arms crossed. "I was just about to hop into the shower."

He ran his hand through his damp hair. "Me too."

"It's your place. You first." I sidestepped toward my room, in search of that robe.

"You're my guest. You first." He flipped on the bathroom light and snagged a hand towel from inside to wipe off his face.

"No, really. I insist."

"No, *I* insist."

"Brooks—"

"Hannah," he cut in, a tipped smile carving into place. "There's a solution that's a compromise."

I made a face as I ducked behind the bedroom door. "From the look on your face, I don't want to know."

"We could save water and shower together. Simple solution to both of our problems."

My stomach did the weird sensation thing again. Likely due to lack of sleep and drinking coffee on an empty stomach without my usual breakfast of butter and chocolate. "More like an endless supply of problems with that solution."

He chuckled before ducking into the bathroom, the sound of the shower cranking on following. "Fine, if you're not down with companion showering, then you get first dibs."

I could have kept arguing, but it wouldn't have gotten either of us any further in the compromise department. Plus, the hot water would run out and we would both be late to work.

"I'll be quick," I said after grabbing my shower stuff from one of my bags. At least, what I'd managed to toss inside in the chaos of last night.

His mouth lifted higher on one side. "Oh, I know."

Pretending not to understand what he was getting at, I snatched my "fetching" robe and jogged toward the bathroom. Once I was in the bathroom, I double-checked that I'd locked the door, then I actually looked around the room and behind towels to make sure there weren't any hidden cameras. Perv might not have been Brook's MO, but I wasn't taking any chances. Not that he didn't already know what I looked like naked . . .

I took my frustration out on my scalp as I shampooed and conditioned my hair. It had never been so squeaky clean. I managed to get my legs and armpits shaved and my hair and body washed all in under five minutes. That had to be in the running for a world record.

After swiping the towel up and down my body, I wound it around my hair and slipped into my bathrobe. I could do the rest of my morning ritual in the bedroom so he could hop in the shower next.

Brooks was in the same place I'd left him, coffee cup in one hand, newspaper in the other. He didn't look up when I moved down the hall.

"Next," I said, pausing outside his bedroom door. No lights were on, but there was enough natural light to illuminate the inside. His bed was so neatly made it was as though no one had ever slept in it, and the surfaces were bare of personal effects save for one frame propped on the dresser. "Is that your mom?"

Brooks made an "Mm-hmm" sound.

"She was beautiful."

"She was," he said, resting the newspaper at his side. "In every way. And her husband still left her. That's not the happy ending she deserved."

"That has to do with your father's nature, not love's."

He shook his head. "Love is a chemical in our brain. It's not some thing of whimsy or written in the stars or the thing of fate and providence. It comes. It goes. Sometimes it lasts. Sometimes it doesn't. It isn't a guarantee—it's a risk." As he moved by me, he closed the door of his bedroom before heading toward the bathroom. "I'll see you at the office."

My hand clutched the top of my robe. "I can wait for you. If you want?"

"I figured you wouldn't want us to arrive together. You know, in case anyone from the office noticed." He paused in the middle of peeling off his wet shirt.

My eyebrows pinched together. The two of us arriving together, for someone at the office to see, for anyone who recognized us to see, should have been what he wanted. It aligned with his whole objective of getting me to fall for him. He should have been jumping at the idea of the two of us climbing out of a cab and heading up to the *World Times* together.

So why was he suggesting something else?

"See you later." Turning, I rushed into my room to finish getting ready.

It took all of my willpower to keep my brain on the task at hand and not wandering to other pressing matters. Like the condition of my apartment. Or what I was going to do tonight for accommodations. Or why Brooks was behaving the total opposite of how I expected him to act. Or why my body was betraying me at every turn whenever he looked at me a certain way or said my name in just the right tone.

Since I'd been racking up taxi fares lately, I elected to take the subway to work that morning, which meant I didn't have time to grab my usual breakfast. When Quinn texted to ask if I wanted anything, I requested she grab an extra chocolate croissant. And might have suggested she channel Beyonce in "Run the World" and seal the Justin deal already.

She ignored my last text.

Unlike most Friday mornings, I was one of the last to arrive to work, and I was slightly annoyed I'd missed my chance at peace and quiet to get caught up on some work.

Conrad had let both Brooks and I know that we could lighten our workloads given the time suck *Romance Versus Reality* had become, but neither of us seemed to be taking him up on his offer. We clearly both put a priority on our work and weren't easily brought to crying *Mercy*.

"What the what?" Quinn greeted the moment I collapsed into my chair. "You look like you didn't sleep a wink last night."

"Ugh. Yeah. I had a bit of an emergency last night and am running on fumes." I shot her an apologetic look, and she plopped a familiar brown paper bag on my desk. "Thanks for grabbing my breakfast of champions for me."

"What's going on?"

Tearing off a chunk of my breakfast, I debated how much to tell Quinn. I told her everything, but I wasn't sure I should tell her this.

"My apartment flooded last night and I had to leave." I peeked across my cubicle to make sure someone hadn't sneaked into his chair yet.

"Oh my god. No way. Why didn't you call me? Why

didn't you come over?" Quinn stopped, her eyes narrowing on me. "Where did you go last night?" When I didn't answer right away, she added, "A hotel?"

"A *kind* of hotel in that it's temporary and impersonal."

Recognition dawned on her face. "You spent the night with him? *Him?!*" She glared at Brooks's empty workspace. "You could have had a slumber party with your best friend and you choose him over me?"

"It wasn't like that." My head fell back. "It was late, I didn't want to wake you, and I knew your living quarters are already cramped. I didn't want to impose."

"We are best friends. Therefore, there is no such thing as imposing." She stuck out her lower lip. "I can't believe you called him instead of me."

"Shhh," I hissed, glancing around the office. It was buzzing with noise, but I did not need anyone finding out about my current living situation. "His place is huge, and if I'm going to impose on anyone, I'd rather it be him over someone I actually like."

Quinn gave me a suspicious look as she chewed her fingernails. "You swear to make his life miserable while you're there? I'm talking leaving dirty dishes in the sink, putting an empty carton of milk in the fridge, leaving your hair all over his shower walls?"

I crossed my finger over my heart. "Promise."

She took the chunk of croissant I offered her. "How long before you're able to move back into your place?"

"I don't know. I'm hoping to know more today."

"Okay, well, if it gets to be too much or too long, my bed is yours. I will sleep on the floor if it means protecting my friend from that leech of a *Homo sapien*."

"Gee, Quinn, I thought you were starting to warm up to the guy."

She dropped her face in front of mine. "I was. And then my best friend choose him over me in a moment of crisis." She sneered at the empty cubicle across from me. "Come on. Let's go get some coffee. Bowers was just making a fresh pot."

"When in doubt, coffee." I followed Quinn toward the break room, where quite the crowd had assembled.

"Okay, whose birthday is it and where did the cake come from?" Quinn shouted into the crowd before realizing the herd hadn't assembled for a slice of red velvet, but were fixated on the television in the back corner.

Getting a sinking feeling in my gut that some kind of natural disaster or worse was being streamed, I wove through a wall of bodies so I could see the screen. Short people problems.

My eyebrows came together when I saw what was playing. It was one of those national morning shows, the perky host interviewing some distinguished-looking older woman.

"If you're just tuning in, I'm talking with body language specialist Judith Reeves on what physical signs we give off when we're attracted to someone."

Quinn managed to shoulder her way up toward me and stared at the television the same way I was—with confusion. "What's so enthralling about this?"

My shoulders were just rising when a clip played on the television screen behind the host. "Oh . . ."

"Fudge," Quinn snapped as footage from Brooks' and

my first date played.

"If you're one of the few who haven't heard about the new reality television experience to hit the airwaves, *Romance Versus Reality*, the show follows the lives of two journalists who have differing views on love. In fact, you might have read one or two of Ms. Romance or Mr. Reality's advice columns. In a social experiment that's got the whole nation talking, the *World Times* is attempting to answer, once and for all, is love real or fake?" The host motioned at the guest across from her. "Dr. Reeves has been viewing the show and selected a few clips to give her opinion as to how things are progressing between these two."

"This isn't real." My hand snapped out to take Quinn's. "Tell me this isn't real."

Her throat cleared. "This isn't real?"

"Your confidence is overwhelming," I grumbled, as "Dr." Reeves paused the clip. It was when Brooks and I had been at the restaurant, and no matter how hard I looked, I couldn't see anything that gave away any feelings other than disdain.

"If you take a close look here, you'll see Miss Arden's pupils ever so slightly dilated." The clip zoomed in on my face as Reeves rose to point at my eyes.

"Surprise, lady. It was dark inside that stuffy place. Last I checked, our pupils dilate in the absence of light." My foot tapped as I resisted the impulse to toss my heel through the television screen.

"You see the way she's fully angled toward him? Not leaning away or angled to the side? That's another indicator of attraction."

Around me, my co-workers' heads turned toward me,

gauging my reaction.

I supposed the one I was giving wasn't very subtle. "Bombshell number two, Witch Doctor. I was sitting at a table *across* from him."

Quinn was speechless, grimacing as they moved to the next footage clip. This was one from our picnic in the park when we were both sitting on the blanket and talking after lunch. There was literally nothing that body language charlatan could infer from that scene that would suggest I was head-over-heels for Brooks.

The host and doctor watched what was maybe ten seconds of footage, but it felt like an eternal damnation in hell from where I was standing smack in the center of dozens of colleagues. God, this was humiliating. Knowing I was being filmed for an audience was bad enough, but having to watch it and have my eye movements and body placements be dissected on morning television was beyond the inner circle of shame and embarrassment.

"And if you'll notice right here—" The doctor forwarded the clip a few seconds before pausing it on me again. And zooming in. Again. "Notice the way Miss Arden pushes her hair back over her shoulder, tipping her head, exposing her neck, subconsciously releasing pheromones meant to attract a potential suitor."

My stomach roiled as I grabbed Quinn's arm. "My life is over."

Quinn patted my hand. "Click your heels three times and keep saying 'there's no place like home.'"

"Again, watch the neck. Here she touches it and again here . . ." Reeve's voice trailed off as she forwarded the clip to the next instance of me touching my neck for no apparent reason. "Yet another indicator that, in some way, Miss Arden is attracted to him."

More heads turned my way. Even the ones I couldn't see I could feel burning holes through my back. After today, I was never touching my neck in Brooks's presence again. I didn't even realize I touched it that much.

"Okay, so we've talked about Miss Arden." The host recrossed her ankles. "What about Mr. North? Any body language cues to give away what he's feeling?"

My shoulders relaxed a little. At least I was out of the hot seat and didn't have to worry about her reading my upper lip for signs of attraction.

"Mr. North is a tougher read actually." Reeves moved to another clip, waving the remote at the screen where Brooks was frozen. "His favorite expression seems to be this one. In fact, this flat façade is present in more than half of the air time."

"What does that tell us, doctor?"

"It doesn't tell us much. It could mean contempt as much as it could mean attraction. It's impossible to know in a person who's perfected the art of indifference as Mr. North clearly has."

Quinn huffed. "That's not indifference. That's what having a heart as black as coal does to a person."

A few chuckles circled us from Quinn's expert opinion, so I moved closer to the television so I could hear what was being said. Now that it wasn't about me, I wanted to hear every word.

"However, I did find certain instances of dilated pupils, raised eyebrows—especially when Mr. North first saw Miss Arden—and quite a few examples of manspreading."

I imagined my expression matched the hostess's. "Manspreading?" She chuckled, a nervous tick to it. "I'm not sure if that's a medieval form of torture or the latest craze in male hygiene."

"You and me both, lady," I muttered.

The doctor shook her head, smiling. "Manspreading as related to body posture is taking a position of power. Making oneself as big as possible. Legs spread out, shoulders open, arms held out at one's side a bit." She skipped to a few more clips where Brooks was in this "manspreading" position. "If you look at it from a strictly evolutionary perspective, it's how a male attracts a mate. By proving himself strong and large enough to protect her. It's a sign of virility, a nod at confidence."

"More like arrogance," I whispered to Quinn, who'd shouldered up beside me again.

"Can you believe this lady? What universities actually give doctorates for this kind of pseudo science?"

"Our time together is almost up, but I have one last question for you, Dr. Reeves. One that seems to be on the minds of the millions of viewers who have been bitten by the *Romance Versus Reality* bug." The hostess leaned in like they were about to share a secret. "Which of these two, in your opinion, is more attracted to the other?"

My stomach felt like it had dropped into my feet.

"If we were to just go off of body language cues alone, in my opinion, it would be Miss Arden."

"Please tell me everyone else has left the room," I whispered to Quinn.

Quinn glanced behind us with a grimace. "Ignorance is bliss, baby."

A rattling exhale trembled past my lips.

"But as Ms. Romance, she's trying to prove that attraction can't be created with anyone other than one's true soul mate. If anyone should be showing signs of attraction, it would be Mr. Reality, whose one point is to get us to believe attraction can be created with just about anyone given the right circumstances and state of mind." The hostess perfected the right degree of head tilt to strike the precise balance of confusion and curiosity.

"That is true. It seems, in this instance, what we would assume about each of their attraction levels has been reversed. However, body language is only one piece of the puzzle when getting to the bottom of attraction. There're voice cues, word choice, heartrate—a plethora of other measuring sticks, if you will."

"A *plethora*," I repeated, loud enough that more than just Quinn could hear me.

The hostess and doctor went on to say goodbye, after plugging her latest *New York Times* bestseller.

"I need to get some fresh air." I shot Quinn a reassuring smile before heading out of the break room, trying to make eye contact with as few people as possible. It felt like every one of them was trying to lock eyes with me, some offering comfort, others more accusatory.

"I'll come with you." Quinn was on my heels, snapping in a few colleagues' faces who were the worst staring offenders.

"No. I just want to be alone for a few minutes. Thank you though."

"Misery loves company," she said quietly, nudging me.

"Pretty sure this pit in my stomach is from humiliation, not misery, and it loves exilement." I gave her arm a gentle squeeze. "I'll touch base later."

Quinn stopped, letting me leave the break room without her. "You know where to find me."

As I rounded into the hall, I noticed a tall figure just outside the break room. I recognized his shape from the corner of my eyes and braced for whatever he was going to say, something that would no doubt drive that shame several layers deeper.

He remained quiet.

My head turned his direction to find him watching me with an expression that was hard to read. It wasn't flat, as it had been on "more than half of the footage," but it wasn't readable either. Our eyes held for a couple of moments, but I couldn't help noting the size of his pupils. The height of his brows. The gradual pull at the corners of his mouth.

I caught my hand just as it was lifting. It's target: my neck.

Damn Doctor Judith Reeves and her voodoo science. I would never interact with another human being in the same way again, and it would make my interactions with Brooks that much more uncomfortable.

Once I'd made it to the hall, my feet picked up speed. I played deaf when I heard him call my name, the sound of his footsteps following.

I needed air.

Suddenly, a door flew open in my path. The door to

Mr. Conrad's office. His expression was downright jolly, and became even more so when he saw me. And who was following behind.

"Arden. North. The very two people I was about to come looking for." Conrad clapped, stepping in front of my path.

My gaze went over Conrad's shoulder as Brooks caught up.

"Do either of you have plans tonight?" Conrad asked, barely waiting for us to answer. "Cancel them. Cancel whatever plans you have for the rest of this experiment."

My eyebrows drew together. "Why's that?"

"I'm upping the number of dates you two lovebirds go on. Three a week. Maybe four if ratings keep skyrocketing." Conrad's smile lines were carved deep as he continued. "We gotta strike while the iron's hot, and in my fifty years of journalism experience, let me tell you, the iron's never been hotter."

My tongue worked into my cheek as I attempted to think logically while ignoring the man hovering beside me. "Tonight I have plans with my friends."

"Sorry, Arden. They're going to have to take a rain-check." Conrad pointed inside his office where his television was playing the same morning show my dignity had just been dissected on. "Viewers are going to be rabid for fresh footage. New viewers are going to drop what they're doing to tune in. Sharing fruity drinks with your besties is going to have to wait."

My blood heated, but before it could spill out into words, Brooks beat me to it. "We'll do something tomorrow. Tonight, Hannah has plans."

Mr. Conrad blinked at the two of us. "I can't believe what I'm hearing. My two best writers are behaving like a couple of bench warmers instead of stars." His finger waved between us. "Tonight. The two of you. Together. I don't care what you do so long as it's being filmed."

Leaving no room for negotiation, Conrad disappeared back into his office, not only closing but locking his door. My shoulders slumped. It was barely nine in the morning and this day had already hit the top ten chart of worst days ever.

"Shrewd businessmen have nothing on Charles Conrad." Brooks tucked his hands in his pockets as he moved beside me. "I'll check back with him in a bit, after he calms down. See if I can convince him tomorrow night's better than rushing tonight. You know, to really amp up viewer anticipation."

"Thanks, but he's not going to budge."

"How do you know?" he asked.

"Conrad's immune to budging." My head turned toward him, and I instantly felt that heady, tingling sensation. Crisp white shirt, light gray slacks, still-damp-from-the-shower hair, just the right amount of stubble to make a girl imagine what it would feel like scraping along the insides of her thighs . . .

"You're flushed." Brooks angled toward me, concern creasing the skin between his brows. "Are you okay?"

My eyes sealed shut. "Yeah. I'm just hot. *Warm*."

"You want me to grab you some water or something?" He stepped closer, his arm brushing mine, not helping my "hot" situation at all.

"Brooks, I'm fine. Thank you, but we should probably nail down tonight so we can both get to work. I've got two thousand words to drum up by three o'clock." I made sure to take a couple steps back before opening my eyes again.

"What time were you meeting your friends?" he asked.

"Seven."

"Where were you meeting?" His expression was still drawn with concern as he inspected me.

"The Latin Fire Dance Company." My arms crossed, anticipating having to defend the venue, but I might as well have told him we were meeting at the pizza place around the corner.

"Fine. I'll meet you there at seven." He was turning to leave when he paused. "If that's okay with you."

"You, *you*"—my hands thrust at him—"are volunteering to meet five single women at a dance hall for an introduction to Latin dance?" I waited for the punchline.

"Five women. One guy." He held up his fingers as he listed off each number. "Why *wouldn't* I be okay with that?"

"When you put it that way . . ."

He gave one of those easy smiles as he backed away. "And maybe there might be this one girl I'd love the chance to tango the night away with."

My feet shifted. "I don't tango."

His smile tipped up on one side as he tapped his temple. "Not from what I recall."

CHAPTER
Eleven

"**D**o you really think he's going to show?" Quinn asked as she struggled to get the special dance shoes the center had loaned to us strapped to her feet.

"He said he was." I pulled the strap a little tighter before securing it. I didn't need these puppies flying off when I flicked my cankle. "If he doesn't, Conrad will probably shit his gallbladder."

I looked down the line at the three other friends who had signed up for this Latin Dance experience over a month ago. Everyone was wearing a dress that was showier than any of us would ever wear out in public—except for Quinn, who'd gone with a sensible pair of slacks. As we finished strapping on our shoes, Quinn's phone pinged in her pocket. I gave her a look as she pulled it out; most everyone who'd text her after work hours was here.

"Who's—" My eyes went wide when I glanced at her screen. "Is that *the* Justin? The one who peddles our morning fix and you've been pining over for months?"

Quinn angled her phone out of my eyesight as she punched in a response. "We don't know any other Justins. So yeah, it's *the* Justin."

"And what is The Justin texting you about?" My hand dropped to her knee. "Wait. How does he have your number to begin with?"

"I gave it to him," she said as she seemed to be typing the longest text in recent history.

"He asked for it because . . . ?"

Her eyes flicked to mine for a second. "In case he got some more basketball tickets and couldn't find anyone else to go with him."

My eyes lifted. "In case he wanted to ask you out on a date."

"As friends."

"As friends who have a secret crush on each other," I mumbled, checking the door for Brooks.

"He doesn't have a secret crush on me."

"Of course not. That's why, in a city brimming with single women who would auction a kidney to go on a date with The Justin, he asked for your number so he could ask *you* on a date."

Quinn studied her phone's screen. "He isn't asking me on a date. He's asking me to a basketball game."

My hands covered my face as my head shook. "How can you be so clueless?"

"Having Ms. Romance for a best friend is really obnoxious sometimes." Quinn rose from the bench, immediately holding her arms out like she was balancing on a tightrope. Or a pair of high heels. "And I'm not the only clueless one apparently, because neither of us have tallied up a whole lot of dates in the past couple of years."

My eyes narrowed at her in feigned anger. "I've been on plenty of dates lately."

"Fake dates," Quinn stated. "Which is worse than no dates."

"You. Suck." As I rose, I found myself experiencing the same problem Quinn had with balance. I wore heels, but not the kind with a point so narrow it might as well have been a toothpick. And how was one supposed to walk in these? Let alone tango?

The two instructors at the front of the room winced as they watched Quinn and I take our first steps. Maybe we would have been wiser to attend a line dance lesson.

The sound of a door opening drew my attention. Along with the rest of the females in the room.

"Slap me stunned." Quinn wobbled toward me. "He showed."

Jimmy followed Brooks, already fiddling with the camera strapped on his head.

"And that man does not suck in a suit." Quinn's elbow jabbed my arm like I hadn't noticed how very not sucky he looked in his tailored dark suit and crisp white dress shirt, walking in like he owned the place. And the planet.

As Jimmy ambled toward the instructors to explain and get the okay to film, I did my best to look at Brooks without staring. It was difficult. Only made more so when I realized how many people I'd looked at in my lifetime without stressing over whether I was staring, inspecting, or regarding.

Brooks headed toward me, his eyes roaming my dress

with an expression that hinted at approval. Not that I cared. Not that I wouldn't have preferred disapproval where his opinion was concerned.

"You came," I said when he stopped in front of me, the scent of him as dumbfounding as the sight.

"You sound surprised."

"It's an introduction to tango with a roomful of women." I motioned around the room. In addition to my friends, there were a good dozen other single women ranging from my age to knocking on funeral home doors.

"What man has ever frowned upon a roomful of women?" Brooks angled in closer, his eyes sparking mischievously. "And some guys might not enjoy dancing, but they likely didn't have a mother who loved to dance and begged her teenage son to tag along with her to dance classes on Thursday nights."

My eyebrows lifted. "You? You took dance lessons?"

"I was coerced, forced, begged, and bribed, but yes, I took dance lessons." Brooks checked over where Jimmy was still chatting with the instructors.

"Wow." My hand circled him. "This whole severe image of you I have is beginning to crumble."

He sighed, looking as though he regretted divulging his secret. "I'm more surprising than I am predictable. You know, in case you're planning on leaping to any more conclusions regarding who I am."

I tapped my temple. "Noted."

Brooks stepped back, his gaze roaming me again as his chin dimple made an appearance. "I like that dress, but I love it on you."

Warmth seeped into my limbs as I struggled to maintain my unfazed expression. "They said to dress femme fatale, not like I was showing up for an interview at an escort company." Pulling up on the neckline, I simultaneously pulled down on the hem. I hadn't felt this uncomfortable when I slipped into the dress earlier; why did I feel half-naked now?

"Femme fatale." His arms thrust at me. "Personified."

"Really?" I asked, still pulling at my dress every which way.

"Really. Escorts don't dress like this."

"How would you know?"

"Most of the entire female population loathes me based on my relationship ideology, so the only way I get any these days is if I pay for it." He dropped his mouth to my ear. "Or I find a woman in a hotel bar to take pity on me."

"You really pay for sex?"

One corner of his mouth twitched. "We all pay for sex. Some people are smarter than the rest and choose to exchange cash instead of sentiments. Money for sex is cheaper in the long run."

"Until you get the clinic bill," I said under my breath as the instructors announced the start of class.

A chuckle rumbled in Brooks's chest as Jimmy started toward us. The instructors talked for a few minutes, giving demonstrations of the beginning steps we'd be practicing, but I didn't hear a thing.

When we were instructed to pair up, Riley nudged me. "Introduce us."

Friends. Introductions. Reattach spinal column to brain.

"Brooks, these are my friends," I started, going down the line. "Riley, Sybill, Annie, and Quinn, you know from work."

Quinn was the only one who didn't smile as she was introduced. She went with the opposite.

"I'm not sure what the protocol is for the one guy at a dance lesson in a roomful of women." He leaned into me. "I'm going to need a little guidance."

"You dance with us all," Sybill chimed in, stepping in front of Brooks. "Hannah won't mind," she added when Brooks glanced at me.

I forced a smile instead of yanking out a chunk of my good friend's hair like my inner demon suggested. "Hannah doesn't mind."

Brooks's head angled toward mine. "Hannah really doesn't mind or is just saying that when she really does mind?"

My back stiffened. "She really doesn't mind."

"She's sure? Because she kind of has that violent gleam in her eye that makes me nervous for my manhood and its ability to create offspring if I partner up with a bunch of other women on our date." Brooks's finger tapped the corner of my eye, his touch sending a ripple of sensation through me.

I stepped aside at the same time I pushed Sybill closer to him. "You have nothing to worry about there. I will not be coming anywhere close to your manhood, to damage it or otherwise."

Jimmy shot me a wink as he adjusted himself so the camera was aimed at all three of us. If he was hoping to catch a catfight in the making, he was focused on the wrong women.

Brooks turned his attention to Sybill, his hands gliding into place after guiding hers where they were supposed to be. He said something that made her laugh before leading her around the dance floor, Jimmy doing his best to keep up with them.

"Come on." Quinn hobbled in front of me, holding up her arms. "I'll be the Johnny to your Baby."

I stepped into her arms and placed my hands where I guessed they were supposed to go. "You're a sad substitute for Patrick Swayze."

"And you're no Jennifer Gray, sweet cheeks. Just dance." Quinn winced when we moved and I stepped on her foot. "And pretend we're having the time of our lives . . ." She sang the last few words as we tripped, clomped, and stomped our way around the dance floor.

The instructors stopped by at first to give us some pointers, but their intervention fizzled out when they accepted Quinn and I moved like drunk elephants instead of budding dancers.

"You're staring. Again." Quinn pinched my waist, spinning us so my back was to him.

After Brooks had gone through all of my friends—save for Quinn, who smiled through telling him she'd rather dance with a human-sized arachnid—he was now making it through the rest of the single women in the place. Women who held no kind of allegiance to me. Clearly. The last woman had been attempting a different kind of tango with him.

"I'm just seeing where Jimmy's at. I hate when he sneaks up on me with that camera."

"I don't know how you deal with that. I'm freaking out I've got a booger sticking out of my nose every time he aims that thing toward us." Quinn sniffed, rubbing her nose. "I guess it will all be worth it when he loses and you get the promotion."

Brooks moved back into my line of sight again. "Totally."

"Ouch!" Quinn yelped, hopping on one foot as she rubbed the one I'd stepped on. Again. "I'm over it. This expanding our horizons and branching out stuff is for the birds." She peeled off the heels and limped over to the benches where a few other dancers had called it quits.

She was right, at least where tonight's experiment in trying something new was concerned. Bowling had been fun, country karaoke had been tolerable. Hell, even water aerobics at the retirement center had been Oscar-worthy compared to tonight's soiree. Though my opinion on the matter might have been swayed by the fact I'd watched Brooks dance with every other female in this room, including the instructor, except for me, the woman he was dating.

"Where do you think you're going?"

I jolted. Brooks had an annoying talent of being able to appear out of thin air. "As far away from this dance floor as I can get."

"But we haven't danced yet." Brooks crept in front of my path, forcing me to stop or crash into him.

Braking to a stop, I shot him a look. "I'll be sure to shed some tears for that later. When I'm asleep."

"Someone's notably grumpier now than they were earlier." His eyes narrowed in an investigative kind of way. "Methinks you weren't totally forthcoming about you minding if I danced with other women."

Jimmy was leaning in, our ever-present third wheel, but I didn't feel the need to lower my voice. "Methinks you were onto something when you expressed trepidation over your manhood's functioning properties after tonight."

Brooks let out a low whistle. "Under the right circumstances, those words, from that mouth, would be such a turn-on."

"The right circumstances being what? Your standing appointment with a dungeon and a dominatrix?"

One dark brow lifted. "Bad kitty."

"No. Grumpy cat." I circled my face before going around him.

His arm whipped out, cinching around my waist to draw me back to him. "Let's see if I can help with that." His hand found mine, lifting it, while his other secured at my back, bringing me closer. And closer.

And . . .

"Brooks," I hissed, remembering the camera before I put into words what I'd just felt.

He didn't appear the slightest bit fazed. "What was that about my functioning manhood?"

"I don't want to feel it digging into my stomach when I'm trying to focus on tangoing."

"Then you shouldn't have worn that dress."

"And we'll lump that in the category known as victim-blaming," I muttered, trying to ignore the hard swell rubbing against my midsection.

"It's not your fault my dick has a thing for your dress." Brooks didn't lower his voice at all. "It's his fault, one hundred and ten percent. Total case of dick-blaming right here."

My mouth worked to keep from smiling, but it was impossible. What person could talk about reproductive organs like they were discussing their weekend plans? Who casually mentioned their hard-on like they were reciting their lunch order?

Focusing on something, anything other than a certain part of him pressed all-too-close to a certain part of me, I reminded myself to dance. Or attempt the closest rendition I was capable of with the case of grace impairment I had. Somehow, the man managed to lead me across a dance floor without making me look like a three-legged giraffe.

"You have to let me lead," he instructed when I stepped on his toes.

"Okay, please." My eyes rolled as we danced, Jimmy creating his own kind of fluid movement to keep up with us. "You guys always say that, like that's going to solve the whole dance problem. How do I let you lead when I don't know where we're going?"

His hand at my back pressed in a little deeper. "By trusting me."

I exhaled out loud. "Trusting the man trying to trick me to fall in love with him? Trusting *him*?"

His hands moved as he bowed me back. So far I was certain he was aiming to hit my head against the floor. His eyes hovered above mine, the look in them making my throat dry. "You're really hung up on that, aren't you?"

"Wouldn't you be if our positions were reversed?" I whispered.

Drawing me back into a vertical position, he was quiet. Contemplative. "Let's attempt something different then." His voice was quiet as he guided me across the floor, away from Jimmy. "Let's try dating without all of the people watching?"

I checked to make sure Jimmy was out of hearing range. "Like a real date? Not one live-streamed to the masses?"

"The very kind."

My fingers curled into his shoulder. "Conrad wouldn't like it."

"Conrad won't need to know."

Jimmy was almost beside us when Brooks took a surprise turn and practically carried me in the opposite direction.

"And you won't tell anyone?"

His head moved beside mine. "Not a soul."

"You can keep a secret?"

"Have I told anyone about your present living situation?" His brow lifted. "Or that one night in Chicago?"

My teeth fretted at my lower lip. "What's your agenda with these real dates?"

"To get to know the real you. For you to get to know the real me. For us to see what's really there."

"And what if there is?" I asked. "Something there?"

"Then we can decide where to go from there." Brooks shot Jimmy a grin as we rushed by him again, Brooks moving more like a world-class sprinter than a ballroom dancer.

"It can't go there." I put my face in front of his. "A proclamation of love. A declaration to the world."

"Why not?"

I blinked at him. "Because you bet my boss you'd get me to fall in love with you with a job at stake."

His shoulder rose beneath my hand. "And what if the job isn't important anymore? What if I had the option to choose between the job and you?"

My eyes lifted. What in the world were we considering? "Well, that wouldn't happen and you wouldn't choose me. With the situation we're in, the stakes what they are, I can't ever trust what you say to me when it comes to feelings." My head throbbed in conjunction with my feet, and I cast a look over Brooks's shoulder to see where Jimmy was. Poor guy was having a tough time keeping up, and he couldn't exactly jog without making viewers feel like they were on a trampoline. "I don't think it's a good idea. It will only complicate things. Which are already complicated."

"Let's try it," he said, knotting his fingers tighter around mine. "If nothing else, by the end of it, I might manage to convince you I'm not the cold-hearted ego-trip you've arrived at."

CHAPTER
Twelve

"**Y**ou think Jimmy suspected anything?" I asked the moment Brooks moved through the door.

"That you're shacking up with me?" Brooks slid out of his jacket and draped it over the back of a dining room chair. "I think it's safe to say not. He'd more likely suspect you of slipping me arsenic in my morning coffee than of willingly moving in with me."

"Yeah?"

"Oh yeah. He's convinced you despise me with every fiber of your being in this life and your next." He rounded into the kitchen and opened the fridge. "Rooftop work for you?"

I slipped out of my shoes. "For what?"

"Our first date."

I paused in the middle of taking off my earrings.

"Our first *real* date," he added, coming out of the kitchen holding a couple of wine glasses and a chilled bottle of . . .

"Is that sparkling cider?"

"Have you changed your mind on the drinking-while-I'm-present issue?" His brows lifted.

"Not even," I replied with a smile.

"Then cider it is." He started down the hall. "Grab a blanket. It can get chilly up there."

After sliding into my slippers, I grabbed the extra blanket in my closet before following him. It was late, we'd already been on one date, and I hadn't exactly agreed to this idea of his, but I couldn't help following him.

After taking the elevator to the top floor, we had to take stairs to the roof. Brooks led the way like he'd lived here for years instead of weeks.

"Spend a lot of time up here?" I asked.

Brooks swung the door open for me. "Written some of my best stuff here."

"You've only published three articles since moving here." I nudged his stomach as I passed. "And those were far from your best work."

"So you read my stuff."

"I *skim* your stuff." A breeze rushed over me as I moved around the roof. "And 'What Women Think They Want' is a freshman attempt at one of your first articles, 'The Female Psyche.'"

"So you've been following my work from the beginning then?" Brooks's footsteps echoed closer as he waited for my response. "I'll let your silence answer for you. And who said anything about my best work being *published* articles? You're just going to have to wait for the good stuff. Stalker." He winked at me before wandering toward the roof edge.

"So. We're here. In real date territory." I sat on the ledge lining the rooftop. Brooks's forehead creased with unease before retrieving a couple of old lawn chairs stacked against the stairwell wall. "What now?"

"First, relax. You're stressing me out with all the questions. And second." He whipped the first chair open and motioned at it. "Would you please put your butt in this? A strong wind comes through and you're going to be doing a backward somersault off this roof."

"That's a physical impossibility," I said even as I moved toward the chair. "I'm too bottom heavy to topple headfirst over much of anything."

"Bottom heavy." He huffed as he opened the second chair for himself. "The crazy runs deep, doesn't it?"

"Pretty sure we're not here to argue my body type. So can we talk about why we're really here?"

He undid his collar button and moved on to rolling up his sleeves. "To get to know each other."

"Don't we already know each other?"

"We know *of* each other. We know our public personas, our views on relationships, our work-centered lives. But we don't know the real person behind all of that." He scooted his chair closer to mine. "I want to know the real you. And I want you to know the real me."

Kicking my feet up on the ledge, I wound the blanket around my shoulders. He'd been right about needing the blanket up here.

"Why?" I asked slowly. "What we do know of one another, we're almost total opposites. We're professional adversaries. We've been forced into this game of dating charades by the forces that be."

"And we came together all on our own before all of this," he interjected as his head turned my direction. "Remove the cameras and our work life and we still have whatever it was that brought two strangers together that night."

The chair whined when I shifted. "You don't believe in any of that chemistry, fate, meant-to-be stuff."

"No, but I believe in attraction. And I was drawn to you that night." I felt his eyes wander me. "I still am."

Goose bumps spilled down my arms, which were thankfully disguised by the blanket. His words were exactly right; it was his intentions that were entirely wrong.

"Well, I declare, Brooks North. You think I'm pretty?" I batted my eyelashes dramatically as I fanned my face. "You must be my one and only. My true love. My prince on the white horse."

"Wow. Drama school drop-out?" He was cringing when I glanced his direction.

"Good for you for recognizing when a woman's faking. You probably have plenty of experience with that."

Brooks snorted, leaning toward me like he was about to let me in on a secret. "Nine out of ten women polled claimed I left them speechless."

"And the tenth?"

He grinned. "Still speechless."

"Cocky much?"

"Only when it comes to my dick and my writing."

My head shook, but I was actually having a good time out on this rooftop, enjoying the view with a man who drove me crazy in just as many right as wrong ways. Brooks was a modern caveman with a big vocabulary. And somehow I found myself drawn to him, enjoying his company, feeling comfortable in my own skin.

"Are we going to spend the rest of our first date like this?" My finger waved between us.

"Thanks for the segue." He leaned down to pick up the cider bottle and glasses he'd placed beside his chair. "Actually, I was thinking we could ask each other one question at a time. As personal or impersonal as we want —nothing is off-limits—the only rule being whoever's answering has to be honest. One hundred percent honest. The three-quarters version isn't going to fly."

I was fixated on one word—personal. I didn't consider myself closed off, but agreeing to answer whatever depraved question an oaf like Brooks might come up with made the air feel thin.

"I don't know . . ." I said, summing up in three words how I felt about all things of a Brooks nature.

"Come on. It's the only way to get to know each other in as quick and truthful a way as possible. Couples take years to learn what we're going to condense into mere weeks." He popped the cap off the cider and poured it into the glasses. "No bullshit."

My fingers drummed across the rusted metal arm of the chair. "No bullshit? Not even the kind that might have an ulterior motive of getting me to profess my love for you on camera?"

His mouth moved as he handed me a glass. "Not even that kind. That's the foulest kind of bullshit. And if it makes you feel any better, we can each have one veto to whatever question we don't want to answer. Sound fair?"

Taking a drink of the cider, I stared at the city lights as I considered my answer. The idea of getting to know him beyond the online research and biased observations was appealing. The thought of him getting to know me, whatever he wanted to know, was paralyzing.

"Let's do this." I clinked my glass to his while my insides glitched, one part at a time.

From his temporary silence, I knew I'd surprised him. Hell, I'd surprised myself.

"First question." He bowed his head at me. "You get the honors."

My brain hiccupped, not realizing we were starting this hive-inducing game of Q&A a half second after agreeing to it. *Question. Question. What do I want to know about Brooks North?*

"What was your kindergarten teacher's name?" The words exploded from my mouth, followed by my face drawing into a wince. Of all the questions, *that* was the one I led with?

Just paint a giant L on my forehead. For lame.

Brooks covered his mouth—probably so he could silently laugh into it. "Mrs. Spears. The most patient person on the planet."

"She would have had to be to put up with a five-year-old version of you," I muttered, adjusting in my chair to get comfortable. "Okay. Your turn."

"How many times had you hooked up with someone before that night with me?"

I was already wincing in anticipation, but his question shifted my expression into shock and awe. "Uh oh. No way. I just asked you what your teacher's name was and you ask me how many guys I've hooked up with in my life? Not fair."

He lifted his shoulders. "You wanna use your veto?"

"No," I half-shouted. "Because if that's your first question, I don't want to imagine what your fiftieth will be."

"So?" He blinked at me with the least innocent look humanly possible. "How many?"

I dropped my feet from the ledge. Then I placed them back there. Crossed my ankles. Crossed them the other way. "Before you?" God, my voice was about an octave and a half too high.

"And after, if you want to add that in too," he replied before taking a lazy sip of his cider.

"Taking in college experiences, subtracting life-like dreams, not counting leap years, rounding to the closest number . . ." My eyes narrowed as I calculated my answer, shifting yet again in my seat. "That would be none."

He was quiet long enough I glanced his way to make sure he hadn't fallen asleep.

"None," he stated.

I inhaled. "None."

A shorter pause this time. "None?"

"And there's that word again," I gritted out. "You seem to be struggling with it. Let's try another. Zero. No one. Nada. Zip. Zilch. Nil."

Brooks set his glass down and leaned forward in his chair. "Really? Never?"

"No." I shot him the same look he was giving me. "And why are you looking at me like I'm some kind of mutant because I'm picky when it comes to who I fall into bed with?"

"Picky?" A single laugh rattled in his ribcage. "You spent all of three hours getting to know me before—"

"Thank you. I remember what followed."

A whirlwind of emotions played over Brooks's face while I second-guessed my decision to agree to this slow form of torture.

"And after?" he asked.

"That's two questions." My head shook. "And it's barely been two months since my first random hook-up, so I'll let you read between the lines there."

"So none after either," he said, clasping his hands. "Your turn."

My forehead creased from the abrupt shift. Confessing I was a hook-up amateur to firing off the next question.

"How many women before me did you have a one-night stand with?" I asked without hesitation. No more teacher-name quality questions.

His eyes locked on mine. "I invoke my veto power."

My nose crinkled. "What?"

"Ve-to," he enunciated slowly.

My eyebrows rose into my hairline. "You seriously just used your one and only veto on the very first *serious* question I asked you?"

"I'd rather veto right up front than keep thinking 'damn, I wish I hadn't answered that question.'"

I stared at the city, considering his approach before deciding it was not for me. "And I'd much rather save my veto for one of the last questions, in case you ask something totally inappropriate."

Brooks tucked the blanket higher behind my neck. If he noticed the goose bumps scattered across my skin, he gave nothing away. "You're more likely to ask the most important questions up front."

He was right, making me wonder if he already had a very good idea who the real Hannah Arden was. Maybe I knew him better than I thought I did too.

"And you're most likely to save those for last."

CHAPTER
Thirteen

My phone chimed while I agonized over the last sentence of my article that was due in twenty-three minutes. Not the ideal time to let myself get distracted.

Checking the screen, I squashed my smile before it formed. The message from the mysterious DC (two guesses what that stood for) read: *How would I know you were lying?*

It was his turn to ask the next question after he'd answered mine last night. I'd asked if he had any food allergies so I could, naturally, make sure to include that in the next meal I made for him.

I considered ignoring his question until I'd finished my article, but now that I was thinking about it, I couldn't turn it off. Swiveling around in my chair, I considered my answer. How did I act when I lied? What did I do? How did I look?

Of course I realized he was asking so he could call me out if he caught me lying to his face. So maybe I should have kept my answer vague . . . but that flew in the face of our Q&A's one cardinal rule: be honest.

I typed in a quick response and reread it before sending. *My voice gets a little high, and I can't make eye contact. I throw in more ums and yeahs than usual too.*

A moment later, I heard a chime from the cubicle in front of me. We never asked our questions out loud when we were at work; we relied on email and texts. In the evening when we were at his place, we could spew as many verbal questions as we could fit in before we crashed for the night, but here we had to keep a careful distance.

A minute later, Brooks rose from his chair. "So you must think I'm a pretty amazing guy by now, right? A real catch? One in a billion?" He adjusted his tie, giving me a burning look I managed to play ignorant too.

"Um, yeah, sure," I said, pitching my voice a few notes high. "I'd, um, agree. Yeah."

"That's what I thought." He chuckled as he wove out of his cubicle. "You want a coffee?"

I nodded as I got back to my article.

"Extra cream, extra sugar?"

"You always ask that. Do you assume one day I'm going to change how I like my coffee?"

"I don't assume. I just want to allow you the option of changing your stance on how you like your coffee." His light eyes sparked. "Or anything else for that matter."

"Wishful thinking," I called after him, loud enough a few heads turned my way.

Brooks and I already drew enough attention as it was in the office, thanks to the increasing popularity of our dating experiment, and I knew neither of us should be giving anyone more reasons to speculate in whispers in cube alcoves.

After getting back to my article and feeling confident I'd stiff-armed that last sentence into shape, someone stepped into my space.

"That was quick," I said before spinning around to discover it wasn't the person I thought it was.

"What was quick?" Quinn asked, stabbing her pencil through her messy ponytail.

"Sorry. Thought you were someone else."

"Nope. Just your uber awesome best friend here with a friendly reminder that the cafeteria downstairs is closing in fifteen minutes." She tapped her wrist where a watch might have been if she wore one. "Time to scavenge what we can before it's another meal compliments of the vending machines."

"Perfect timing," I said as I hit Send on my article to Mr. Conrad.

"Perfect timing would have been twelve thirty for lunch instead of two forty-five." She wove her arm through mine and steered us toward the elevators.

Most days we scored lunch from the cafeteria on the second floor. Quinn usually got something from the fried section while I scouted the grilled section, then we shared our loot. With how busy I'd been the past six weeks, our lunch dates had been infrequent at best.

Plus with my new living situation, the subway no longer spit me out at the stop right by Flour Power. Quinn had been gracious enough to snag my morning sustenance and bring it into work for me, but I missed my breakfast dates with her.

"How're you holding up?" Quinn asked as we waited at the elevators.

"Not too bad. You?" I fired off a quick text to Brooks letting him know I was grabbing lunch but he could leave my coffee on my desk. I might have angled my phone so Quinn couldn't see it, since she was still convinced he was one of Stalin's blood relatives.

"You don't have to keep up the façade with me. It's got to be exhausting going on all of those damn dates, having Conrad pull your strings while millions of people are watching you live. And having to keep up with your duties here as an actual writer on top of it all . . ."

I patted her hand as we stepped onto the elevator. "Considering everything, I'm doing good. Real, non-façade answer. I swear."

"Oh my God, and your apartment on top of it all. It's taking forever for them to get it fixed up." Quinn's head fell back, patting my hand faster. "Having to endure breathing the same air as him in that sterile haunt he calls home."

"Actually, it's not his home. He's just renting the place."

Her head whipped back into place, those dark eyes narrowing on me. "You're defending him." Her face got in mine. "Why are you defending the demonic parasite?"

"I'm not." I internally cringed when I registered how high my voice was. "I'm just stating that he's only temporarily residing there until I prove my point and become editor in chief. I'm sure his real place in California is much worse. So sterile you can actually smell the joy being sucked out of you."

Quinn pinched my cheek. "There's my girl." After I swatted her hand away, she hip-checked me. "How many more days until you can move back into your place?"

"Andre called this morning and said the cleaning crew is almost done and I should be able to move back in by next Monday." My shoulders slumped for some strange reason. Why wasn't I psyched about getting to move back into my own space and out of Brooks's soulless dwelling?

"Any way they can speed things up? It's practically been a month." Quinn led the way off the elevator when the doors chimed open on the second floor, toward the smell of fried food that had been wilting beneath heat lamps for hours. "Your landlord should compensate you for having to move out, or at least give you a break on your rent. Not to mention toss in some Benjamins for the therapy you're going to require after spending all that time with a turd like Brooks North."

"Yeah, not sure they're going to go for that, but thanks for looking out," I said as I steered toward the grill while Quinn sauntered to the fryers.

"Eh. Anything look edible over there?" Quinn tapped her foot as she inspected the selection of goods under the heat lamps.

"This coming from the woman who ate half a hot dog that I'd forgotten in my purse the day before?" I touched the wrapper of one of the few burgers left out, confirming the bun was about as hard as a Frisbee. "Think we're going to have to settle for the salad bar or risk breaking a tooth biting into one of those things."

"Salad bar? Did those words just come out of your mouth?"

I felt Quinn's hard stare aimed at my back. "Just an idea." I touched the wrapped chicken sandwiches. Instead of rock hard, the buns felt soggy.

"People die from eating at salad bars."

"Aren't fresh vegetables good for us?"

"Not if they're packed with E. coli." Quinn held up a tray with a couple of corndogs that were cracked from spending hours under a heat lamp. Taken as a whole, a questionable meat substance wrapped in dried-out corn bread was the best option.

"Works for me," I said, snagging a few packets of ketchup before paying for our just-edible lunch. After we'd selected a table, I squeezed my ketchup into a blob on the tray. "So I've been waiting for you to bring it up, but since you don't seem in a hurry to . . . what's the latest Justin news?"

Her failure to make eye contact alerted me *something* had happened. "We went to that basketball game."

The noise my corndog made when I dropped it sounded like it was made of wood. "When?"

Quinn shifted. "Last night."

My mouth fell open as I lowered my head toward hers. "And you were going to tell me about this when?"

Quinn swirled her corndog into her mustard. "There's nothing to tell. He got some tickets, asked if I wanted to go, we went, that's all."

My fingers rolled across the table. "That's *all* all?"

"I don't speak Ms. Romance."

A sigh escaped me. "No long stares, no arms draped over shoulders?" The corners of my eyes creased. "No good night kiss?"

"No. Definitely no." Quinn gave me a look that suggested she was offended by my question.

"Why definitely no? Don't you want him to kiss you?"

Quinn tore off a bite of her corndog. "Maybe."

"So why act like I'm criminally insane for speculating there might have been a good night kiss?"

"Because he's not into me like that," she said, still chewing like the lady she was. "He sees me more like some other dude than a chick you make out with."

Clue. Less.

For ten thousand please, Alex.

"What makes you think that?" I asked, realizing if Quinn was incapable of picking up Justin's signals, she was going to die alone.

"I don't know. I just don't seem like his type?" She shrugged.

"The sports aficionado who has so much to offer it makes heads spin and is a beauty that doesn't require the aid of face spackle and paint to make her so?" I waved at my best friend, wondering on what planet she didn't consider herself a high-ranking candidate to just about every straight, red-blooded male out there.

"The Justins of the world end up with the Jessicas." She twirled her corndog like it was a wand before ripping off another bite.

"The Jessicas?" I slid my lunch aside because no amount of hunger could get that brick down.

"You know, the hair-flipping, eye-batting girls who came out of the womb with the talent to accessorize and abstain from anything containing sugar." She frowned.

"The Jessicas."

My hands flattened on the table. "Justin is not looking for a Jessica." I blinked at her, wondering when her wires had crossed. "Justin is looking for a Quinn Rivers, a.k.a. *you*."

Half of her face pulled up with a doubtful look, which left me flabbergasted. How could she be so blind to the obvious? To what was literally right in front of her, practically flashing in neon lights?

Suddenly, her eyes focused on something over my shoulder. "Um. Fan club alert." She cracked open her can of Sprite after finishing her last bite of corndog.

"Fan club?" I repeated, twisting in my seat.

It took me a moment to process what I was seeing through the windows of the cafeteria. A group of people had their faces pressed to the glass, phones raised, chattering excitedly to one another. They were tourists—the comfortable walking shoes, backpacks, and newly done nails gave it away—but I couldn't figure out what they were doing standing outside this building instead of the one where the *Today* show was filmed.

"Those shirts are new. I'm going to have to pick myself up one of those." Quinn waved at the spectators with Sprite in hand.

"'I'm With Her'?" I read.

"Except for that chic. She's with him." Quinn's pinkie finger indicated one of the younger woman whose shirt was a different color—blue, and it had exchanged the *her* for *him*.

"People still hanging onto those after the election?"

Quinn shook her head at me. "Those have nothing to

do with politics. At least not the governmental kind."

Someone might as well have clocked me across the face for the realization I had then. "They're talking about us, aren't they?" I gaped at the shirts. "'I'm With Her' means they're with me, and 'I'm With Him' means they side with Brooks."

Quinn banged an invisible drum. "Next, the street vendors will be selling dolls with a lifelike resemblance to Ms. Romance and Mr. Reality, and let's not forget about scrapbooks for signatures and photos taken in the same locations you two had your dates."

Silence settled in, winding deep. I'd been kept abreast of the rising number of viewers and advertising spaces being sold thanks to Conrad's manically gleeful updates. I'd even been recognized a couple of times on the subway, though one person thought I just looked a lot like Ms. Romance and wasn't really her.

My life had taken no direct hit due to the show, other than having to carve out the time—and dignity—to attend the dates.

Until now.

When a dozen tourists with shirts showing their support watched me pick at a rubber corndog across from my best friend, whom I'd been lecturing on her own love life disasters.

"I don't know what to do," I whispered to Quinn, as though they could hear me through the glass.

"I don't know. Just smile, wave, and evacuate the premises." Quinn's chair screeched across the tile floor as she rose.

Doing as suggested, I plastered on a smile and moved

my hand back and forth in a way that made a robot seem personal before following her out of the cafeteria.

"Might I suggest evacuating swiftly?" She nudged me as her pace picked up. "Before those fangirls bust into the building to tackle you. That one chick with the feather ear-rings is tipping the stalker scale of considering skinning you to make into a handbag."

My heels had no problem keeping up with her sneak-ers after that warning. "I'm a writer, not a celebrity. If I wanted fame and phones in my face, I wouldn't have gone into a career where I get to hide behind my computer screen for a living."

"Better get used to it." Quinn punched the elevator button a few more times, eyeing the front entry doors. "Because I don't see viewership going down anytime soon."

"Now every time I leave the house, I'm going to be paranoid I have lipstick on my teeth or my dress tucked into my tights."

When the elevator doors whirred open, we both jumped inside.

"You're going to have to hire one of those big, beefy security guys with a dark suit and sunglasses. The kind of guy who can crush you with his stare." Quinn chugged what was left of her Sprite. "My best friend is a celebrity, tearing up the Twitter trending models."

"Your best friend is not a celebrity, and the only thing I'm tearing up is the Chinese takeout menu at Lee Ching's tonight to self-soothe my anxiety."

I trudged out of the elevator, feeling overwhelmed. Brooks aside, the real dates, the fake dates, all of that I'd figured out a way to deal with. In my own quirky way. But this? The public scrutiny and not being able to go out for milk in my jammies at midnight without fearing recognition made me downright spastic with stress.

"Don't freak. You've got six more weeks before you prove to the world love lives, slide into your dream job, and say goodbye to Brooks Who? forever." Quinn made a face in the direction of Brooks's cubicle. He wasn't there, but I could make out my coffee resting on the cube wall between us.

"You sound so certain it's all going to work out," I said.

"That's because it *is* going to all work out. This is you we're talking about. You set your mind to something, I fear the person who tries to stand in your way."

My neck cracked. "What if—"

"Don't you even think about dropping a what if on me. That's the gateway to failure."

"What I was going to say before you jumped in is . . ." I paused to see if she was going to be so bold as to interrupt a second time. "What if we're both right? What if he has a point as much as I do?" My teeth worked at my lip from hearing myself out loud. "You've said so yourself a few times."

Quinn tossed her Sprite can in the closest garbage can before grabbing my shoulders and giving me The Look. "I've changed my mind. Taken a total one-eighty in light of new evidence brought to light. If you're right, he can't be right. If he's right, you can't be right. One person can't say the sky is blue and another claim it's orange and both of them be right."

I sighed, feeling more confused than I had before this conversation. "But depending on the time of day, the sky can be blue. Or orange."

CHAPTER
Fourteen

L ast night's "date" had brought in a staggering number of viewers. Or if you were me, a paralyzing amount. So much so, I could not make myself repeat the figure out loud or in my head. As popularity spread, street teams had assembled, blasting out on social media any sightings of Brooks or me, some so hardcore they could be found waving posters on the sidewalks outside the *World Times* building, showing support for whichever side of the love debate they found themselves on.

I'd even heard whispers that advertisers were spending upward of six figures for a fifteen-second advertising spot parsed in at the bottom of the screen during the live dates. It was a circus, and Brooks and I had become the main attraction. Merchandise had gotten out of control, expanding beyond T-shirts and pins and bleeding into every department imaginable. When I'd caught sight of cupcakes in a local bakery that had leapt onto the *Romance Versus Reality* bandwagon, I considered boycotting them.

Until I noticed the fresh lemon bars being placed into the display and sidelined my principles for five minutes.

It had gotten to the point where I'd actually considered asking for a body guard or some surly-looking giant who would flank me whenever I took to the streets, because mixed in with the harmless diehard fans were a few who gave off the psycho vibe. Or as Quinn had put it, the ones who'd rather skin me and carry me as a handbag than ask for a photo with me.

"You about ready in there, Hannah?" A staccato of knocks sounded outside my bedroom door as I pulled on my last boot.

"One sec," I replied before swiping on a fresh coat of lipstick and raking a brush through my hair. When I threw open the door, Brooks was standing right outside it, which made me flinch.

He chuckled. "You'd think you'd have gotten used to that by now."

"Used to what? Having someone plastered against my door with a creepy look on his face?" I waited for him to step aside, but he didn't budge. Discreetly, I shifted back.

"You can't go out like that." His brows pulled together when he took a good look at me.

"Excuse me? I can go out however I want." My eyes skimmed down my outfit. A light jacket, jeans, and boots. It was casual at its best, but it wasn't like we were heading to the Four Seasons.

"If you do, we're not going to make it two steps outside the door before being recognized." He retrieved a paper bag from the floor before coming inside and upending the contents onto my bed. "Incognito in a bag."

He selected a pair of wide-rimmed glasses from the stash and slid them on. When he held out his arms and did a slow spin, I collected a few other items for his disguise. It was like taking Superman and putting dorky glasses on him though; not exactly a convincing disguise.

"Are you sure this is a good idea? Going out in public like this?" I stepped into him, lifting onto my tiptoes to position a ball cap on his head. "We've always done these things in private."

"These *things*?"

"You know what I mean." Shuffling through the pile of goods, I found something I couldn't resist.

"It will be fine. That's why I went to the costume store and stocked up like I was considering a career change into the secret agent field." He frowned when I tore off the sticker backing of the fake mustache.

"What? It's not like you bought this for me," I said, pressing it into his upper lip before smoothing it out. Even pasting a fake mustache onto him, my body wasn't immune to the warmth of his breath on my wrist or the way his throat moved when I touched him.

"How do you know? Plenty of women have mustaches."

My hands dropped when I realized they were frozen against his jaw. "Yeah, except red-haired women usually don't grow black mustaches."

"Case of the drapes not matching the carpet?" He shot me a wink, twirling his fake mustache.

My hand shoved his stomach. "Stop acting like a pubescent boy. It's too predictable."

"Who said I'm acting?" He nudged me as he passed

by to sort through what was left on my bed. "Okay, my turn." Grabbing an emerald-green silk scarf, he wound it behind my neck before knotting it tight.

"Because my neck is so recognizable." My fingers rolled across my hip as he gathered up a few more things. When he held up the dark brown wig styled straight with a blunt cut, I stepped back. "I don't think so."

But he was already gathering up my hair, twisting it on top of my head. "You put a predator stache on my face. You're getting off easy with a wig."

"I hate wigs. They make my head itch like crazy," I argued, though I stood still when he slid the heinous thing into place. "And I don't look good with short hair. Makes my cheeks look like two balloons about to pop."

Brooks exhaled, moving the wig around a bit before stepping back. "Nah, you can pull off short hair." He plunked a pair of huge sunglasses on my face, fighting a smile when he took in his masterpiece. "Though I do like you better as a redhead."

"Yeah, and I like the non-predator look on you better too," I grumbled as I grabbed my purse from the door-knob. "Actually, no, you look more like an 80s porn star with that stache."

Brooks followed me toward the front door, a wicked smile creeping into place. "And how would you know what an 80s porn star looked like?"

"Oh, please. Nice attempt at entrapment there, Hugh Cox." I tipped my cat-eyed sunglasses at him. "For your information, I've never watched 80s porn. I'm more a fan of the 70s era."

The keys in his hand dropped as he was about to lock the door.

I played it cool, waiting for him at the elevator bay.

He was jogging, from the sound of his footsteps.

"You look flushed," I noted.

He recovered instantly, that unfazed expression going into place. "It's not every day a man comes across a fellow aficionado of the golden age of porn."

We were both holding back laughter as we climbed onto the elevator.

"Your apartment still going to be ready to move into tomorrow?" Brooks asked as we watched the floor buttons light up in descending order.

"So long as my upstairs neighbor doesn't forget to turn off her bath again tomorrow, it's all set."

"Yeah. That's good," he said, but there was no conviction in his voice.

I knew the feeling.

Spending the past few weeks in the same living space as Brooks had been eye-opening. Not only that, it had been easy; both of us had settled into a pattern that I'd never experienced before when living with a roommate. Usually, increasing one's level of tolerance was required for sharing a space with another human being, but this felt less about tolerance and more about harmony. We moved through our daily lives as though it were a dance we'd learned in another life and were performing unconsciously in this one.

"Like I said before, don't feel like you have to help me get settled back in. It's only a few bags of stuff. I can manage on my own no problem." When the doors opened,

Brooks waited for me to get off first. "Besides, with all of the time we've been spending together, you could probably use a break from me."

Brooks tipped his baseball cap an inch lower before he shoved open the outside door. "A break from you? What would I do with myself then? I don't like all of that peaceful, quiet stuff."

I glared at him through the dark lenses. "Not sure insulting your date is the best approach to getting her to view you as something more evolved than your ape ancestors."

He made a few blaring ape calls, swinging his arms around like a brute.

"I thought the idea was to *not* draw attention to ourselves," I said, indicating the people wandering the sidewalk with us.

"You make a good point." His arms went back at his sides. "This one time."

My eyes lifted. He was already getting on my nerves and we hadn't even arrived at our destination. "Where are we going?"

"Not far."

"Not far as in a few blocks or a few miles?" I motioned at my boots. "Because I am not the superhuman triathlete who doesn't break a sweat until mile ten."

His mustache pulled at the corners from his smile. "Good of you to finally acknowledge my superhumanness."

"I meant super more in the vein of abnormal."

"Thank you again."

"Can a person say anything to you without you taking it as a compliment?" I asked, my fingers twitching from the urge to itch my head.

"Doubtful."

"I guess I know where everyone's lack of self-confidence got filtered to."

He shrugged without a hint of shame before dodging in front of me to swing open a door. "Not far," he repeated, waving me inside the bustling joint.

"McGregor's?" I said, reading the rusted metal sign hanging above the door. I'd never heard of the place, but rowdy Irish pubs weren't the worst place to spend an evening.

"Trust me. You'll love it."

"As who? Hannah Arden or Trixie Derriere?" I stepped up to the door, the scent of beer and fried fish rolling over me.

"Would you get your stuffy little derriere inside before I throw you over my shoulder and volunteer you to stand on the bar and recite a limerick after chugging a car bomb?" He nudged me inside just enough so the door could close.

"Whatever. Hugh."

As I made my way inside, it was refreshing to find no one really paying attention to anyone else. Everyone was too occupied with their own conversations, their beers, or their games of darts.

It was a unique mix of people stuffed in a place that looked and smelled like it had been around since before any of the skyscrapers. McGregor's appeared to be the watering hole for just about every breed of person one could find on the diverse island of Manhattan.

"Quick!" Brooks had to shout above the noise, pointing at a small table in the back where a couple were getting up and leaving.

"It's just a table. Not the cure to cancer," I shouted back.

"Yeah, well, finding an open table at this place on a Friday night runs about the same odds as finding that cure." Brooks pumped his fists as we barreled into the empty seats.

"I'm kind of regretting keeping this date a secret." When I went to lift the sunglasses onto my head, he slid them back over my eyes. "It would do the world good to see just how imbalanced you really are."

He pointed into the crowd of people acting more like it was the last night on Earth instead of a Friday night in April. "Makes me relatable. They'll only love me more."

I ignored him and scanned the crusty menu. I wasn't a snob when it came to places I'd visit, but I had standards for hygiene. "This does not seem like your kind of place."

His forehead creased. "Why not?"

I stared at him for a minute, wondering if he was actually expecting me to answer that. "Oh, I don't know. Take a look at the way you keep your apartment. Or the way you dress . . . any other time but tonight." I eyed his T-shirt and casual slacks. It was like he'd been possessed. "Even the way you organize your fridge. That picture does not align with this one," I finished, eyeing the scene at McGregor's.

"My goal isn't to be congruous and predictable in every facet of my life, you know?" His attention diverted to the bar, where he lifted two fingers at a guy who looked like he benched redwoods for a warm-up.

"Then what is your goal, Mr. Suddenly Stoic?"

"To be unpredictable. To surprise myself. To change, evolve, that kind of thing. How boring would it be to be born, live, and die the exact same person, believing the exact same things?" He lightly pulled on the ends of my bob-cut wig.

"That's a romantic's way of viewing life," I said.

"No, that's a realist's view. To imagine we can go through life without changing is a fool's doctrine."

A waitress with corkscrew red hair and a face full of freckles set a couple of nearly black beers in front of us.

Lifting my glass, I clinked it against his. "Like your soul?"

He tipped his beer at me before taking a sip. "And my heart."

"And your stache," I added, setting my beer down without taking a drink.

"Still too scared to drink in my company?" He flicked my glass. "Afraid of what might happen after if you lower those unscalable inhibitions of yours?"

"Oh, to have the delusions of an ego-bloated psychopath."

Relaxing into my chair, I took a few minutes to survey the scene. I'd always been a people-watcher; that was part of what drew me into writing. Observing, without interacting. Being the fly on the wall. I'd learned more about humans from watching than I ever had from conversing.

When my gaze returned to Brooks, I'd forgotten about his "disguise." A laugh spurted from me when I noticed one corner of his mustache had curled away from his lip.

"We look ridiculous," I said, re-adhering the corner to his skin.

"Well, you do. I look distinguished."

When I slugged his arm, he rubbed it. "Okay, my turn." He cracked his knuckles and leaned in. "Would you rather marry someone who wasn't 'the one' or spend the rest of your life alone, waiting for said solidarity?"

My head rolled as I groaned. This question-and-answer game had remained a practice in torture. At the same time, I could appreciate its merits. In a handful of weeks, I felt like I'd gotten to know more about Brooks than I knew about most people in my life. The carte blanche to ask any question and the stipulation to answer honestly meant those skeletons in the closet eventually toppled out.

"Alone and waiting," I answered. "No question."

Brooks contemplated that with another drink of beer. "Really? You'd rather miss out on a chance at a family and everything else that comes with marriage for the gamble your one true love is out there?"

"A family is possible without the traditional method. Welcome to the twenty-first century." I patted his hand. "I'd just rather spend my life hoping than resigned. Wouldn't you?"

"Is that your question?"

My eyes rolled. "Sure."

"No, I would not," he said emphatically. "I would rather marry someone who might not set my life on fire, but had the potential for feelings to mature, than spend my whole life alone." Half of his face pulled up. "That sounds like a terrible way to waste your life."

My fingers skimmed beneath my wig to scratch my head. My hair follicles were suffocating. "A waste of a life is spending it with someone you learn to tolerate."

Brooks huffed. "Next question." He rubbed his hands together. "Would you rather marry me or . . ." He held up his finger when I started to protest. "*Or* that manchild from your apartment building who has been calling or texting you every day since you moved out?"

"How do you know he's been contacting me?" I asked, my mouth falling open.

"Your phone." He shrugged, all innocent-like. "That you keep on counters as though you're inviting any passerby to check out."

"I'm not even surprised," I said as he circled his hand at me, waiting for my answer. I eyed my beer, actually considering chugging it before answering this question. "I'd rather marry you." I glared at the smirk growing on his face. "Because at least we've already figured out one important component to making a relationship work."

His smirk only deepened. "We had no problem figuring that out, did we?"

"I meant living together," I exclaimed, scooting my chair away from him. "We've figured out how to *live* together."

He stared at me over his beer. "That too."

Lowering my sunglasses so he could see my eyes, I ran with the streak of bold that had surged inside. "Would you rather marry me . . ." I paused long enough to give him time to interject, but he stayed quiet. "Or the girl in layout who's always hovering by your cube?"

Brooks gave me a funny look. "Easy. You."

I pursed my lips when I felt the smile coming. "Why?"

"Sorry. That's two questions. I already answered your first."

My shoulders fell. "Really? You're going to play all 'by the book' like the good rule-follower we both know you aren't?"

"When it comes to you encroaching on my question territory, yes, that is how I'm going to play it." He twirled the corner of that nasty stache again, able to make me laugh even when I was annoyed with him. "Uh-oh. Two o'clock. Pretty sure we've got some diehards who aren't buying the disguises." Brooks tipped his hat a bit lower, his gaze flickering to a few ladies pressed up against the bar, whispering to each other as they kept glancing back at our table.

"Or they could be discussing the atrocity that thing on your face is." I slid my beer beside his empty one since I wasn't going to drink it.

"That might be possible, if they weren't all wearing a certain pin on their jackets."

Seeing what he was talking about, I nodded. "I like them."

"The phones are coming out," he said, taking my arm to guide me out of my seat.

"They don't recognize us. You're overreacting."

He took my hand and wove through the crowd toward the door. The women's phones followed us.

"It physically pains me to say this, but I think you're right," I said, adjusting the bangs of my wig so it covered as much of my face as possible.

"Sweetest words I've yet to hear." He shot me a grin when we were about halfway to the door, but that was when things went south.

The trio of women had defied the laws of motion and somehow gotten in front of us, blocking our escape. The one in the middle had an *I'm With Her* pin on her jacket, but her eyes were gushing *I'm With Him*.

"You're that couple, aren't you?" she asked us. Well, she asked Brooks. Brooks attempted to scoot around the woman wall, but they moved with us. "Don't you even think about sneaking past without posing for a picture with us."

My teeth worked at my lip for a moment. "Only if you promise not to post them publicly. For your eyes only, okay?"

I didn't want to fathom what Conrad would say if he found out Brooks and I had been sneaking out on private dates.

"Our eyes only," the woman with the bright pink lipstick said, drawing an X across her chest.

As the women staggered between us, Brooks gave me a look, double-checking to make sure I was good with this. I answered by winding my arms around the women closing in and smiling at the camera phone they'd convinced someone at the nearby table to take a picture with.

"You are just hard all over," the older woman of the bunch cooed as her hand moved from Brooks's side to capping behind his shoulder. "Your thoughts on romance might not align with mine, but I'd be willing to take a temporary hiatus to the dark side with you."

My eyes lifted behind my dark glasses as the other

women rocked from their snickers.

Brooks shot me a flash of a grin before the person holding the camera gave the "say cheese" prompt. The three women around me stuck out their chests and smiled like they were vying for Miss America. In contrast, my posture wilted at the same time as an indigestion bubble burst in my throat. Great. I probably looked like I'd just swallowed a cat. Alive and clawing.

After the picture, the women took their time thanking us for our time, probably because they were hoping Brooks would take them up on their dark side foray offer. If these were my so-called followers and he'd managed to change their minds with a porn-star mustache and a hard body, I was in trouble. Where were the diehard romantics? The ones who were immune to a sharp jaw and eyes so expressive they could make a girl blush with one look?

When Brooks managed to whittle his way through the women toward me, his hand circled my arm before we carved a path toward the exit. But with the commotion from the pictures, a crowd had formed, phones raised and flashes going off from every direction.

"Think if we ask real nice, they'll all agree to keep those pictures to themselves?" I said to Brooks, even as I noticed one girl pulling up her Instagram app one hot second after snapping a pic of the two of us.

"I'm more concerned with how I'm going to explain this mustache to my grandkids one day." Brooks scooted a guy blocking the door so he could get a photo out of our way.

"Grandkids? That requires you to actually like a woman long enough to procreate. Which, Neanderthal, doesn't follow your relationship creed."

Brooks's arm swung behind my back, partly speeding me up, partly shielding me as we shoved through the pub's crowded doorway. "A man wanting to sow his seed is as base instinct as it gets. Of course I want offspring."

"Offspring. Sowing seeds." I pretended to fan myself. "If that doesn't turn a girl on . . ."

A noise rumbled in his chest as we finally burst free of the pub. Fresh, cool air spilled around me, and it was so refreshing I had to take several long breaths.

"Hey, Double-oh-Seven, your disguises suck." I ripped off the wig and glasses, stuffing them in my purse.

Brooks had already torn off the mustache but left the ball cap on. He was about to say something when a group of guys staggered out of the pub, immediately making bowing motions at Brooks. They must have been drunk. It was the only explanation for why they'd be pretending to worship the man with a red patch of skin in the shape of a mustache on his upper lip.

"I think you're being deified." I tipped my head in the direction of his admirers.

"Deified by a gang of drunkards. Not exactly my life's calling." Brooks slung his arm around my shoulders to steer me down the street when a chorus of whistles sounded.

"You're the man, Mr. Reality!" one of them called. From his voice, he'd achieved puberty all of one week ago. "No way I'm letting a chick trick me into a life sentence of monogamy."

Sighing, I gave Brooks one of my looks he'd gotten used to by now.

In response, he gave me one of his I'd gotten used to as well.

"You go on and live your best life there, chief." Brooks shot the band of bros a thumbs-up and kept going.

"I bet you've scored some serious tail. Some serious-ly *hot* tail." The sound of footsteps echoed behind us until the most sober of the bunch managed to catch up. The one with a beer T-shirt nudged Brooks after giving me a once-over. "Kinda dropping down a few leagues to prove your point though, eh? But whatever it takes, man. Take one for the team."

My mouth was opening to breathe fire when Brooks blinked a few times as though he'd been roused from a nap. "Sorry, I missed all that." He barely glanced at the kid as he picked up our pace. "I was too busy wondering how many times your mom has cursed herself for not insisting your dad pull out when you were conceived."

A confused look pulled at the guy's expression before he fell behind, the jeers and laughs of his friends echoing into the night.

"Mr. Reality, keeping it real!" a different voice shout-ed, followed by more laughter—except for who I assumed was Beer Shirt, cussing them all out.

My arms wound around me as my head swam with a dozen different emotions.

"Forget what he said." Brooks slid closer, his arm staying around my shoulders. "That guy wouldn't recog-nize a good woman if he had ten lifetimes to try."

My head shook. "It's okay. I'm used to it."

"Used to what?"

I pulled at the scarf knotted around my neck, combing

through the tangled mess that was my hair. "Being told to stick to my league." I motioned back at the ensemble of ding-dongs who'd moved on to harassing a couple of young women with unoriginal catcalls. "In high school, it was when the captain of the basketball team asked me to winter formal. The cheerleaders weren't having that. In college, it was when the guy with the nice car and smile asked me to a frat party. The sorority girls practically staged a revolt." I felt my mood aiming south from the mere mention of those miserable moments. "I learned a long time ago not to tie my self-esteem to some jerk-off's opinion."

Brooks was watching me as we strolled down the dark sidewalk. "Well, can't say I don't understand their motivations."

"Whose motivations?"

"The guys. And the girls. It doesn't take a genius to recognize the whole package when a guy sees one. That being you." Brooks tipped his head in my direction. "And those girls clearly felt threatened and would rather run you off than be forced to up their game and maybe improve themselves."

Thinking back to the girls who'd teased me to tears, it was almost laughable to consider those air-brushed-to-perfection specimens feeling threatened by me in all of my baby-fat-and-frizzy-hair glory. "I've certainly never considered it that way. I just wrote it off to the world being full of beautiful mean girls, their sole mission in life to make the awkward, chubby girls feel as pitiful as possible."

Brooks made a pfft sound. "Pretty on the outside. Ugly on the inside. That only gets a person so far in life for so long. Where do you think those girls are today?"

"Are you asking the petty me? Or the higher ground me?"

"Like you even need to ask."

I clapped a couple of times as I conjured a scene of payback. "Festering in some rusted-out trailer, getting their sanity unspooled by four insufferable kids under five, waiting for the husband to bring home the case of beer and pork rinds but knowing he's likely giving it to the widow hillbilly three trailers over."

When I glanced over, I caught Brooks giving me an impressed look. "And look where you are now."

I thought about that. Where I was. In New York City, vying for my dream job, already in possession of an impressive career. But I was alone, never having come close to a relationship that parlayed into a walk down an aisle. My career life was on point. My love life was non-existent.

"What about you? What were the high school years like for Brooks North?" I asked.

"About the same as yours from the sound of it."

I stopped moving.

"What? I was a late bloomer. Took some time to mature into all of this manly goodness." He waggled his brows at me, grinning when I laughed. "You think you've got horror stories from those days? Not even. The first time I asked a girl I thought was in my league to homecoming, she laughed in my face. Then she told her friends and they all laughed in my face. For the next three years of high school."

My eyes narrowed at the sidewalk. "You? A nerd?" I tried to envision it. I couldn't.

"Nerds had more status on me. I was more a . . . disease." Brooks's hand tightened around my shoulder. "Then college rolled around and I ditched the glasses, put on fifty pounds of mass, and testosterone decided to finally give me a jawline. After that, I never had any issues getting dates. In fact, I'd leave a party with a dozen new phone numbers. Now, why did I go from zero to hero in a few short years?" He glanced at me, waiting.

"Hero might be an exaggeration . . ."

He gently pulled my hair before continuing. "Nothing about my personality changed—"

"You mean you were just as charming then as you are now?"

"My looks. Those changed. If that isn't evidence that humans are shallow, I don't know what is."

"So that's yet another reason why you believe what you do? Because high school girls avoided you and college girls couldn't get enough of you?"

One of his shoulders lifted. "What would you infer from that?"

"Your pheromones went into overdrive, making you irresistible to any red-blooded female?" I spurted off. "Because you're not *that* good-looking."

He gave me a look that told me he knew I was lying. "When you strip any of us down, you'll find us all either heeding or lying to ourselves about survival of the fittest. Looks, status, money—it all equals survival. That's all this relationship dance is about, Hannah. I know it isn't pretty, but the truth usually isn't."

Even as he finished, Brooks drew me closer, his fingers absently playing with the ends of my hair. Survival or not, instinct or more, the connection forming between us could not be denied.

"Hey, North?" My head dropped to his shoulder. "I would have gone to homecoming with you."

"Hey, Arden?" His mouth floated to my ear. "That would be the only reason I'd consider going back and reliving those years of my life."

CHAPTER
Fifteen

"**A**rden! North! Your asses in my office!"

That was the sound I, and everyone else in the office, was greeted with on Monday morning.

"If I had a dime for every time I heard that . . ." The chair across from mine whined as Brooks rose. He waited for me outside of my cube. "Let me take the lead on this."

I took another chug of my coffee. "Gladly."

Brooks's expression flattened. "Was that you agreeing with me? No argument?"

"When it comes to this, no argument," I said, starting the journey to Conrad's office, Brooks right beside me.

I knew there'd be some kind of repercussions for this weekend. Quinn and several of my friends had texted me links to the posts and articles outing Brooks' and my "secret" date. I'd been right about me looking like I was in the middle of swallowing a cat. Beside me, even with that butt-ugly mustache, Brooks looked like the rebel god thrown from Valhalla.

As predicted, Quinn grilled me to the n'th degree as to why I'd agreed to such an arrangement and what was our motive behind the secret dates. I'd given her enough to mostly satisfy her, and not a hint more.

"Think he's wanting to congratulate us on our latest articles?" Brooks nudged me.

I scooted away discreetly. We'd nudged, shoved, and pushed each other to no end, but lately, those touches felt different. "Well, maybe to congratulate me on mine. Yours was a snoozer."

"But you read it."

"I skimmed it."

Brooks erased the distance I'd put between us. "Liar," he whispered, right as we rounded into Conrad's office.

My feet froze when I saw the look on Conrad's face. I'd never seen a face achieve that shade of red. Even the vein running down his forehead was bulging.

"What the hell do you two have to say for this?" Conrad didn't wait for us to close the door before tearing into us, whipping around his laptop with a picture of the two of us enlarged on the screen.

It wasn't one of the photos I'd seen. It was one someone had snapped before we were officially outed. Brooks and I were sitting at our table, closer than I remembered. His hand was reaching out to brush back my hair, but it looked like he could have been caressing my cheek instead. The caption with the picture read: *Your Daily Dose of Romance Versus Reality.*

"I want an explanation and I want it now!" Conrad's hand blasted down on his desk.

Brooks stepped forward. "It was my idea. *All* my idea."

His confession did nothing to diminish Conrad's anger. "And what led you to believe this idea was a good one?" He jabbed his finger at the computer screen while I stared at the photo of the two of us.

God, did we really look like that when we were together? A real couple?

"We're two different people who believe two different things. I thought if we took the time to get to know each other off camera, it would make our on-camera time less stilted." Brooks's posture was relaxed, his tone unapologetic. He was wearing the gray suit he'd worn the first day he showed up here. I should have rued the sight of it; instead I found myself imagining what it would look like crumpled up on my bedroom floor.

Because that wasn't an inappropriate thought right now . . .

"I thought it would up the 'production value' if Hannah's and my relationship ran deeper than just rivalry." Brooks peaked his brow, throwing Conrad's own term in his face.

Conrad was quiet, his fingers drumming across the desk. "How long has this been going on? These private meetings?"

I swallowed.

"They just started," Brooks answered, staring him straight in the eyes.

My tongue worked into my cheek and I kept quiet. Sure, they'd just started. If you considered three weeks "just starting."

"And they're just ending too, understood?" Conrad slammed his laptop shut, giving us his notorious Conrad stare-down.

Brooks was already angling toward the door. "Understood."

He paused at the door, waiting for me. I scurried out of that office as quickly as my wedges would carry me. Once I was in the hall, I let out the breath I'd been holding.

"So? Did I handle that well?" Brooks winked at me.

"It pains me to admit it, but yes, you handled that very well." I waved at the office that had gone uncannily quiet, half of my co-workers gaping at us like they were surprised our heads were still attached to our bodies.

"Just look at us, would you? Day one, we were at each other's throats, and here we are two months later, the god damn dream team."

I didn't mention that our actual day one, we'd been at each other's something else, because that memory was better left in the forgone and forgotten pile.

"Who would have thought we could be this close and not sparring insult for injury?" I made an okay sign at Quinn, who was lingering in the break room.

"Funny the way life turns out." His sleeve brushed my arm, causing actual tingles to erupt down my back. "You think you know the story, you can almost see the ending, then all of that goes to hell."

We slowed as we approached my cube. "Sometimes you might think it's all falling apart, when really, it's all just falling into place."

Brooks stood there for a minute, contemplation knitting together his expression. Then he shrugged. "Maybe," he said, backing into his own cube. "We still on for Operation Move Hannah Back into her Apartment?"

My shoulders lowered as I thought about it, when I should have been flipping cartwheels that I was no longer stuck sharing the same living space as Brooks North. "Yeah. I talked to the apartment manager again this morning and he said it's all ready for me."

"I'm going to squeeze in a quick run after work, then I'll meet you at your place to help."

"A quick run? Let me guess, that's, like, eight miles for someone like you." I shot him a look as I fired up my laptop. I had another article due in a few days and all I'd completed so far was opening a new document for it.

"Actually, it's ten." He shot me a grin before turning his attention to his own laptop.

"Ugh. Your stamina is sickening."

"Why thank you. And good to know you've spent some time considering my stamina."

I grumbled. "Can we go back to pretending to be arch rivals who can't stand the idea of exchanging a single word with each other?"

"You got it, boss." Brooks was already typing, his keys chattering away like his article was spilling out of him. It was like his muse had gone into overdrive since our dating experiment started, while mine had become mute.

The passion. The fervor. The conviction. All of that had waned into extinction over the past few weeks. I couldn't consider the reason why. It was off-limits territory. It wouldn't only spell the doom of my career but of my entire view on life.

No man was worth that sacrifice. Especially not one

who had everything to gain if I admitted I'd fallen for him.

I'd already let him get too close. I could not risk letting him any closer.

I stared at the blank page on my computer screen, it practically mocking me while the sound of one hundred words a minute echoed across from me.

CHAPTER
Sixteen

"**I** don't remember you showing up at my place with this much stuff," Brooks said, the top half of him hidden behind the stack of boxes and bins in his arms.

"And I wasn't expecting to spend twenty-five days at your bachelor pad either. A girl can't get by on one bag of goods alone." After unlocking my apartment, I paused with my hand on the doorknob. I was wincing, bracing myself to find musty, water-damaged carnage inside.

"Are we going to hang out in the hallway all night, waiting to be recognized, which will no doubt lead to a stream of questions as to what we're doing together without a camera in our faces?"

Brooks's prompt gave me the motivation I needed to push the door open. No foul odors seeped out—promising, I thought as I flipped on the lights. My whole body relaxed when I got a good look at my apartment. It looked exactly how it had pre-flood. With the exception of the ceiling and floor, nothing had changed. My furniture, area rugs, curtains; everything had been dried, cleaned, and replaced how I'd had them.

Brooks had to maneuver through the door sideways to fit without knocking the boxes out of his arms.

"You got your cardio and your strength workouts in," I said as I unloaded the top boxes from his pile.

"And now I need a nice massage." The hopeful look on his face made me laugh.

"There's an Asian spa of questionable repute just down the block. They keep night hours."

He followed me to the dining table I was stacking boxes onto. "Every massage come with a complimentary happy ending?"

"That depends on your definition of happy."

He leaned in as he set down the bins in his arms. "If you want to be my masseuse, I can help demonstrate what makes me happy."

Taking a breath, I held my palm in front of his face. "My hands are all chapped."

He surprised me by pressing his cheek into it, his stubble scratching the soft flesh. "Good. I like it rough."

My hand dropped back at my side as I distracted myself by heading into the kitchen. "You want something to drink?"

My voice was off, but so was everything else. Having him here in my apartment. The front door closed and locked. Late in the evening, my willpower and inhibitions worn to the point of snapping. I shouldn't have accepted his offer to help. I shouldn't have let him burrow so deeply into the contours of my life.

But here he was.

And here I was.

Whether fate or circumstance had led us to this moment, I knew it was not coincidence.

"I'm good, thanks." His footsteps echoed through the apartment. "Your place is exactly how I expected someone like you would keep her living space."

I rummaged through the cupboards as a diversion. "I can't tell if that's an insult or observation."

"Actually, it's a compliment," he said, his footsteps coming to a halt. "You know who you are and aren't trying to change that to fit a generic mold."

My fingertips rolled along the counter. "Thanks?"

He chuckled as the sound of shuffling came from the living room. "Good god. *Pride and Prejudice* on the top of the pile. Both DVDs and books." Brooks grunted. "What is it with women and Darcy?"

After forcing myself from the kitchen, I mustered up as much composure as I could. Which wasn't much. "I don't know." I watched him turn over my worn copy of the book, the DVD I'd watched with my friends a couple of months ago in his other hand. "He's a reluctant hero. This guy who seems like an egotistical ass but turns out to save the day in the end, without attempting to take any credit for it."

"But he does take the credit in the end. And he gets the strong, spirited Miss Bennett."

My mouth worked as I removed the book from his hand and set it back where it belonged. "That's what makes it a love story and not a tragedy."

"Ah, that's the distinction." Brooks wandered to the wall where I had a couple dozen photos in ornate, mismatched frames. "As opposed to the guy who does not get the girl or get the credit for his heroic act."

"Correct."

"But isn't that romantic as well? Giving up the woman you want so she could be happy with someone else? Staying the anonymous savior instead of basking in the glory of recognition?" The corners of his mouth twitched when he studied the photo of me as a toddler with my parents. Chubby and wild-haired—the story of my life. "I'm asking you because you're the expert. I'm in uncharted territory where the romance phenomenon is concerned."

After sliding my sandals from my feet, I padded closer. "I suppose so. In its own way. But it's hard to imagine Elizabeth being happier with anyone besides Darcy."

"But like you said, Darcy's an egotistical horse's ass."

"On the surface maybe, but what hides behind all of that is what matters. And he loves her."

Brooks leaned in to make out where I was in my senior class photo. "So you're saying that's enough?"

My fingers combed through my hair as I attempted to sum up what point I was trying to get across. "I'm saying love is a good start."

"There it is again. The L word."

"It scares you," I stated.

"How can it scare me when it doesn't exist?"

"Why are you so sure it doesn't exist?"

The floor creaked as he moved toward the next picture; the one with Grandma and me at my high school graduation. "Because I have no evidence to prove its existence."

"Evidence?" I sighed. "It's literally all around you."

"Says the woman dubbed Ms. Romance."

"But if you're wrong, you've sacrificed a lifetime of potential intimacy and commitment. If I'm wrong, I've spent my life believing in a fanciful dream."

He leaned in closer to the picture, shaking his head. "No, I'd live my life free with the truth. You'd spend yours chained to a lie."

A puff of air rumbled out of my lips. "I know where this conversation is going. Nowhere." Grabbing one of the bins from the table, I carried it toward my room. "I'm going to save my energy for unpacking instead of arguing a pointless battle with you."

"But pointless battles are my favorite." He wrestled a box under each arm and followed me to my bedroom.

My heart about seized when I heard his footsteps right behind me. My room had been tidy when I left, but who knew what shape I might find it in. Hopefully any signs of unmentionables or items of a personal nature wouldn't be spread out on my comforter in plain view.

"More pink. And flowers. And sparkle. And lace." Brooks gave me no time to give my room the once-over before his gaze moved from one corner to the next, not missing a thing. He fought a smile when he got to my fancy vanity, half of the surface covered by pretty perfume bottles.

"What? I, unlike some people, like to surround myself with things that bring joy. Instead of self-loathing."

He huffed, peeking inside my dark closet when he passed by. "This room is some cross of a little girl's, a Hollywood starlet's, and a great-grandmother's." He paused beside my bed, his fingers reaching for my nightstand drawer. "But I bet there's some stuff hiding in here that isn't so innocent."

"Brooks!" I exclaimed, lunging over the bin I'd been about to open, hauling ass to intercept him before . . .

He must have been expecting me to put on the brakes, because he didn't move, his eyes widening a moment before I crashed into him. We collided with a loud slap, our bodies careening onto my bed. Somehow, I wound up on top of him, my legs tangled around his, my chest moving fast from the exertion and mini panic attack I'd given myself from thinking about him finding what was tucked into that nightstand drawer.

His arms had found their way around me as we tumbled, but they refused to unwind now that we'd landed. His throat moved when my eyes found his, one side of his mouth lifting high.

"Not so innocent at all," he said as his eyes skimmed down the length of my body covering his.

Heat wound up my spine. Before I gave myself a second to reconsider, I rolled off of him, tumbling onto the empty bed beside him. I focused on the ceiling, trying to regulate my breathing. The mattress whined when he rolled onto his side toward me.

"Brooks," I breathed. "Stop."

"I'm not doing anything." He was watching me, waiting for my attention. It only made me stare at the ceiling harder. "Hannah?"

"Please. Don't."

"I'm not touching you." As he said it, my instinct was to scoot farther away from him. "Is my presence offending you now?" He motioned between us. "One minute I think I know what you want from me, and the next I realize I don't have a damn clue." His voice grew with every word as he went to crawl off the bed.

Out of nowhere, my hand reached for his, pulling him back down beside me. The next thing I knew, I was pressed against him, my mouth crashing into his as my hands grabbed hold of whatever firm place on him I could find.

If he was surprised, he didn't show it. He shifted below me so our heads were perfectly aligned, his mouth rising with mine, and falling together. He tasted like cinnamon and need, and the harder I kissed him, the more I wanted of him.

When the rest of my body went to cover him, my hands slipping beneath his shirt at the same time, Brooks went still.

"Wait." His breathing was uneven, strained, as his fingers formed vises around my wrists to draw my hands out from beneath his shirt. The warmth of his skin lingered in my palms, the firm planes of his stomach imprinted on them.

"For what?" When my mouth molded into his again, ever so slightly sucking at his bottom lip, he trembled.

"You are not making this easy." He didn't sound like himself at all, as his body went tense.

"I'm not trying to make it easy." My own voice was nearly unrecognizable as that black hole of want reappeared. I'd only experienced it once before, that night he and I had shared together. It was a feeling that overwhelmed me, alarming in its magnitude.

"Check," he breathed, his hands twisting around my wrists tighter when I tried to pull free.

When my hips slipped over his, gently rocking against him, he cursed under his breath. "Hannah."

His eyes opened into mine, his chest beginning to calm. He felt so solid beneath me; the kind that suggested no force of nature could get through him.

"What's the matter?"

He released one of my wrists, resting his hand on the bend of my neck. "The first time we met, I had you in my bed after a few hours. And I lost you." A deep line creased between his brows. "This time, I'm going with a different approach."

My mind struggled to keep up with what was happening. From wanting to jump his bones to hearing him confess he wanted to . . . *wait?*

"I'm lost," I breathed. "I don't know what you're trying to say."

"Three hours after meeting, we fucked. This time, it was almost two months to a first kiss." His fingers curled into my neck as he lifted his head off the pillow, his lips finding mine. Gentle and slow, yet strong and swift.

My lungs collapsed before he ended that kiss.

"I don't plan on losing you again." His breath was warm against my skin as he pulled away.

My body. My heart. He was doing everything right to appeal to them both.

I had to remind myself this was Brooks North. Mr. Reality. Everything he was saying and doing could have been to manipulate me into falling for him. I *knew* that. Yet something in his eyes told me this was no ruse.

"Why wait?" I asked, knowing he wasn't the type of man who did or had to wait to get a woman into bed.

He combed my hair back from my face. "Because you're worth it."

"You've already had me."

"I've had your body," he said, drawing my head to his chest, holding me against him. "But now I want the rest. I want it all."

CHAPTER
Seventeen

Jimmy gave a low whistle across from us in the limo. "That was one hell of a shoot, you two."

Brooks rubbed his mouth. "Good to know."

"I mean, the chemistry was, like, off the charts. You've gotten good at selling it, Hannah." Jimmy winked in my direction as he settled the camera gear beside him on the seat. Conrad had decided to upgrade the camera gear a few weeks ago—you know, for added production value. "You too, Brooks. I wouldn't have thought the stone-cold reality guy could be so . . ."

"*Not* stone cold?" Brooks suggested.

Jimmy shook his head. "Romantic. Didn't think you had it in you, North."

I had to bite my tongue and look out the window to keep from laughing. Our public dates had been different ever since that night in my apartment, and even though we both tried to keep what happened off-camera from trickling on-screen, it was impossible.

"Either Conrad forced you two to take some acting

lessons or he's pumping aphrodisiacs into your coffee, because seriously." Jimmy's finger waved between Brooks and me keeping a measured distance between one another in the back of the limousine. "That was scorchin'."

"Good to know we figured it out a day before the three months is over." Brooks's head turned to look out the other window, trying to ignore me like I was trying to ignore him. I wondered if we were at all convincing, or if it only made it more obvious that something was going on behind the *Romance Versus Reality* façade.

"So tomorrow night." Jimmy clapped. "We'll pick you both up at seven sharp, but you'll be riding in separate cars to the venue. Conrad is having some formalwear delivered tomorrow morning for you to wear."

"Why can't we wear something we already own?" I asked. A.k.a. something comfortable.

"Because this is the final night. Conrad wants to make it big. Fireworks. Twelve-person ensemble. Designer gown and tux. The whole bit."

Brooks and I blinked at Jimmy.

"It's the last night of a social experiment, not a presidential inauguration," Brooks said.

"Maybe. But almost as many people will be tuning in tomorrow night as do during the actual presidential inauguration."

My palms, sweaty from thinking about what was in store tomorrow night, rubbed down my jeans. Brooks and I had become pros at skirting around our positions as public guinea pigs for romance. Our unsaid motto was to take things one hour at a time and to ignore the elephant looming between the two of us.

"Any other spoilers you can share about tomorrow night?" I asked.

Jimmy wrestled two beers out of the mini fridge, holding the extra out toward Brooks and me. When we both declined, he swung it in the direction of the two bodyguards sitting ramrod-straight in their seats, laser-focused on their "clients."

"Sorry, that's right. On duty." Jimmy set the extra beer back inside the fridge and twisted the cap off his. "Let's see. Spoilers, spoilers." He took a pull of his beer. "It's going to be like the final rose ceremony meets *The Hunger Games*." He grinned, looking proud of his analogy. He noticed me gaping and held out his arms. "You both can't win, you know?"

Brooks shifted in his seat, getting back to staring out the window.

"Oh, and Conrad decided to let the viewers decide who wins tomorrow night."

Jimmy had said it so quickly, in such a straightforward tone, it took me a minute to catch up to what had been said.

"Wait—"

"What?" Brooks cut in, looking angry instead of distraught like myself.

Jimmy kicked his feet up on the seat across from him. "After the finale, voting lines will be open for viewers to call in with their vote as to which one of you two love-slash-anti-love birds comes out the champion. I think each number can vote five times. Or maybe it's ten. I don't remember."

"That wasn't part of the original agreement," the

words tumbled from my mouth.

"The agreement you all had written up, notarized, and signed in blood?" Jimmy clucked his tongue. "Come on. We all know Conrad is an asshole who's going to do whatever he thinks is best for the company, screw the employees working for it."

Brooks's hand brushed mine, as though he'd been about to take my hand and caught himself at the last moment. "This isn't fair," he said.

"Hey, man, you're the one who quoted that letting fairness be the guiding compass for life is for the suckers." Jimmy took a swig of his beer. "It sucks man, I'm with you on that, but that's what's going down tomorrow night. Might as well make the best of it."

Inside, a thousand protests were rising, but I stifled them all, knowing, as Jimmy did, nothing would change Conrad's mind on this. The viewers would decide who won tomorrow night—Brooks or me—and a part of me already knew the final result. "I guess I shouldn't be surprised. Conrad has done everything in his power to make this a bigger spectacle whenever the opportunity presented itself." I blew out a slow breath. "It doesn't matter. A person would have to possess the emotional intelligence of a grasshopper to believe I've actually fallen in love with Brooks North."

Beside me, Brooks huffed.

"Daaamn. Ice cold." Jimmy chuckled. "I love it."

"Miss Arden." The security guard, Dean, who had been assigned to me a few weeks ago when getting to work without being mob-rushed had become a challenge, said as he reached for the limo door.

My apartment building was outside, and Dean was scanning the sidewalk like he was protecting a foreign diplomat in a hostile country.

"I'm going to hop out here too."

As Brooks moved, his security guard, Sven, got up to follow. Brooks shook his head, and Sven instantly fell back into his seat. I didn't know where the paper had gotten these security guards from, but my guess was that they were half machine from the way they behaved.

"Dude. Your place is miles from here," Jimmy said.

"I'm meeting some friends at a bar down the street."

"You've got friends? People that actually like you and seek out your company?"

Brooks grunted. "Hilarious, camera boy."

"You should bring Sven though." Jimmy scanned out the windows. "You're going to get lady-mobbed if you step foot in a public place."

Brooks laughed. "I'm the guy trying to prove love is a fallacy. The mob slings pitchforks at me, not bras."

"Pretty sure those pitchforks can do more damage than lacy bras," Jimmy called as Brooks climbed out of the limo behind me.

"I've got a thick skin."

I glanced back at Brooks. "Try an impenetrable shell."

"Good to know I've fooled some." His blue eyes found mine, holding longer than they should have.

"Well. Good night, Brooks." My posture straightened, attempting to sell how formal I felt where Brooks was concerned. "I'll see you tomorrow."

Something sparked in his eye. "I'll see you tomorrow."

Clutching my purse, I turned to head into my apartment building. From the corner of my eye, I watched him meander down the sidewalk. God, were we fooling anyone? It seemed so obvious to me, as though we were holding billboard-sized signs proclaiming our secret relationship.

Dean stayed at my side, swinging the door open and checking the lobby before indicating it was safe for me to enter. Half the time, I thought Dean forgot he was protecting me and not T Swift.

Once we made it to my apartment, he took his position outside my door, hands clasped in front of himself. The paper had insisted on the security detail, Conrad no doubt behind that decision. Not because he was concerned for my well-being in the sense of human decency, but because I was an investment he couldn't afford to have out of commission.

His social experiment had achieved everything he'd hoped it would, and more. Millions of viewers tuned into every episode of *Romance Versus Reality,* and the paper was capitalizing on it in every way imaginable. From random trivia about Brooks' and my lives, to posting exclusive extra questions Jimmy asked us leading into each date, the *World Times* had secured the crown of hybrid news conglomerate. Half *People* magazine, half *New York Times*, everyone from CEOs to stay-at-home moms found some reason to make the *World Times* their premier news source.

Dean wasn't here to keep Hannah Arden safe. He was here to protect the asset labeled Ms. Romance.

"Do you want anything to drink?" I asked him the same question I asked every night before slipping into my jammies.

"No, thank you, ma'am," he answered, his exact reply every time.

"If you change your mind, just knock down my door or something. That seems well within your skillset." I paused to gauge his reaction. Nothing. Not a muscle movement, no eyelid flicker. Okay, he was more like ninety-percent machine.

Once I was inside, I flew into my bedroom, ripping off my shirt as I went. After tearing through my closet, I changed into a come-hither dress and slid into a fresh pair of underwear that were not cotton solids. Then I lit some candles and turned down the lights. All in under five minutes. I kicked on the pair of heels still lingering at the doorway from yesterday and pulled the door open. Dean did not blink, his gaze still aimed forward.

"I just remembered I'm out of creamer. Need that for my morning coffee unless all of New York wants to experience the female version of King Kong."

Dean's face didn't register an emotion even close to the amusement scale. "I'll grab some for you," he announced, already marching down the hallway. "I'll be back in ten minutes. Lock the door and don't answer it for anyone."

"Maybe the mayor?" I teased.

No response as he jogged down the stairs. Going through the motions, I closed my door and locked it, then leaned into the wall behind me, waiting. It wouldn't be long, based on past experiences.

A soft trio of knocks echoed outside the door a few minutes later. My stomach knotted as I reached for the handle, both in anticipation and trepidation.

Brooks' and my relationship was still undefined, lurking in murky waters. That wasn't strictly because we'd dodged having that conversation with each other, but because I'd shirked having it with myself. I had feelings—I felt emotions—but if I didn't assign them a name, I could spin whatever theory I wanted based on the outcome. Would our story wind up a fairy tale? Or a cautionary one? As long as I kept things vague, I could accept either without being crushed. Or at least, that was what I told myself.

"That was fast," I greeted upon opening the door.

Brooks looked fine. He smelled fine. That silver glimmer in his eyes was beyond fine. "Too fast? Should I leave and come back? I don't want you thinking that I'm overeager or anything."

When he backed away from the doorway, I grabbed his arm and yanked him inside. "Why don't you want me thinking that?"

"Because I don't want you to see me as some kind of Red Zone Clinger. Even though one might lurk just below the surface where you are concerned." The pads of his fingers brushed against mine when he moved closer.

"Red Zone Clinger? Is that a label you're going to share with your readers?"

"No way in hell."

"Why not?"

"The man who bites his thumb at commitment coming out of the closet as a clinger?" He shot me a look as he rolled up his sleeves. "Can you imagine the blowback?"

"Nice story." My hands planted on his chest, shoving him into the wall behind him. "When do we skip to the part that comes next?"

His expression changed from amused to aroused. His head fell toward mine, his breath warming my cheek. "Next."

My fingers curled into his shirt, my lips finding his. A low sound rumbled in his throat as I pressed my body into his.

"This is the kind of hello a man could get used to." His mouth collapsed into mine for a moment. His eyes opened like he'd just remembered something. "By the way, nice dress."

"*Nice* dress?"

One brow lifted. "Nice is short for a million other things I could say about this dress and what seeing you in it makes me want to do to you, but to save time . . ."

"Nice works," I said, a smile pulling at my mouth. "Instead of saying what it makes you want to do to me, why don't you just show me?"

Brooks's arms wound behind my back; a moment later, I was lifted into the air as he carried me into the living room. "Your wish." His voice outside my ear sent a tremble down my back. "My command."

My ankles crossed behind his back, my arms tying at the base of his neck. His strides were purposeful, moving as though he knew exactly what he wanted and was not in the business of waiting for it. I loved that about Brooks; he knew what he wanted, and he wasn't afraid to go after it.

"I've got a perfectly good bedroom back that direction," I said when he paused beside the sofa. "With one of those bed things."

He kicked off his shoes, still holding me close. "Too much temptation."

I fought the urge to groan. "What's so wrong with that?"

Brooks flung us onto the sofa, him on top, me below him. My whole body throbbed with desire, the weight of him pinned against me fanning the flame.

"I thought you didn't want to have a conversation."

My hand slid lower, skimming beneath his shirt. "I don't."

The words were hardly out before his mouth returned to mine, his large hands gripping the back of my dress. I lost whatever thread of restraint I'd been clinging to as his weight settled deeper into me, the pressure building between my legs as I felt him hard against my stomach.

My breath was strained as our kisses deepened, tongues dominating then yielding. The ache had become a throb that had turned into an overpowering swell. It was my body, but at that moment, I was not in possession of it.

As my fingers scrolled further beneath his shirt, I swore his skin heated from my touch. It went from warm to scalding in a few strokes. My hand grappled with his shirt, peeling it up his back as I contemplated ripping it from him if it took longer than a few seconds to remove.

Brooks shrugged, dipping his head to make it easier. The shirt wound up in a crumpled heap at our feet. When he collapsed onto me again, the air in the room changed.

Anticipation had given way to resolution. Doubt yielding certainty.

My legs fell open wider to meet him at the same time my hands lowered to his belt.

"Slow down." His mouth left mine, his eyes sealed closed almost like he was in physical pain.

It took me a few moments to formulate a reply. "Slow down?" A few more to catch my breath. "We've been making out like a couple of church-going teenagers afraid of eternal damnation for weeks. How much slower can we possibly go?"

Brooks's face twitched with amusement as he planted his hands beside my head to better hold his weight. "What's the rush?"

I blinked at him. "What's the hold up?"

His head tipped as a familiar expression moved into place. I knew what the hold up was, and he was waiting for me to acknowledge it.

"No proclamations, remember? No designations to whatever this is. That was part of the agreement." Sighing, I gave his chest a shove as I adjusted my legs into a less inviting position.

His forehead pressed into mine. "What is this, Hannah?"

"Why do we have to give it a name?"

"Because tomorrow night, the world is going to force us to."

My eyes closed when I thought about the future. The near and distant. With Brooks' and my relationship, one hour into the future was too far to plan out. "We don't owe the world an explanation."

"Fine. But we owe ourselves one." When he exhaled, his warm breath broke across my face. "So what is this? Us. Behind closed doors. Off camera. What are we?"

God. That face. It was as flawless up close as it was at a distance. What presided from the neck down was no different. But what dwelled past the surface was perhaps the sexiest component of Brooks North.

As much as I wanted to tell him how I felt—to assign a title to whatever this was—I wasn't enough of a fool to do so before the show was over.

"No. Designations," I enunciated slowly.

Sliding out from beneath him, I adjusted my dress back into position since he wasn't going to be taking it off in the near future. Or maybe even the distant future. The one-night-stand man had become the wait-for-marriage type, and I'd never wanted to give irony the bird more.

"Slow down doesn't mean stop." His arm wrung around my stomach at the same time his teeth grazed my earlobe.

"But slow down does mean probable cranium eruption from the female equivalent of blue balls, so yeah, I'm gonna stop while I'm still breathing." Gliding away from him took the ultimate feat of willpower.

"I bet I could give you that release you need . . ." Brooks's hand at my stomach skimmed lower, his fingers slipping beneath the hem of my dress. "Without removing a single article of clothing."

My hands balled into fists when I felt his fingers grazing the insides of my thighs.

"Just lie back . . ." His teeth sank into my earlobe at the same time his fingers reached their destination. "And let me . . ."

In the background, I heard a noise.

It wasn't important. It could have been a rocket launcher bursting through my kitchen wall and it wouldn't have been more pressing than what Brooks was doing to my body at that very moment.

When the same sound echoed in the apartment again, Brooks paused. "Are you expecting anyone?"

My head shook. "Nope."

"Someone's knocking at your door."

"It's probably one of my neighbor's doors. Definitely not mine." My hand rested against his cheek as I made eye contact, hoping he could read that I was literally two finger strokes away from blastoff.

Then came the voices hollering outside my door, accompanied by the knocking.

"Still think it's someone at your neighbor's door?" Brooks gave me a cocky smirk, knowing exactly what he'd done to me in all of ten seconds.

"Yes." I frowned even as I heard my friends shouting my name.

As he pulled away, my head banged against the back of the sofa a few times before I rose to see why my friends were surprising me with a visit at the most inopportune time possible.

"Hey. Did you forget I'm here? Shirtless on your couch and still nursing a hard-on?" Brooks's voice followed me as I marched to the door. "Unless you're ready to admit to your friends—"

My eyes went wide when I realized the sticky situation I was in. A half-naked enemy was lurking in my apartment after hours, not a camera in sight. My friends would not rest until they'd dragged the truth from me. "You've got to hide!"

"Where?" Brooks gave me a look as he reached for his shirt. "Under the table? Think they'll see me."

"My bedroom." I motioned frantically for him to follow as I rushed into my room, spinning in circles as I searched for a hiding spot that would conceal one-hundred-eighty pounds of muscle and bravado. "The closet." Grabbing his hand the moment he padded into my room, I shoved hangers to the side to make some room for him.

He broke to a stop when I tried pushing him inside. "I can't hide in there."

"Afraid of the dark?"

He glanced at the space I was trying to squeeze him into. "My dick wouldn't fit in there. My *flaccid* dick."

"Aren't you the optimist?"

"*Realist.* Mr. Reality, remember?"

My eyes rolled as I planted my hands into his chest and shoved him into the closet. My friends' knocks and shouts were only getting louder. "Just get in there with your giant dick already."

He winked as he backed into the warzone that was my closet. "I appreciate your confirmation."

"Yeah, yeah, now get in there and be quiet. I don't need my friends finding out I've been clothed-screwing the enemy on the eve of the big finale."

"It's better than naked-screwing." We both made a face when he said that. "Never mind. Nothing's better than naked-screwing."

My hand went to my hip as I slid the door closed. "Says the man who refuses to get naked with me."

"Touché." His voice was muffled once the sliding door was shut.

Turning off the bedroom lights and closing the door, I rushed to let my friends in before every one of my neighbors called in a noise complaint.

"You kept us waiting long enough," were the first words out of Quinn's mouth when I threw open the door. "Were you taking a crap or something?"

I swore I heard a muffled laugh coming from the direction of my bedroom. So much for not making a peep.

"Sorry. I was in the shower." I stepped aside to let in the trio of friends.

"The shower?" Annie gave me a look as she passed by. "Does your hair dry instantly or something?"

"And you put on a sassy dress right after?" Sybill added.

My head shook as I reminded myself to edit my answers before verbalizing them. "I was *about* to get in the shower. Had to throw my clothes back on when I heard you all making a ruckus like it was New Year's Eve in Times Square." I shot Quinn a look, knowing she was the volume instigator. I'd heard the level this woman's voice could achieve at sporting events, and it had to come close to tipping a world record.

Dean was just coming down the hall as I was about to close the door, the carton of cream tucked stiffly under his arm.

"Thanks," I said as he handed it to me. "You're a lifesaver. Figuratively *and* literally."

My clever remark got nowhere with him. "I told you not to open the door for anyone."

"Um, I didn't. They more like pounded the door down." I disappeared into my apartment, letting Dean settle into a stance that indicated he was ready to battle The Hulk. "Thanks again for the cream. Have a nice night."

My friends burst into laughter once I locked the door.

"That guy is not your everyday rent-a-cop," Annie said. "He acts like he's working security detail for the Queen of England or something."

Quinn set down the paper bag she was carrying and unloaded a goldmine of snack foods. "Have you seen Ms. Romance's online following lately? Pretty sure she's close to Buckingham Palace status."

My nose scrunched up. "Don't remind me. I just want a few precious hours where I can forget all of that and pretend my life is as mundane and predictable as it used to be before all of this craziness."

Quinn ripped open the container of guac and a bag of tortilla chips. "That's exactly what we're here for." She licked a glob of green goop from her thumb. "Moral support, in the form of junk food and chick flicks, on the eve of what is to be one of the highest-viewed, most-talked-about shows in modern history."

My stomach spiraled. "Your moral support needs some work."

"How's this for work?" Quinn said as she launched a box of Raisinets at me.

It hit my stomach and fell to the floor.

"Sorry. Forgot you couldn't catch a felt ball if you were covered in Velcro."

"Moral. *Support*," I grumbled as I picked up the Raisinets, my gaze traveling to my bedroom door. With the amount of snacks these chicas were strapped with, Brooks was in for a long night in the closet.

When Quinn came toward me, Annie took over the snack unpacking detail, spreading out a cavalcade of every food item I wanted included in my last supper.

"How's this for moral support? I agreed to sit through the entire, grueling five hours and twenty-seven minutes of your favorite version of *Pride and Prejudice*. I've even promised not to pepper any snarky commentary throughout." Quinn slung her arm behind my neck. "And you know I would rather endure the full Brazilian, cat to ass, than sit through Colin Firth P&P silently."

"I thought you've never done the full one."

"I haven't. The basic bikini wax was enough to convince me I'm good with embracing what nature gave us down there." Quinn winced as though she was reliving that torturous day two summers ago.

"And you really think you'd rather endure the full cat to ass instead of watching *the* best version of *Pride and Prejudice*?" I shook some Raisinets into my hand as we meandered to the sofa. Which still had the indents of Brooks' and my bodies smashed into the cushions.

Quinn bumped her hip against mine. "It's over quicker."

As the other two finished prepping for the snack apocalypse, Quinn selected a familiar DVD from the stack and popped it into the player. Unable to contain the sigh as she did.

"How are things going with Justin?" My eyebrows

bounced at her. "Still glad you took my advice to make the first move?"

Quinn's answer came in the form of a reddening face.

"With the pace you two were going, you might have achieved first-kiss status in eight and a half years."

"What's wrong with taking things slow?" she asked.

"Nothing. If you're both intentionally taking it slow. It's different when you're going a snail's pace because two human beings are scaredy-cats and second-guessing the other's level of interest."

"Well excuse me, Ms. Romance, for believing the guy should be the one to make the first move." Quinn grabbed the remote and plopped down beside me on the couch. "Isn't that kinda the definition of romance?"

"The definition of romance is defined by the two people in the relationship. *That's* what romance is."

Quinn's head turned toward me, her mouth open. "That kind of talk sounds more like the ideology of the enemy. What are you gonna tell me next—romance is as romance does?" She huffed as she shook her head. "You've been spending way too much time with that douchecanoe. He's rubbing off on you."

I had to bite my lip to keep from laughing at the irony of that sentiment. If only my dear friend knew what he'd been rubbing off on me, on the very place she was seated, minutes ago, she would probably start looking into ways to have me involuntarily committed.

"Don't start it until we're in there!" Annie warned as she wrangled a couple bags of chips and a package of assorted licorice that was big enough to put us all into sugar comas.

"Don't worry, we won't," Quinn mumbled. "It's not like you haven't all seen it so many times you could recite every line in your sleep."

Annie dropped the licorice bag in my lap, knowing my weakness, before sprinkling the remaining items around on the coffee table in front of us. Once she and Sybill were settled in their seats, snacks in hand, Quinn punched Play with a dramatic flair.

Other than our usual spots we ooohed in, and the same spots Quinn usually stuck a finger in her mouth at, we passed the time in silence. At least other than the couple bags of chips we crunched through. When we were an hour in and I had yet to consume a single piece of licorice, Quinn called me out on it and I dutifully nibbled a few pieces.

I was too stressed to think about food, even my all-time favs. Brooks was one room away, stuffed in my closet, while three of my closest friends were here to provide moral support over the three months of torture I'd been exposed to at the very hand of the man in my closet. If they found out . . . if they knew Brooks was more to me than some annoying obstacle in the path of my dream job . . . what would they say? What would they do?

Would they stand by me, supporting me as they had through it all? Or would they label me a hypocrite, as I guessed the rest of the world would if they found out I'd fallen for the very man whose whole objective was getting me to fall for him?

When it was time to put in the second disc, I lifted my arms above my head and let out an overdone yawn. "I have to get some rest. We'll finish the second half the next time we get together. Thank you all so much for doing this. It was exactly what I needed tonight." When the three of them started to clean up the snack mess, I waved them off. "Don't worry about that. I'll take care of it. You've all done more than enough, and it's way past all of our bedtimes."

Quinn wasn't the only one to give me a suspicious look. She knew something was going on, that I was keeping something from her, but lord knew even her most unlikely guesses weren't half as bad as what it really was.

"You sure?" Annie asked.

"So sure," I answered, smiling at her as I started toward the door.

They took a minute to grab their bags and slip on their shoes, all meeting me at the door with expressions that suggested they were visiting me in an ICU.

"You've got this, Hannah." Sybill pulled me into a hug, holding me a couple beats longer than was standard. "We're all rooting for you."

"That department head title is going to look oh so fine below your name." Annie stepped in next, another embrace that hinted at goodbye. The eternal kind.

Quinn elected for a different kind of farewell. Clamping her hands over my shoulders, she dropped her face in front of mine. "Twenty-four hours, and this is all over. You never have to see that piece of camel dung ever again." Her fingers kneaded my shoulder muscles like she was sending me into the ring for round seven. "Tomorrow night, you show the world what you've been telling them for the past eight years."

I worked up the most convincing smile I had in my

arsenal as I swung open the door. "I've got the best friends a girl could ever ask for."

"Eh, yeah." Annie waved at me as they passed through the doorway. "Obviously."

Sybill jumped when she passed Dean, her hand moving to her chest. "I forgot he was here. He's like a ninja with a high-and-tight."

Of course that would be the one comment that would garner an amused reaction from my stonewall of a bodyguard.

"You're going to be out of a job with Hannah here soon." Sybill wagged a finger at Dean. "Whose door will you stand guard at next?"

Was that an actual facial expression? A brow lifting, a maybe twinkle in his eyes?

"Maybe yours, Miss Sybill."

She looked as surprised as I was that he'd responded, in words and everything. It took her a moment to realize he'd called her by her name. "How do you know my name?"

Dean's hands clasped in front of him seemed to relax. "I make it my business to know the names of people who come within two feet of my client."

"So when Hannah is no longer your client, I'll be back to another no-name face?" Sybill's head tipped as she waited for his answer.

Dean had no problem holding eye contact. Unblinking, penetrating fixation. "When Hannah's no longer my client, I'll call you Sybill."

"Why?"

One side of his mouth crept higher. "Because I also

make it my business to call a beautiful woman by her name."

Once Sybill realized what he was getting at, her eyes went wide. Beside her, Quinn and Annie fought smiles as they wound their arms through hers to steer her down the hall.

"She's single, you know." I clucked my tongue at Dean as I watched them round the corner.

"Of course I know." Dean morphed back into high-and-tight ninja.

"That's right. It's your business to know." I lightly tapped his arm before stepping into the apartment. "Have a good night."

"You too."

My fingers flinched on the lock. It was the first time he'd ever said anything to me when I offered a good night or a goodbye or hello. We were making progress—on one of our last nights together.

I couldn't help thinking of how that sentiment applied to another man tucked away inside my apartment. We'd made so much progress, but now we were at the end. And progress, without a resolution or goal in mind, was nothing but wasted effort.

Charging into my room, I threw open the closet door, having no idea what kind of mood I'd find Brooks in.

He was standing in practically the same position I'd left him, the look on his face more playful than anything.

"Sorry about that," I breathed, stepping aside so he could break free of the two-by-six cell I'd jailed him in the past few hours.

Instead of coming out, his arms crossed and his brows raised. "You. Owe. Me."

"I know."

"Like, *really* owe me." If it wasn't the way he said it, his expression had me picking up right where we'd left off earlier.

"Did you have anything in mind particularly?" My hand dropped to his belt, encouraging him closer. "I never like to be in anyone's debt for long."

Brooks let me pull him from the closet, his smile making my chest tight. "I have something in mind."

"Care to share that something with me?"

A gleam flashed in his eyes as his hands wound behind my elbows. "I'd try explaining it, but I think I'd get my point across better with a live demonstration."

When my calves bumped into the edge of my bed, my throat ran dry. Maybe I should have tried locking him up in a closet weeks ago.

Before I knew it, Brooks had me on my back, his mouth covering mine as his body pressed me into the swells of my comforter. "How's this?"

My legs braided around his, my bare feet dragging down his pants. "I love live demonstrations."

"Too steep a price to ask for a few hours hiding in a closet?" Even as he asked it, his hand sank into my backside, lifting it until my hips locked against his.

An uneven breath escaped us both at the same time.

"Ask for more," I panted, letting my body find a rhythm that suggested we were making love had it not been for the folds of material keeping us apart.

Brooks's hand in mine balled into a fist as my hips

rose and fell against his, his face indicating he was being tormented in the best kind of way.

"If you say . . ." His voice was so deep, it rattled my chest. "After being locked in a small cell with heaps of clothes, I've got a bit of an aversion to them now." His mouth dropped to my collarbone, sucking at the tender flesh as his fingers slipped beneath the shoulder of my cardigan.

Finally. Sweet baby Buddha. After all of this waiting and heavy making out, we were going to have sex. Never in a hundred million years would I have guessed the one guy I'd shared a one-night stand with would turn out to be such a pussy-tease the second time around.

When my fingers worked the top buttons of my dress undone, Brooks stiffened. One of his hands enveloped both of mine, tying them above my head as he stared at me. "Just the sweater for now."

As he worked the cardigan down my arms, I stared at the ceiling with confusion. Once he'd tossed it aside, before he got back to kissing me, I interrupted him.

"Next?" I slipped my dress straps off my shoulders, giving him the chance to take care of the rest.

He exhaled. "Hannah . . ."

My head fell back. "Seriously, Brooks. What is going on?" I didn't pause long enough for him to respond because I needed a good, long rant. "We've been dating for weeks now, and the farthest we've gone is one shirt and now one sweater removed. I mean, damn, I might understand the hold up if we hadn't already had sex, but we have." My eyes had to close in order for me to concentrate on what I was saying, instead of getting distracted by what

I was feeling. "I guess I just don't get this whole reverse order thing. I'm ready—I've *been* ready for a while now. And you're not exactly the guy who's waiting for his wedding night, so can you help me understand what it is I'm missing? What part of this I'm not realizing?"

Brooks was quiet, waiting for me to spew whatever else I needed to get out. But for now, I was good.

He rolled off to the side, staying close but not so close it made critical thinking difficult. "You're right. I'm not waiting for marriage. If that night in Chicago didn't make that clear." His throat moved when his eyes found mine. "I'm waiting for *you*."

I felt my eyebrows knit together. "I just said I'm ready—"

His head shook. "Not for that."

"Then for what?" I asked, sitting up on my elbows.

His mouth opened, but a sigh came out of it instead of words. "That night, I didn't really know you. Or I guess you could say I knew enough to realize I wanted to get into bed with you, but I didn't know *you*. The real Hannah Arden I've spent the last three months learning about." He shifted on the bed, his eyes narrowed in concentration. "That girl I was content to share a night with, no expectations, no conditions, no commitment—but the girl beside me now, I want more from. I *need* more from."

My leg slid out from beneath his. "What more do you want?" My voice was cool, encroaching on cold, as I digested what he was implying.

"I want you to know exactly how I feel about you," he said, his eyes reading a rare innocent. "And I want to know exactly how you feel about me too."

"I care for you. But you already know that."

"The woman I met in Chicago deserved more than a one-night stand from some guy afraid of commitment. That woman deserves everything a man can give her." His forehead creased. "I need you to know that while I care for you, I feel so much more, Hannah. The word catches in my throat every time I try to say it, but you know what that word it is. You know how I feel about you."

When his hand reached for mine, I couldn't move to accept or reject it. Instead, my hand rested limply in his, as though the bone and muscle had dissolved from inside.

"And even though I might not deserve it, I need to know if you feel the same." The words stuck in his throat, his eyes closing in an attempt to free them.

"Don't, Brooks. Don't say it."

I didn't know if he heard me as he finished. "I need to know if you love me."

A bolt of ice shot down my spine. That word.

In every other context, the L word was my purveyor of hope and happiness, the pillar of my profession, but coming from him . . . on this night . . .

"I told you not to bring that up. I made you promise you wouldn't pressure me with such a loaded word." My hand came back to life, yanking out of his as I shot up from the bed.

"Wait." He blinked as he sat up on the bed. "You think this is still about some stupid job? That everything I've done, everything I've just said, is part of some master scheme to score a promotion?" With the look he was giving me, it was as though I'd just sentenced him to death by a million paper cuts.

But truly, how could he not consider I'd arrive at that conclusion if he brought up the love word? Brooks was neither dumb nor naïve. Not to mention, I'd warned him no fewer than a dozen times never to push me to confess certain feelings or to assign designations to our relationship; not until this whole *Romance Versus Reality* circus was behind us.

"Last I checked, you hadn't bowed out of the running for the job."

"Look around you. There are no cameras. No spectators to prove anything to. It's just you and me and the moment when it's time to define exactly what this is." His finger circled the room as his voice grew. "I'm able to put into words how I feel—I just damn well did. Now it's your turn."

My feet carried me farther from him, not sure if I wanted to throw a bottle of perfume at his face or myself at him. He was saying everything I wanted to hear . . . at precisely the worst possible time.

"No cameras?!" A burst of air exploded from my mouth. "Maybe not tonight, but there sure as hell will be cameras tomorrow. Cameras catching every moment of our last date together, and on the other end, millions of viewers will be ready to cast their vote as to who proved their point."

He inhaled slowly, as though he were taking his time to gather his thoughts. "This, us"—his finger motioned between us—"has nothing to do what any of that."

"No, Brooks, this has everything to do with that." My arms crossed when my vision blurred. "You're here because of the job and the show and because you're Mr. Reality trying to prove to the world that you're right."

"Yeah, maybe that's what brought me here, but that's not what's kept me here." His hands clasped as he stared up at me. "You. You're what's kept me here. My feelings for you are what's kept me here."

"Kind of convenient this is all coming to light the evening before the show's finale, isn't it?"

His brows lifted. "I thought it was a better time than bringing it up tomorrow night."

"Unbelievable. You promised you wouldn't do this to me. You swore—"

"Do you love me?" he cut in. "It's my turn to ask a question, and this is the one I'm asking. You know the rules—be honest, no bullshit." His neck rolled as he searched my eyes. "Do you love me?"

Tears burned in my eyes as I backed away. "Veto." When his head fell, a heavy breath falling from his lips, I added, "I knew you'd save the worst question for last."

"The worst for last? Is that really what you think of me confessing that I love you and wanting to know if you feel anything close to the same for me?" His voice broke toward the end, the pain carved into his face so real it almost convinced me.

But I remembered he was playing a part, an actor reading a script. This wasn't real. The man I'd fallen for wasn't real. His professed love wasn't real. Not even the ball in his throat was.

But my broken heart, my tears, were very real.

"I can't believe you're doing this." My head shook as I started for the door, grabbing my sweater. "I can't believe I was stupid enough to think you actually cared for me in a way that extended past your career ambitions."

"Hannah!" He shot up from the bed, coming after me, but he stopped when I gave him a warning look. "I don't give a fuck about the job or proving my point or whatever else you think this is about. I care about you. I *love* you."

The words rebounded off of me, feeling cheap and hollow. "Liar."

"What am I lying about?"

"Loving me." I forced myself to look him in the eyes. It wasn't fair. A man shouldn't be able to appear so convincing when he was lying. "You don't believe in love, remember?"

I didn't wait for whatever his reply might have been, because as soon as I slid into my shoes, I was out the door, Dean falling into place a step behind me. As I noticed quiet tears creeping down my face, I felt this unfamiliar sensation deep in my chest. As though something inside was being torn apart, a little at a time.

Maybe love really was a big sham. A façade only the naïve fell victim to. What the hell did I know? I was the woman who'd gone and fallen for the very last man on the planet I should have.

CHAPTER
Eighteen

This was almost over with. All of it. The show. The cameras. The stress. *Him.* In a few hours, I could file it all away in the history compartment.

The viewers would be the ones to decide who'd proved their point, but on the off-chance Mr. Reality was voted the winner, I had a plan. One that involved handing in my resignation to the *World Times* first thing Monday morning and looking for work elsewhere. Preferably far enough away I'd never have to run into Brooks North on the sidewalk in passing.

A frown was all I was capable of as I stared at my reflection. The red formal gown the studio had sent over for the big finale made breathing, not to mention walking, a challenge.

When the knock on the door came, I sucked in as much a breath as the stitching would allow, then checked my teeth to make sure I didn't have any red lipstick splashed across them. That would be my luck—to be remembered as the lipsticked-teeth girl who wrote about romance and love and was responsible for proving them dead.

My lasting legacy.

Stuffing my phone into the small clutch, I headed for the front door, repeating to myself that the sooner this got started, the sooner it would be over.

"The car's downstairs waiting for you, Miss Arden." Dean stepped aside to make room for me, having exchanged his standard dark suit for a tuxedo.

"You clean up nicely," I praised while I locked the apartment.

"Not as nice as you." He cleared his throat as he gave my dress a brief scan. "Shall we?"

"I suppose I'm in too deep to attempt an escape now."

"Doubt you'd make it far if you tried." This time, Dean stayed one step in front of me as we passed down the hall. "Your face has got to be almost as recognizable as Oprah's by now."

"Except her face is synonymous with philanthropy and mine is with fraudulence."

Dean's head slightly tipped back at me. "You've made a believer out of me."

"You don't need to give me a pity pep talk." I worked up as much of a smile as I could. "But thank you all the same."

"That isn't pity, Miss Arden. You've confirmed your point to this disbeliever."

I patted his arm. "It's nice to know some good will have come from this hellish experiment."

Dean was silent the rest of the way, opening doors and scanning shadows as we made our way to the gleaming black car waiting outside the building.

Two hours. Maybe three. That was all I had to endure before the cameras would finally be turned off for good. I could hold my emotions in check for a handful of minutes if that was what it took. Amiable meets distant, that was my goal for the night. The less emotion the better, because feelings were not what I wanted viewers to pick up on. I needed to prove love was real. I had to show my life's work, not to mention my worldview, was not some epic lie.

"Wow. I mean, really, wow." Jimmy blinked at me as I climbed inside the car.

"Thanks, Jimmy. You have a real way with words."

"You're the writer, not me." He flashed a smile as he prepped the camera on his head. "You ready for this? Last line-up of questions. I bet you're going to miss it, right?"

"Like a boil on my ass in the summer." When Dean and Jimmy's heads flicked toward me, I shrugged. "I have a way with words."

Jimmy grunted in acknowledgement before giving the countdown with his fingers. As he did, I encased myself with the numbness I felt on the inside, praying it was thick enough to prove impenetrable.

"We are live for the very last time with Ms. Romance, Hannah Arden, on the season finale of *Romance Versus Reality*," Jimmy started, while I reminded myself to smile. "We're on our way to meet Mr. Reality and have a few minutes for some questions. These ones we pulled directly from our viewers." My back tensed, but the smile held. "Our first question comes from Callie in Houston. She wants to know what's been the best part of the *Romance*

Versus Reality experiment."

I didn't need a moment to consider my answer. "That it's almost over."

When Jimmy mouthed, "Whoa. Harsh," I capped my response with a chuckle. One that suggested I might have been teasing, but might not have been.

"Okay, moving onto our second question leading into the blockbuster last date." Jimmy checked the notes on his phone. "This one comes from Rachel out of Cleveland. She wants to know how your opinions on love have changed throughout the course of the show."

"They haven't really," I said, my hands wringing in my lap. "If anything, this all has only further confirmed my beliefs where love is concerned."

Jimmy rolled his eyes; my response hadn't budged from the first time I'd been asked it. I wondered if he could hear the deceit in my voice, see the lie in my eyes. The truth was, my views on love had changed, but if I admitted that, I lost. And I'd already lost so much, I couldn't bear to lose my chance at my dream job.

"You are just tearing through these questions, so we've got time for a few more."

My nails dug into my palms. *Talk slower. Add a bunch of fluff.* Whatever it took to keep me from answering any more of these god-awful questions than necessary.

"The next question comes from Gus in Seattle. He wants to know if you were the last woman on the planet, Brooks were the last man, and the fate of civilization rested on your shoulders—"

My hand raised as I waved. "Bye-bye, civilization."

Jimmy's chest rocked with a contained laugh, and he

checked outside before consulting his phone once more. "Kaitlyn in Brooklyn would like to know why you dislike Mr. Reality so much."

"Why I dislike him?" An endless stream of answers flooded my mind—right before it all went blank.

When my silence stretched, Jimmy rolled his hand at me, looking as surprised as I was that a torrent of answers weren't spilling from me.

"For one, we have totally different views where relationships are concerned."

"Yes, but does that mean you dislike everyone who has an opposing view as you?" Jimmy asked.

"No, not at all," I said, rethinking my answer. "It's just that Brooks is so conceited, so unwilling to even consider the possibility that he might be wrong."

"And you're not?" An angelic smile formed on his face when I shot Jimmy an annoyed look.

I allowed myself to take a breath before replying. "It's one thing to be passionate about what you believe in. It's another to insist you're infallible."

From the way Jimmy lifted his eyes, I guessed he wasn't impressed by my answer. "And we have just enough time for one more quick question as we roll up to the surprise location of our last date." Jimmy motioned for Dean to stay put as the car pulled up to the curb. "Lexie in Tulsa wants to know one valuable lesson you've learned from this experiment."

Dammit, Lexie. Thanks for the sucky question. Why couldn't someone want to know what my sign or my favorite color was?

"I suppose I've learned to trust my instincts." I

cleared my throat. "To go with my gut when I feel conflicted."

Jimmy allowed a few moments of quiet to let me expand, but I wasn't adding one more word. "Let's get this date rolling and find out, once and for all, who will be the victor in the final episode of *Romance Versus Reality*."

On cue, Dean threw open the door and scanned the surroundings before waving me out. Jimmy followed as I inspected what was around me to attempt to figure out where I was. It didn't take long. We were parked in front of one of the more iconic skyscrapers in the city, standing like a silver pillar stretching into the night sky.

Dean held open doors, examining every square foot as we whisked toward the elevators. Jimmy stayed in his position a few feet behind me, not making me self-conscious at all.

My teeth worked at my lip as I watched the numbers light up in ascending order. He must already be there. Brooks was waiting. After last night, I wasn't sure what would happen when we saw each other. He'd in so many words issued an ultimatum, and I'd stormed out.

I'd confessed I cared for him. He claimed he felt even more for me. The man who was a stout believer in the lie of love wanted me to believe he felt that very thing for me?

He was a liar. A manipulator.

And I was a sucker. A fool.

As I rode the elevator to the top floor, I reminded myself not to show any emotion, to not give away anything that might make viewers question my sentiments for Brooks North.

"Nervous?" Jimmy asked, as though he'd forgotten he had a camera on his head that was being streamed to millions of screens around the nation.

"Not one bit," I said, though if someone had pressed their fingers to my neck, my pulse would have told a different story.

When the doors finally opened, I found a scene straight out of a romantic's fantasy playbook. Strands of lights ran along a path, creating an aisle that led up a bay of stairs, creamy white rose petals sprinkled along the floor.

Pushing through the door, I found myself standing on the roof of one of the most recognizable buildings in the country. The décor made the hallway scene seem lackluster by comparison. The volume of lighting and flowers rivaled even the most lavish of weddings I'd attended; it was a dream.

A dream encapsulated in a nightmare.

It didn't take long for me to notice the tall figure waiting in the shadows, the whites of his eyes targeting me the moment I stepped onto the rooftop. I couldn't help thinking back to the last time he and I had climbed the stairs to another roof, our first private date feeling like another lifetime ago.

When Brooks stepped into the fringe of the light, the breath siphoned from my lungs, little by little, until I felt lightheaded.

No man—especially one who believed as he did— should have this effect on a woman.

As Jimmy swiveled around so he was in front of me, I cleared my expression and focused on putting one foot in front of the next. I might have felt like my insides were melting from the way Brooks was staring at me, but all the viewers would see was a woman bored with the charade.

Brooks stayed frozen in place as I moved toward him, a swish of red silk and veiled spite. It wasn't until I was within a few feet that I registered the look on his face.

Where I was hiding everything, he concealed nothing.

Not that the awe ironing out his face could be taken as truth—it was some last-ditch effort to trick me into buying he truly was in love with me.

When I stopped in front of him and he stayed silent, I waited. I wouldn't be the first to speak.

But the silence became too uncomfortable to bear.

"You're staring," I said, trying to ignore Jimmy as he prowled around us, searching for his angle.

Brooks finally moved when he exhaled. "Because I have no words."

My arms twitched at my sides, desperate to cross, but I held them in place. No reactions. Stone cold. Robotic aloofness. Those were my marching orders for the rest of the night.

As more silence crept between us, Jimmy waved a notecard at us, keeping it out of the camera's view. It looked like a schedule of events for the night, penned in Conrad's blocky letters.

I caught myself right as I was gearing up for an eye-roll. Conrad couldn't have devised a more cliché date if he'd tried.

Brooks cleared his throat after scanning the notecard, getting right after item number one. "Would you like to dance?"

One of my eyebrows lifted at him. "Would I *like* to?"

Dodging my loaded question, he stepped into my space, his arms carefully enveloping me in a way that suggested he was holding a bird with a broken wing. Sensation spilled down my spine, so I braced my hands on his chest, keeping him at a measured distance.

Music played in the background. It wasn't until I'd spun around that I realized the notes weren't coming from a sound system but from an actual string orchestra tucked against the ledge of the roof.

Brooks's arms cinched around me right before he led me across the roof at a pace that suggested we were racing instead of dancing. It took Jimmy a moment to figure out what had happened. Not stopping when we came to the stairway door, Brooks threw it open before steering me inside.

"What in the hell are you doing?" I shouted as he slammed the door behind us.

When I moved to shove through the door, he blocked my path. His eyes locked with mine. "Attempting to save something we both know is pretty fucking rare."

A huff rolled from my mouth. "A guy pretending to love a woman for an ulterior motive? Not so rare at all."

"You're really hung up on that aren't you? The show? The promotion?" Brooks's voice echoed down the stairwell, reverberating off the walls. "What if I march out there right now and tell the whole damn world that I love you?"

The door started to pull open from outside, Jimmy getting the faintest glimpse of us before Brooks slammed the door shut and held it closed.

"Brooks, please. Millions of viewers are on the other side of that camera lens, each one twitching to cast their votes for one of us." My arms crossed as I backed away from the incarnate daydream in a good-fitting tux. "This has nothing to do with what you say tonight, but what I do. You can profess you love me until you're blue in the face, but all viewers are going to be watching is my reaction."

Jimmy was now pounding on the door, but Brooks ignored him, all of his attention on me.

"What difference does it make if you say you love me for all the world to know?"

He shifted his weight. "Someone once told me it made *all* the difference."

My throat tightened, foiling my plan to stay as emotionally vacant as possible tonight. "If that's true, that you really do love me, you won't say it tonight. Or any other night. Just leave me alone after this nightmare is over." I stormed toward the door, but his hand wound around my forearm as I was about to throw it open.

"I found your number. Last night." He reached into his jacket pocket to retrieve his phone, then scrolled through his contacts list before pausing on one. "Snowstorm in Chicago?" His throat moved as he read what I'd typed into his phone before the break of dawn one February morning.

I stared at his hand molded to my arm. It looked right. It *felt* right. My heart told me one thing, while my head said another. A heart could be tricked, but a mind not so easily.

"It seemed like a better idea than tucking a piece of paper with my number on it into your pocket." I unwove my arm from his grip. "You were the one who made it a point not to use names, so I got creative."

He stared at the number for another moment before tucking his phone away. "I had a better shot at dialing random numbers in hopes of getting you than thinking you might have punched your number into my contact list under a pseudonym. And what number is this anyway? It's not the same number I have for 'Hannah Arden' in my contacts."

I tried to back away from him, but I was frozen in place. "The number you have for me is my cell phone. Snowstorm in Chicago's is my landline."

"Landline?" He blinked at me. "You've got to be the only person under seventy who still has a landline."

"I like having a back-up," I said, motioning at him. "When I don't want to give a guy I just met carte blanche to my cell phone."

His mouth twisted with a hint of amusement. "You gave me your landline number instead of your cell? After the night we spent together, all that earned me was some archaic means of communications?"

My head shook as I finally succeeded at pulling away from him. "It doesn't matter. My number, that night, our real dates, our fake ones—it just doesn't matter anymore."

His head angled toward me. "It matters to me."

My feet faltered from hearing the rawness in his voice, from seeing it in his eyes. He was a skilled actor, a seasoned manipulator. "You don't show your love to someone when they're walking away. You prove it before they even think about leaving."

His posture wilted at my words, finally letting go of

the handle when I shoved the door open, letting me go. Jimmy fell back a few steps, the look on his face leaving no question as to how he felt about Brooks's latest camera-evading stunt.

"I've had enough dancing for one night," I said as I whisked past Jimmy. Behind me, Brooks's steady footsteps echoed. "What's next on the schedule?"

Jimmy gave a silent sigh as he retrieved the agenda from his pocket.

Dinner.

Fabulous. That would go quickly as well, since I had zero appetite.

As I approached the table, Brooks swept in front of me to pull out a chair. When he motioned at me to take a seat, I skirted around the table to take the other chair. He didn't say anything, instead settling into the chair he'd pulled out once I was seated. Rolling his neck a few times, he pulled at his collar as he reached for the glass of water in front of him.

To distract myself, I inspected the table. Short bunches of white flowers were staggered in the center, pale gold linens and china complementing the setting. Truly, the whole sight was breathtaking, and in another context, I would have been wide-eyed and twirling through the enchanted scene. But this was all a Trojan Horse, and I would not open myself up to its sabotage.

"Can you believe this is it?" Brooks asked after acknowledging Jimmy circling his finger in desperation. Finale or not, we were going to bore viewers to death if we didn't open our mouths eventually. "It seems like three months flew by."

"I wouldn't say it flew by," I said, letting my eyes be drawn to the candlelight. "But at least it's almost over."

His tongue worked into his cheek before he reached for his glass of white wine. Lifting it toward me, he said, "To almost having me out of your life, once and for all."

Raising my glass, I clinked it against his, then set it down without taking a drink.

"What's your plan for after all this is over?" Brooks followed his question with another drink of wine, shifting in his seat.

"That depends how this all finishes," I answered, diverting my attention toward the server carrying a couple of appetizer plates.

"How do you hope it will finish?" When the server set our plates in front of us, Brooks leaned aside, keeping me in his view.

"I'm assuming that's a rhetorical question."

"It's not."

"Well, I'm going to pretend it is and leave it at that." Glancing at what was on the plate in front of me, my appetite dipped below zero. It looked like nuclear-green baby food in a fancy bowl.

Brooks appeared as impressed with the puce sludge as I did. He slid it aside, resting his arms on the table. "What do you want, Hannah?"

His question threw me. *What do I want?* That could have meant a thousand things. But I guessed it all led to one—what did I want from him?

"I don't know, Brooks. What do you want?" My eyes met his while my stomach twisted into an infinite knot.

"I know exactly what I want." His stormy eyes

flashed. "Exactly *who* I want."

My back stiffened as I pointed at Jimmy. "Of course you do. The camera's rolling."

His throat moved as Jimmy moved in closer, panning between Brooks' and my faces. No doubt selling the drama for every last nickel it was going for.

Refusing to keep the conversation rolling for the show's sake, I pretended to be interested in the view. Not that a person needed to pretend very hard. Millions of lights twinkled against a canvas of black, the din of the city creating a unique melody.

A few minutes went by, Jimmy imploring us with pleading eyes to give him something more than obstinate silence. I didn't budge. I was done being a puppet and having my strings yanked.

Jimmy's phone buzzed in his pocket. When he pulled it out to read the text, he rolled his eyes, before slowly mouthing, "Talk to each other" at us.

Brooks glanced in my direction before rising from his chair. "I hear they've put together something for us to watch." Brooks glanced in Jimmy's direction, as though looking for confirmation, before his attention floated back to me. "If you're in a hurry for things to be over."

"I'm in a hurry," I said, rising as the server returned with what looked to be an ornamental beet salad.

My heels made a snapping sound as I followed Brooks to where yet another extravagant scene had been staged. A large movie screen rested in front of an eggplant-colored vintage-style sofa, a mass of hurricane glass containers holding candles of varying sizes. It was gorgeous. It was garish. I wasn't sure which it was more of, or if it my mood was creating my experience of it all.

"What is this?" I asked, my words as hesitant as my steps, eyeing the screen where the bold *Romance Versus Reality* logo was displayed.

"No idea," Brooks replied as he took the glasses of champagne from a different server. He waited for me to take a seat on the sofa first, holding the glass of champagne I guessed by now he knew I wouldn't drink. He set both glasses down at his feet when he sat beside me, his distance not going unnoticed. He was giving me space.

"How bad is this going to be?" I mumbled to him as Jimmy worked to secure the right vantage to film us.

"My guess is it will fall somewhere between appalling and truly heinous." Brooks glanced at me from the side of his eyes, his throat moving as he did.

From a couple of large speakers, a voice narrated as the screen played a familiar scene. "Three months. Two people. One winner. Who will come out on top, proving their case to millions of viewers? We'll find out tonight on the finale, but first, let's take a quick stroll down memory lane."

Brooks and I gave small groans. With as much money as this show was making the paper, you would have thought they could have afforded to hire a decent writer.

From there, clips of Brooks' and my dates played. Sweet mother of mercy. You know how a person hated the sound of their voice being played back to them? Magnify that by about a hundred and that was what it was like watching oneself on a giant screen. Even though the date clips were available to watch online whenever a person wanted, I hadn't viewed a single one. Save for the few frozen stills on that morning show with that witch doctor, I'd refused to watch any footage from the dates.

The first clip had been taken from date one, skipping from one moment to the next, playing back dialogue in such a way as to give a different impression of what had really been intended. From there, a few clips of our second and third dates, skimming through days in seconds. A close-up of Brooks's face. One of mine. A shared laugh. A lingering look.

God damn. It was the Cliff's Notes to a romance novel in five minutes of airtime.

My head fogged as I watched the young woman on the screen in front of me. Was it as obvious to everyone else as it was to me? Was it easy enough to detect in her eyes or her smile or her posture? To Ms. Romance, it was blinding. That young woman was not just participating in a social experiment, nor was she merely putting up with the man opposite her.

All of the clips. The questions. The woman on the other side of that screen was obvious.

She was in love.

I'd missed it. The romance expert couldn't recognize when she herself had fallen in love. I'd accepted that I'd fallen for him, but I'd been blind to what had come after.

Love.

The first man I'd loved was the last one I should have.

The picture became blurry as it came to an end, though it took me a moment to realize it wasn't the picture but my vision that was cloudy.

"What's the matter?"

I looked away when Brooks asked his question, not sure how long he'd been watching me.

"Nothing," I whispered, blinking in an attempt to clear my eyes before Jimmy noticed and zoomed in.

Brooks scooted closer, his forehead drawn with concern.

"Don't," I warned.

"Hannah . . ."

The way he said my name had my lungs straining. It might have been an act for him, but it wasn't for me. It hadn't been for a while now.

I was in love with him.

In love with a man who was betting on me falling in love with him. The irony was cruel. But the reality was worse.

"In a minute, we're going to open up the voting lines to viewers, after one last question posed to you both." Jimmy kneeled in front of us, clearing his throat dramatically. "What is the final thing you'd like to say to one another on live television? Your last words, so to speak."

The sentiment didn't register at first. I wasn't sure what he meant. Our last words to one another? What else did one say besides goodbye? There was nothing left to say, given the situation.

Brooks was the first to move, angling his body toward mine. The corners of his eyes were creased as he stared at the floor, concentrating. I had no idea what he would say —anything from goodbye to divulging that we'd slept together before all of this.

My lungs squeezed when he opened his mouth.

"I'm sorry for what I said. What I did." His eyes held

mine for a moment, allowing a silent exchange to pass. He wanted me to know exactly what he was talking about.

The confession. The proclamation. It really had been an act, the clincher in his playbook. It had been as real as the smile frozen to my face all night.

The creases on his forehead carved deeper. "I'm sorry for everything. You deserve more . . . more than I have given, more than I ever could give you."

I didn't feel the tears forming. But I didn't miss them when they wound down my cheeks.

When Brooks noticed them, he reached for me, his body moving as if it was an instinct. The moment his hands touched me, I jolted out of my seat, backing away from him. My vision tunneled in, focused on nothing but Brooks watching me with a look I didn't have a translation for. It was pinched like regret, but his eyes didn't match. Something else was reflecting in them.

I didn't stop to decipher it. I couldn't. This whole experience had begun as a joke and was ending as a tragedy. I'd sacrificed my beliefs, my career, my standards for this. And I was leaving with all of that destroyed.

"Hannah, wait." Brooks rose from the sofa as though he was going to follow.

"Stop." My voice quivered as I shook my head. He stayed where he was. "Just . . . stop. It's over."

With nothing left to give, I ran toward the stairway, my heels flying off as I went. I didn't stop to collect them. I couldn't afford to pause or turn back now. The only option was forward. It was my one hope for rebuilding the wreck this experience had left me with.

Love. It was responsible for all of this.

Maybe it was easier to believe how he did.
Maybe he was right.
Maybe I'd been wrong about everything all along.

CHAPTER
Nineteen

The aftermath from playing a lead role in the social experiment of our generation had yet to set in. Maybe because I took a sick day Monday and kept my phone, tablet, and laptop powered off.

Rolling out of bed Tuesday morning, I knew better than to think I could get away with faking another sick day. Knowing Conrad, he'd probably show up at my front door with a full camera crew in some ploy to document an "After the Final Date," or some crap like that.

I knew better than to hope if I just hid beneath my comforter for a few weeks, this would all blow over. So I got up before my alarm, took extra time to do my hair and make-up, and slipped into my favorite pink skirt suit. Ms. Romance might be going down today, but she'd be making that descent in her signature color, head high. My grand-ma's pearl necklace finished the ensemble.

Dean was outside my door, not saying anything as he fell in behind me, as though he hadn't been exposed to copious amounts of Death Cab for Cutie and Chinese De-livery the past forty-eight hours.

Before heading onto the sidewalk, I shoved a big pair of sunglasses on my face, hoping they'd conceal my iden-tity just long enough to dodge into a cab and sprint into the *World Times* building.

Dean hailed a cab, swinging open the door for me when it screeched to a stop. Once we were inside, he gave the driver the address and I attempted to relax for the fif-teen-minute drive to work. It might be the last chance I'd get for the rest of the day.

The voting polls had officially closed last night at midnight, so I knew the results would be in. I couldn't bring myself to check the live updates or open the news to find out who voters had deemed the winner.

I already knew.

My actions that last date had sealed my fate. I couldn't have been any less removed, or acted less distant. In the end, Brooks didn't need me to say the words out loud—the unspoken ones carried more weight.

When the cab rolled to a stop, I took a deep breath and prepared myself for everything that was waiting for me on the fortieth floor. Seeming to sense my unease, Dean nudged me. "At least it's over."

I shared a smile with him, thankful for the kind words, despite knowing that, for me, it wasn't over. The show, yes, had filmed its last segment, but the aftermath would stay with me for a while.

The being recognized on the sidewalks, hiding behind sunglasses and floppy hats. The co-workers constant re-minders in the coffee room, the slant of the comments that would accompany my articles. It would be a long time before this was over for me, but perhaps what would last the longest was what cut the deepest.

How could I ever trust myself with another man again? How could I trust that I recognized love when I saw it or felt it? How could I know it wasn't all some fabrication? I'd spent my career proclaiming to be the expert on relationships and love, yet had become the fool where both were concerned.

Those who can't do, teach. The cliché played through my mind as I made my way inside of the building. Perhaps in my situation, it wasn't so cliché.

Waiting for the elevators, I noticed a cluster of women talking in hushed voices, eyes scanning my direction. I waited for the next elevator.

Dean slid in front of me when we climbed onto the next available one, almost as though he were shielding me for as long as he possibly could. I wasn't sure how much longer the company would have Dean assigned to me, but when he left, I'd miss him. Go, figure. I had a soft spot for a robot with a soul.

I took off my sunglasses when the doors chimed open forty floors up, knowing no amount of camouflage would conceal me from my co-workers. I'd arrived early, but not my usual time before anyone else had staggered in. My palms started to sweat the moment I set foot in the lobby, not sure what I'd find waiting for me. Would my co-workers lead with the overly-supportive vibe? Or the pretending like nothing had happened front? Would Conrad call me into his office before I had a chance to sit down? Would a certain counterpart still be working from the cubicle across from mine? And if so, how would we act around each other now that the experiment was over?

The stream of questions were about to give me a headache so I concentrated on the tile floor, making a game out of not stepping on any of the cracks as I meandered through the office.

The soft din of noise dissipated with every step I took, figures in my periphery vision freezing to a halt, heads angling toward me. When I'd worked up the courage to return some of their stares, I found faces formed in varying phases of pity and sympathy.

My knees gave a wobble, but I pushed through it. I might have been a romantic and adored pink more than was appropriate for a woman my age, but I was strong, god dammit. I'd survived my parents dying at a young age, and I'd endured three months of being followed and filmed, having every blink analyzed. Confronting my co-workers after all of the votes had been tallied was nothing.

My eyes jumped to Quinn's cube, knowing I was going to be in deep trouble with her for dodging her calls and texts the past couple of days. I still hadn't turned on my phone to see what messages I'd missed, but I knew my best friend well enough to guess she'd tried getting ahold of me a good three dozen times.

Maybe more.

I'd offer to buy chocolate éclairs and coffee for the next month and that should mollify her a little at least.

My desk was exactly how I'd left it Friday evening, save for the newspaper resting on top of my keyboard, a neon green sticky note pressed over the top headline on the front page. It was familiar handwriting; my best friend's small, precise letters.

Setting down my bag, I dropped into my chair as I read the words she'd scratched onto the post-it: *Maybe he's not such a douchecanoe afterall.*

Automatically, my eyes lifted to the space across from me. There was no head bobbing above the cube wall, no keys beating wildly, no foot-tapping when those keys went silent as he contemplated his next words.

He wasn't coming back. At least not to that desk. He'd earned the big fancy one in that coveted corner office. He'd earned it by doing exactly what he vowed he would three months ago at that conference room table.

My vision blurred as I peeled the sticky from the newspaper. No tears, I reminded myself. I'd already humiliated myself enough without turning into the woman who melted down at her desk on Tuesday morning.

The headline was printed in big, black letters, front and center. *My New Reality.*

In much smaller letters, I read who the article was written by. Brooks North. Not Mr. Reality. I'd never seen him attach his given name to an article.

When I picked up the paper to begin reading, my hands were trembling too much to make out the small words, so I set it back down. I had no idea what this was about, and maybe I shouldn't read it at all, but I couldn't stop once I started.

Readers know me as Mr. Reality. Viewers know me as Brooks North. However, as I sit down to write this article sometime before sunset Sunday morning, I have no idea who I am anymore.

I stopped. I reread that first paragraph again. He had no idea who he was anymore? Make that both of us.

When I signed on with the World Times to take part in this "social experiment," I had one goal: to succeed. Based on the way the polls are looking as I write this, it looks as though I will accomplish exactly what I set out to do. Win.

But all I feel is loss instead.

Loss of self. Loss of belief. Loss of purpose. Loss of

. . .

Her.

Readers know her as Ms. Romance. Viewers as Hannah Arden. Me? I know her as an adversary. A thorn in my side to begin, who would become my Achilles Heel, who is now the woman I love.

My heart stopped, stalling for a few beats from the unexpectedness of his words. Certain I'd read them wrong or there was a typo, my eyes scanned that last sentence again. And again. And eleven more times.

Love.

That was the word. It wasn't a typo.

I guess I proved my point. I suppose I was right about relationships and love. That's what the results from the show have demonstrated. Maybe I was correct the past eight years of penning articles about the reality of relationships, and what I believed for years before that from my own life experiences. Love is a lie. Soul mates are nonsense. Happy endings are for the mentally deranged.

Maybe I was right.

*But I **know** I love her. It's the ache in my chest when I watch her walk away, it's the pit in my stomach when she's not near. It's written inside my very soul, the nuance of my essence, the center of my existence. Her. She's there. She feels more real to who I am than I do. She has become—she is—my reality.*

I am still a realist. You can still call me Mr. Reality on the sidewalks and it won't offend. But my reality has shifted, a new truth rising in its place.

Ready for the big reveal? Make sure you're sitting down first.

(drum roll begins playing in the background)

You don't find a soul mate. You become one.

You don't fall in love. You create it. You live it. You shape and mold and build upon it until it has become the sacred thread tying two unlikely souls to one another. An unbreakable bond that defies meaning, refusing to be lumped into a definition one can pen into words, or fit into a box.

She is the one. My one.

I love her. Not because I wanted to. Or tried to. Or even consciously thought to. I love her because I had to. There was no choice. No fight I could muster that would result in victory.

I fell in love with her the way one breathes: unconsciously.

Yet I will stay in love with her the opposite: consciously, exactly, precisely, concentrating every fiber of my being on protecting it.

I was love's greatest cynic, and now, it's most infa-

mous casualty.

Ms. Romance, Hannah Arden, was right about love, in all its intricacies and idiosyncrasies. She achieved the impossible in proving it to me.

I believe.

A ragged exhale spilled past my lips as my vision tunneled in on the last couple of sentences. My hands were still trembling, now joined with the rest of my body as I contemplated what I'd just read.

Another lie?

A satire?

A prank?

The truth?

Before I could give it too much thought, my phone's speaker buzzed. "Arden. My office."

Conrad didn't add another word before the speaker buzzed off.

As I stood, I touched the newspaper. An attempt to ascertain its existence. It was real as far as I could tell, but there was no telling. My mind could have drug me into an alternate reality with the way the past couple of days had gone.

As I headed down the hall toward Conrad's office, I ignored the stares of my co-workers.

Setting aside the mind space Brooks's article was taking up, I stepped inside Conrad's office without knocking.

"Close the door," he greeted, not looking up from his computer.

And this was where he jabbed the pin into my dreams, causing them to burst. The promotion I'd wanted since the day I finished writing my first article in the junior high newspaper would remain just that, a dream.

"Congratulations, kid." Conrad's gaze found me after I closed the door.

My eyebrows pinched together. "Congratulations? For what?"

"You, Hannah Arden, are going to be the new department head of the Life and Style department."

My hands reached out for the chair back. "You mean, the votes . . . I won?"

A single laugh-snort shot from Conrad. "Hell no. You lost by a landslide, barely thirty percent of the votes for Ms. Romance."

"Then why am I getting the job? The winner, the one who proved their point, was supposed to get the position."

"Exactly. Except when I called the winner up last night at twelve-oh-one after the polls closed to congratulate him, he informed me he was removing his candidacy from the position." Conrad shook his head as he waved at the chair I was standing behind. I didn't move. "Therefore, you get it."

"By default."

"However you want to look at it, Arden. You still wind up with everything you wanted."

My chest squeezed. "Not everything," I whispered, more to myself than to Conrad. "Where is he?"

"Where's who?"

My eyes lifted. "Brooks. Where is Brooks?"

"Like where is he exactly at this exact moment?" Conrad slid on his reading glasses before opening his copy of the morning paper. "How should I know? Somewhere in San Francisco. That's about as specific as I can give you."

My fingers curled into the chair back. "He went back to California?"

"That's what he told me. If he wasn't going to take the job, what reason was there for him to stay?" Conrad paused, his brow drawing together. "Unless . . ." His pointed look aimed my direction gave no mistake as to what he was referring to.

"Mr. Conrad, how quickly can you requisition a private plane and get Jimmy to meet me at the airport with that stupid camera?"

One bushy brow lifted at me. "You might think you're hot shit because you landed this job, but in my twenty years as Editor in Chief, I never once got a green light to fly a private plane at the drop of a hat. Nice try, kid."

"And what if I could guarantee you something that would make the Romance Versus Reality finale ratings seem like a made-for-TV movie?" Moving out from behind the chair, my arms crossed as my plan formed. "You get Jimmy and me on that plane this morning and I will give you a show that will make your ratings-fixated head spin."

"What could be better than you subliminally showing everyone you'd fallen in love with Brooks North on camera?" Conrad's fingers rolled along his desk. He was considering my request.

I marched closer, until I'd run into his desk and was staring down at him. "Saying it out loud."

CHAPTER
Twenty

I was in San Francisco by three that afternoon. Jimmy and camera equipment in tow.

I'd had a layover in San Francisco once, but never actually stepped foot in the city. It was vibrant and beautiful and everything that made my tourist's heart go soft and melty, but I was not here to see the sites. I was here for him.

Now I just had to find him in this metropolis filled with seven million people.

Thankfully, Quinn had managed to find a personnel file and text me his address mid-flight, so I had a starting point. If I didn't find him there, I wasn't sure what I'd do other than wait, or begin searching the city, one grid at a time.

"When do you want me to start filming?" Jimmy asked as we climbed out of the cab in front of Brook's apartment building.

"Whenever you want. I don't have any idea for how this is going to go, and we don't have a detailed itinerary from Conrad. Go with whatever your cameraman gut tells you." I stood outside of the building, smiling at it. This was where he lived. His home.

"How are you going to get inside?" Jimmy lifted his chin at the entry door.

"Just like this," I said, rushing to grab the door when someone shoved through it.

"You know, maybe you just should have called him before showing up at his doorstep like this." Jimmy flashed a peace sign at the middle-aged woman who'd come through the door, giving us a suspicious look.

"Too late for second guessing myself now," I said as we began climbing the stairs to Brooks's apartment on the third floor. As we went, I gave my outfit a brief onceover. My skirt was wrinkled from the flight, my jacket reeking of the Sprite I'd dumped on myself mid-flight compliments of turbulence, matched with an undertone of body odor thanks to nervous sweat. The glimpse I'd gotten of me from the neck up in the plane's bathroom gave the impression I'd spent hard time for something related to meth use.

Let's hope he'd meant what he said in that article, because what I was about to surprise him with, matched with how I looked, would be the gold standard of putting love to the test.

"I can't believe the way this whole thing turned out. Talk about a mind trip." Jimmy elbowed me as we scanned apartment numbers on the third floor.

"Can't imagine a better person to document this mind trip than you." I smiled over at him as we came to a stop outside apartment twenty-one.

My heart started to beat like a hummingbird's as my fist lifted to knock on his door. I wasn't sure what he'd think or exactly what I'd say; I just knew I had to be here.

My hand was still hanging in the air when the apartment one door down opened. A young woman emerged, her eyes landing on Jimmy and me instantly. Recognition lit up her face. "Oh. My. God. You're her, aren't you?" Her feet tapped the floor excitedly. There wasn't time to confirm or deny it before she pointed at Brooks's apartment. "He's not here."

"He left?" My face fell.

"Yeah. But he'll be back. Eventually. He went out on one of those globe-trotting runs of his." Her earrings jingled when she shook her head, chuckling. "Somebody needs to tell that guy that whatever he's running from he left it in the dust ten thousand miles ago."

"Do you have any idea where he might be?" I asked.

She paused for a second, as though she were considering something. "He likes Golden Gate Park. Usually all of his runs wind up weaving through there at some point."

I was already jogging down the hall. "Thank you," I told her as I rushed past.

"Hey, Ms. Romance," she called after me, waiting until I'd stopped before continuing, "You know what I've figured out about those closed-off, removed types? From having lived next door to one for the past five years?"

My head shook. "What?"

The corners of her mouth pulled. "It's not that they're in possession of a black soul, they're just protecting a really big heart."

My chest squeezed. "I think I've recently realized that too."

"Good luck!" she called after me as Jimmy and I thundered down the stairs.

"Maybe you should just wait here until he comes back." Jimmy shoved open the outside door for me. "It's going to be looking for a needle in a haystack out there."

"No. It will be like searching for *my* needle in the haystack. Much easier." I sprinted into the street, flagging the first cab I saw. The driver hadn't come to a full stop before I flung myself inside. "Golden Gate Park!"

Jimmy grabbed onto the overhead handle as the driver sped down the road, seeming to pick up on my urgency. I didn't miss the glances he kept throwing me in the rear-view mirror.

"You're Ms. Romance, aren't you?" he finally said.

"I used to be."

"Yeah. I've been reading your column for years. My wife hooked me." He blasted his horn at the car in front of him when it took half a second to react to the green light. "I was really rooting for you. Voted for you too. Still can't believe so many people thought you fell for that bastard." He huffed, and was quiet for a few minutes while I passed the miles bouncing in the backseat.

"What are you doing in San Francisco anyway?" His brows were pinched as he examined me in the rearview again.

Jimmy cleared his throat, looking out the window.

I met the driver's look and replied, "To confess to that bastard I'm in love with him."

Priceless. The look on the driver's face that followed. I guessed it was a look I'd have to get used to when my diehard fans learned of my betrayal. The accusing brow. The impression that I was a fraud.

But wouldn't I be an even bigger fraud if I didn't admit my true feelings? Denied the way I felt for him?

Whatever it all boiled down to, I was here. Determined.

The opinions of my readers, the masses, the world, didn't matter where this matter was concerned. All I was cared about was his.

"Any special place you want to be dropped at the park?" The driver asked as it came into view.

"You pick."

His forehead crinkled. "This feels like a lucky spot," he said at last, inching up to the curb outside of one of the park entrances.

"Thank you so much," I said as I dug out some money from my wallet.

"My treat. As a way to thank you for all of the advice that has been responsible for making the past five years of my marriage the best." He bowed his head at me. "A forty dollar cab bill is a bargain compared with weekly marital counseling sessions. A steal."

I stuffed the money in his hand, including a hefty tip. "And your readership and loyalty are priceless to me." I squeezed his hand before climbing out the door. "Thank you."

Jimmy followed me out of the cab, but he wasn't expecting me to break into a sprint the instant my feet touched the ground. "Hey!" Twenty pounds of camera equipment on my person. Rein it in, Seabiscuit!"

"I'm going to give you the benefit and presume you're referring to my speed, and not my size, when you compared me to a race horse."

"I like my balls where they are. Of course that's how I meant it," he hollered after me, breathing hard as the clink of camera equipment mixed with the thud of his footsteps.

Once I'd made it a ways inside the park, I stopped, just long enough to scan the area for any sight of a familiar runner, no doubt shirtless. There were hundreds of people on a sunny Monday afternoon, more streaming into the park as the end of the workday neared. Picking him out in this crowd, on the off chance he was jogging through this part of the park during his hella long run was unlikely at best, impossible at worst.

Still, the odds didn't intimidate me.

Jimmy caught up, panting like a dog that had been wandering the desert for days. "Any sight of him?"

My eyes squinted more as I scanned the far distance. My head shook as I broke into another run, heading deeper into the park. Running was not my thing. Even less my thing in a skirt suit and kitten heels. Kicking off the pink pumps, I grabbed them up and kept moving forward. If Jimmy had decided to start filming, viewers were getting quite the show.

As it was, heads were turning as I rushed by them; a panting, barefoot, red-faced woman in pink.

Weaving through a string of cyclists, I caught sight of a bobbing head a ways in front of me. It was hard to tell for sure with the view I had, but it was my gut that confirmed it.

"Brooks!" I belted out, my feet striking the pavement quicker than before.

Jimmy muttered an expletive from behind, managing to catch up but looked like his eyes were about to explode out of his sockets from the effort.

As I continued repeating his name, people were starting to notice what was going on. Beginning to recognize who the crazed woman was and who it was she was yelling for.

Phones were being whipped out, and my name started to be shouted from the crowd. Some people were actually breaking into jogs to catch up, bikes whizzing up beside me. I didn't need Jimmy's camera after all; this was going to be uploaded to YouTube in a hundred different versions in mere minutes.

"Brooks!" I shouted, my legs feeling dead and on fire all at once.

That holler finally cut through, as the bobbing head up ahead rolled to a stop. I kept rushing forward, a cluster of people flanking me as I went, Jimmy positioned at my side with the camera soaking up every move.

Brooks's head slowly began to turn, his body with it. I nearly tripped when his eyes found mine. There it was. Everything I'd been looking for. What I'd been waiting for. It was all there, reflecting in his eyes as he watched me close the last bit of distance keeping us apart.

I crashed into him instead of slowing down, but he didn't stagger back, almost like he'd been expecting it. Bracing myself against him so I didn't collapse, I looked up at him, forgetting about everything else going on around us.

His face was damp with sweat, the ends of his hair dripping, and from the shadows under his eyes, he didn't look like he'd slept in days. A rare shadow of a beard's stubble was even covering his face.

He'd never been more stunning to me than right then. Not fresh from the shower wandering his apartment in a towel. Not clean-shaven and donning his best-fitting suit. Not even that very first night, when I'd stayed awake a few extra minutes to admire the naked man tangled in the sheets beside me in bed.

"Hannah." His mouth twitched, ignoring the droves of onlookers circling in around us.

My index finger lifted when he looked like he was about to say something else. I needed to get this out first.

Unfortunately, my lungs were straining to breathe, let alone speak.

When I started to lean over, Brooks kneeled in front of me. "Where's your inhaler?"

My head shook. This wasn't an asthma attack. This was all the paths my life had taken me down converging into one . . . and it might have had something to do with the way I'd just sprinted the last ten minutes with no cardiovascular endurance whatsoever.

Jimmy crouched beside us, always chasing that perfect angle, but he looked almost as concerned as Brooks that I was about to pass out. That wasn't exactly the kind of blockbuster I'd promised Conrad.

When I tried to speak again, and nothing but a weezy rush of air projected, Brooks's jaw tensed. "You need to lay down and catch your breath." His arm came around behind me, trying to steer me through the cluster of people toward a park bench.

My feet stuck to the ground. "Brooks . . ." A word. Progress. Even though it sounded like I'd been sucking helium. Taking a deep breath, I tried again. I could do this. "I-liv-ju," I puffed out, grumbling when my gibberish reached my ears. This was not the height of romantic proclamations, or anywhere on the scale for that matter.

His eyes narrowed in focus. "What was that?" he asked, still trying to steer me toward the bench.

My eyes closed in concentration as I focused on the words. The heat, the labored breathing, and the dozens of spectators socking in tighter around us was making this a formidable feat.

"Eh . . ." I started, trying to articulate each word, "luv . . . eew."

A frustrated rumble rocked my chest.

"Hannah. It's okay. Whatever you're trying to say can wait—"

"I love you."

The words burst from me, clear and loud enough for half the park to hear. Brooks blinked, his eyes finding mine. "Before I say anything else, I just wanted to confirm those are the words you actually meant to say?"

"Those were the right words." My fingers curled into his arm, my breath evening out.

"You saw my article?"

I took a few deep breaths, letting me heartrate calm, before replying, "I saw it, and hitched a ride on a plane heading this direction two hours later."

"I didn't write it so you'd feel obligated . . . pressured . . ." He shifted, words sticking in his throat.

"I'm here because I want to be." My teeth worked at my lip. "I'm here because I want you. Because I love you."

The skin between his brows creased, his hand finding mine. Everything relaxed as his fingers wove through mine, cementing his palm to mine.

"I was scared. I was a coward. Everything with the show, knowing what you believed and how you'd come into it all, I wasn't sure if I could trust what I was feeling. I didn't know if I could trust *you*." My feet shuffled closer, until our bodies were touching. "My heart knew this was real. My head just took a bit longer to realize it."

An amused light lit in his eyes. "I'm guessing my soul-bearing article on the front page of the *World Times,* and drawing myself out of the running for the job didn't hurt either."

"No, that definitely didn't hurt," I started, my face drawing up. "But you didn't need to do all of that. The article. The job. You sufficiently turned down a promotion at the same time you put Mr. Reality out of commission with what you wrote." My free hand planted against his chest, the sweat and heat of his skin seeping into my palm. "You gave up too much."

"And look what I got in exchange?" His arm wove behind my back, drawing me nearer.

"You knew I'd come?"

"I hoped you would. And someone taught me that hope, is enough to keep even the most outlandish of notions alive."

The crowd had grown so quiet I'd forgotten a mess of people were even here, witnessing it all.

"So, Department Head, would you keep me in mind if you have any paper runner or grunt-level positions that open up? I managed to put myself out of a job." He grinned, brushing my disheveled hair behind my ear.

"Actually . . . I'm going to put myself out of a job too." My nose crinkled as I said it.

"Hannah. What? No. No way. That is your dream job. You'd be one of the youngest department heads ever." Brooks shook his head. "I won't let you give that up."

"It's too late, because I already gave Conrad my resignation. Once this camera is turned off, I'm out."

My hands planted around his neck when he shook his head "That was your dream."

"It was." My shoulders lifted. "But just like everything else, dreams can change. Besides, with Mr. Reality and Ms. Romance going extinct, there's going to be a big hole to fill."

His head tipped. "What did you have in mind?"

"A relationship blog, you and me the writers, contributor, and . . ."—I bit my lip—"the subjects."

He was quiet for a minute, probably considering my crazy idea. "You hate being on camera," he said, lifting his chin Jimmy's direction.

"I do. But there are a lot of misconceptions about love out there. Figured we could maybe clear the air by documenting our experience. The good. The bad. All of the highs and lows and not just the shiny Instagram captures of a relationship. The ugly, really nasty bits too."

His head shook, but he was smiling. "Sounds awful. Where do I sign up?"

I glimpsed over at the camera, waving at the droves of viewers watching on the other end. "You just did," I told him.

"Speaking of cameras, mind telling me why you drug this one with you all the way from New York to document this?" he asked.

My thumb brushed up his neck. "So I could confess to the whole world that I'm in love with you."

"A grand proclamation." He nodded.

"Just following your lead," I replied, my eyes dropping to his mouth.

The corners of his lips lifted, his finger motioning between us. "You and me, this should have been impossible."

I let myself go back to the start, the very beginning. My childhood. My parents. My career. The night we met. The deal, show, dates, heartache and break. This moment.

"Impossible is only a dare."

"Yeah? Then I dare you to . . ." As Brooks leaned in, his hand reached out to cover Jimmy's camera lens as he whispered the rest into my ear.

My legs lost sensation again, but this time it wasn't from physical exertion. "I do," I blurted, laughing at myself. "I mean, yes . . . I will."

"You want to give yourself a second or two to think about that? Kind of a lifelong commitment—at least from what I've read." Brooks lips touched mine, inhaling me before pulling away. "I'm not the prince on a white horse, remember?"

"I wasn't searching for the fairytale." My lips met his once more. "Just my own story."

The End

Thank you for reading
DATING THE ENEMY
by NEW YORK TIMES and USATODAY
bestselling author, Nicole Williams.

Nicole loves to hear from her readers.
You can connect with her on:

Facebook: Nicole Williams (Official Author Page)
Twitter: nwilliamsbooks
Blog: nicoleawilliams.blogspot.com

Other Works by Nicole:

MISTER WRONG

HATE STORY

TORTURED

TRUSTING YOU & OTHER LIES (Random House)

ALMOST IMPOSSIBLE (Random House)

EXES WITH BENEFITS, ROOMMATES WITH BENEFITS

CRASH, CLASH, and CRUSH (HarperCollins)

UP IN FLAMES (Simon & Schuster UK)

LOST & FOUND, NEAR & FAR, HEART & SOUL

FINDERS KEEPERS, LOSERS WEEPERS

STEALING HOME, TOUCHING DOWN

COLLARED

THE FABLE OF US

THREE BROTHERS

HARD KNOX, DAMAGED GOODS

CROSSING STARS

GREAT EXPLOITATIONS SAGA

THE EDEN TRILOGY

THE PATRICK CHRONICLES